"Do you have any other little girls you don't know you have?"

Parker started to choke. He coughed for a few minutes, then cleared his throat. "No, Christie, I don't have any other little girls."

"So, I'm your ownliest daughter?"

"Yes."

She wrinkled her nose, then tilted her head so one of her pigtails brushed against her shoulder. "It would be very nice to have someone to play with. If there aren't other children, I could play with a new puppy."

"Christie!" Erin said sternly.

"Yes, Mommy. I'll be good." She glanced at Parker out of the corner of her eye. "Sometimes I'm a handful."

"I'll bet...."

Dear Reader,

The skies won't be the only place to find fireworks this
month. Special Edition has six wonderful, heartwarming
books for your July.

Babies are fun in the summer, and this July we're
highlighting "the little ones." We begin with RITA-
award-winning author Cheryl Reavis, and our
THAT SPECIAL WOMAN! title for the month,
Meggie's Baby. You last saw Meg Baron in Cheryl's
book, *One of Our Own*. Now Meg returns to the home
she left—pregnant and seeking the man she's never been
able to stop loving. In *The Bachelor and the Baby Wish*,
by Kate Freiman, a handsome bachelor tries to help his
best friend achieve her fondest wish—to have a child.
And the always wonderful Susan Mallery gives us a
man, his secret baby and the woman he's falling for in
Full-Time Father.

And rounding out the month we've got the ever-popular
JONES GANG—don't miss *No Less Than a Lifetime*
from bestselling author Christine Rimmer. Also, it's
time for another of those SWEET HOPE WEDDINGS
from Amy Frazier in *A Good Groom Is Hard To Find*,
and Sierra Rydell brings us a sizzling reunion in
The Road Back Home.

A whole summer of love and romance has just begun
from Special Edition! I hope you enjoy each and every
story to come!

Sincerely,

Tara Gavin, Senior Editor

Please address questions and book requests to:
Silhouette Reader Service
U.S.: 3010 Walden Ave., P.O. Box 1325, Buffalo, NY 14269
Canadian: P.O. Box 609, Fort Erie, Ont. L2A 5X3

SUSAN MALLERY

FULL-TIME FATHER

SPECIAL EDITION®

Published by Silhouette Books
America's Publisher of Contemporary Romance

To my readers—
with heartfelt thanks for the support and
encouragement. You are the best part of writing.

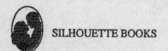

SILHOUETTE BOOKS

ISBN 0-373-24042-2

FULL-TIME FATHER

Copyright © 1996 by Susan W. Macias

Printed in U.S.A.

Books by Susan Mallery

Silhouette Special Edition

Tender Loving Care #717
More Than Friends #802
A Dad for Billie #834
Cowboy Daddy #898
*The Best Bride #933
*Marriage on Demand #939
*Father in Training #969
The Bodyguard & Ms. Jones #1008
*Part-Time Wife #1027
Full-Time Father #1042

*Hometown Heartbreakers

Silhouette Intimate Moments

Tempting Faith #554
The Only Way Out #646

SUSAN MALLERY

makes her home in the Lone Star state, where the people are charming and the weather is always interesting. She lives with her hero-material husband and her attractive but not very bright cats. When she's not hard at work writing romance novels, she can be found exploring the wilds of Texas and shopping for the perfect pair of cowboy boots. Susan writes historical romance novels under the name Susan Macias. You may write to her directly at P.O. Box 1828, Sugar Land, TX 77487.

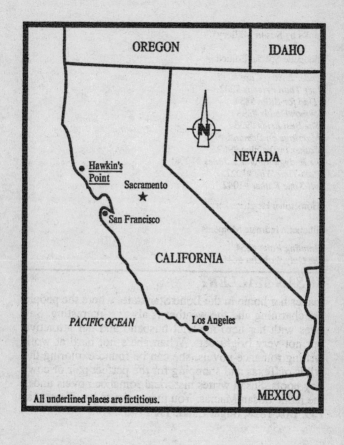

OREGON

IDAHO

NEVADA

Hawkin's
Point

Sacramento
★

San Francisco

CALIFORNIA

PACIFIC OCEAN

Los Angeles

All underlined places are fictitious.

MEXICO

Chapter One

"There's a woman here to see you," Kiki said, sticking her head into her boss's office.

Parker Hamilton wasn't really working, but he didn't raise his gaze from the computer screen. The program wasn't coming together. He couldn't concentrate. Everyone had been telling him to slow down or he would burn out. He shifted in his chair and wondered if he could feel the heat of that even now. He would hate like hell if everyone had been right.

"I'm not interested, Kiki," he said, still not looking at her. "Tell your friend she's wasting her time."

He didn't hear his housekeeper move into the room, but he felt her presence. Sure enough his screen soon filled with her reflection. She was standing behind him, with her hands on her hips. The image wasn't clear enough to see her face, but he knew her expression would be impatient. She'd been impatient with him a lot lately.

"You've got to stop staring at that little screen," she said. "You're going to go blind. Or worse. Your eyes will change shape until they're square, like your monitor."

He punched in the Save command, then spun in his chair until he was facing her. His housekeeper was probably in her early fifties, although she was very coy about her age. As usual, she was dressed in a jogging suit. She must own dozens. Parker had seen a rainbow of colors, all with matching athletic shoes. Today she was dressed in fuchsia. He didn't know they made shoes in that color.

"How is having my eyes change shape worse than going blind?" he asked. Kiki had the most interesting, if illogical, mind.

"Don't try to change the subject. You have a visitor."

"You're the one who brought up my eyes," he reminded her. He flashed Kiki a smile. "I appreciate what you're trying to do. I know you worry about me. But—" He glanced out the window, not really seeing the view of the Pacific Ocean, but instead looking in the black ugliness of the past. "I'm not interested."

Kiki shook her head. Her short blond hair fluttered over her forehead before settling back in place. "You think I don't know that? In the last couple of years I've paraded every single woman between twenty and thirty-five through here. Believe me, Parker, I've given up on you. This isn't one of my friends. I think—" She paused thoughtfully, something she almost never did. "I think you'll want to talk to her."

With that Kiki left.

Parker rose from his chair and started after her. Irritation battled with curiosity. His housekeeper could easily deal with anyone trying to sell something. If it wasn't one of her friends, then who?

He came down the stairs and across the large foyer. The house was large, too large, but he didn't plan on moving. He'd made peace with his surroundings if not with himself.

The front door was open. A woman stood on the porch. She had her back to him as she stared at the wide lawn and the flowers edging the driveway. The back of the house butted up to the edge of the cliffs. Beyond the terrace there was only the drop to the ocean. All the yard was in the front.

He had a brief impression of shoulder-length dark hair, touched with a hint of red. A loose-fitting cream sweater fell to slender hips. Jeans covered her long legs. His gaze dropped lower, and he smiled slightly. Her athletic shoes were white. Apparently she didn't share his housekeeper's compulsion to have everything match.

"May I help you?" he asked.

She turned toward him. Recognition slammed into his gut. Her eyes were hazel and tilted up at the corner. Her generous mouth was straight, but he knew what it would look like smiling. He knew about the dimple in her right cheek and how her laughter sounded. Five years ago, hers had been the only laughter in this empty house.

Regret followed recognition. Regret for how he'd treated her and regret for how easy it had been to let her go. He'd been the worst kind of bastard. Not only had he broken her heart, but he'd used her to forget.

She stared up at him, her hazel eyes searching his as if he were a stranger. Five years was a long time—they *were* strangers. They'd always been strangers.

He took in her clothing a second time. She was dressed more conservatively than he remembered. He raised his gaze to her face. There was something different in her expression. A wariness. He grimaced. Why wouldn't she be wary of him?

"Hello, Stacey," he said quietly.

She looked startled, then shook her head. "Mr. Hamilton, I'm not Stacey Ridgeway. I'm her twin sister, Erin." She held out her hand to him.

He took it without thinking. Her skin was smooth and cool. Instead of releasing her fingers, he held on, as if to keep her from bolting. Not Stacey? Was that possible? "You look just like her."

"We were identical twins." She glanced at the hand he was still holding. "Mr. Hamilton, we need to talk. May I come in?"

"Of course." He let go of her, then moved back, pushing the door open wider.

She stepped inside and gave him a quick smile that didn't reach her eyes. Her eyes. He stared at her. They *were* different. He hadn't been imagining it. Twins. Had Stacey told him she was a twin? She might have. She'd talked a lot, but he'd never listened. The sound of her words had blocked out the pain and that had been enough. It hadn't mattered what she'd been saying.

"This way," he said, motioning to a set of open French doors on the far side of the living room. It was late June and the afternoon sun would be warm on the terrace. Fog rolled in that morning, but had long since burned away.

They crossed the hardwood floors, their athletic shoes barely squeaking on the polished wood. He tried to think of something to say. He hadn't seen Stacy in five years. Had he given her a single thought after she'd left?

On the terrace he held out a chair for Erin and tried to remember that time. It was a blur. He knew he'd felt guilty about what had happened and what he'd said. He also admitted he'd felt relieved when she had left. He'd never thought to go after her, or check on her. Is that what her sister wanted? A piece of his hide for not giving a damn? Five years was a long time to carry a grudge.

Erin sat at the small table and folded her hands in her lap. He took the seat across from her and continued to study her face, trying to see the differences. It was a pointless exercise. He didn't remember enough about Stacey.

"You're probably wondering why I'm here," she said.

He listened to the sound of her words, trying to figure out if their voices were the same. He thought they might be. "I wasn't expecting you," he admitted. "It's been several years since I've seen Stacey."

"Five," she said, confirming his assumption.

She bit her lower lip, then drew in a quick breath. Gathering courage, he thought. But for what?

"Mr. Hamilton—"

"Parker, please."

She nodded. "Parker, I don't know how much you remember about my sister."

"She interned with me for a summer." At least most of a summer. Until circumstances—no, he was determined to be honest with himself if no one else—until *he* had driven her away. He didn't regret her leaving, but he was sorry for how he made her go. "We—" He fumbled for words. Got involved? He hadn't been, although he had a bad feeling Stacey had believed herself to be in love with him.

"There were some misunderstandings," he said at last. "I take full responsibility."

Her gaze met his. "I see," she said. Those two words carried a powerful message. He could tell by the look on her face that Erin Ridgeway knew the details of that summer. She knew what he'd done to her sister.

He resisted the urge to spring to his feet and pace the terrace. Okay, he'd been a bastard, but he hadn't done anything Stacey hadn't wanted. God knows she'd been throwing herself at him for weeks before he'd finally given in. She'd been over twenty-one. An adult.

Sell it somewhere else, Hamilton, a voice in his head muttered. She had been twenty-two and nowhere near grown up enough to handle you. He swore silently at himself and at the voice for speaking the truth.

Before he could think of something to say, Kiki swept onto the terrace. She walked over and set an old polished silver tray on the center of the table. There were two mugs, a coffee carafe, sugar, cream and a plate of brownies she'd made that morning.

"The coffee's fresh," Kiki said. "I ground the beans myself."

Erin glanced up and gave her a polite smile. "Thank you very much."

Kiki nodded. "No trouble. Mr. Hamilton rarely has visitors. I enjoy having people in the house." His housekeeper looked at her and shook her head. "You sure look exactly like your sister." She poured coffee and set a mug in front of each of them. "She was a lovely young woman. Very bright and funny. She brought a lot of life into this old house."

Erin's eyes widened. She'd reached toward her cup, then paused, her hand frozen in midmotion. "Stacey lived here?"

"All the interns did," Kiki said. "There are plenty of bedrooms. Town is too far away for them." She gave an exaggerated shrug. "Those college students always wanted to be working on the computer programs. Morning, noon and night. The world would have ended if they'd had to spend time actually driving back and forth. I would guess half of them never ever noticed the view from their bedrooms." She motioned to the twinkling blue of the Pacific just beyond the terrace. "Mr. Hamilton never notices, either. All he does is work."

She gave him a look that told him she hadn't forgiven him for being so tardy to dinner the previous night that he'd not only ruined her roast, but had also made her late for her date.

"I made the brownies myself," she said, pointing at the plate. "And not from a mix. Eat up." She glanced at him and raised her eyebrows. "You, too, Mr. Hamilton."

With that she walked across the terrace to the far door and entered the small hallway that led to the kitchen.

Parker picked up the plate and offered it to Erin. "Please try one. Kiki is an excellent cook and she gets very upset if she isn't appreciated."

Erin took one of the brownies and set it on a napkin. But she didn't taste the treat. Instead she stared at him. "I hadn't realized my sister lived here."

Parker had to clear his throat before speaking. "Yes, well, there were about six students in the house at the time. She was very well chaperoned." He snapped his mouth shut. Not well enough, he reminded himself, fighting an unfamiliar heated sensation. At first he couldn't figure out what it was, then he realized he was embarrassed. "At the time, it worked out best for everyone. Kiki was right. The interns did work constantly. I never required all those hours, but they would get caught up in their projects. I don't know if you're familiar at all with computer programming, but it can get very intense."

She reached for the cream and poured a little in her coffee. She stirred the mixture slowly. "That's what Stacey used to tell me."

He leaned back in his chair. "Did Stacey send you here, Ms. Ridgeway?"

Her gaze met his. Her eyes widened and her mouth parted in shock. The color drained from her face. "You don't know." Her lips pulled into a straight line. "Of course you don't. How could you?"

Uneasiness settled over him. "Know what?"

"My sister is dead. She died four years ago."

This time Parker gave in to the impulse and rose to his feet. He crossed the terrace to the waist-high stone wall that ran around the perimeter of the open area and stared out at the sea.

Stacey Ridgeway was dead. He probed his emotions and encountered compassion for her family, regret—always regret—for what he'd done and remorse because he wouldn't have the chance to explain or apologize. No sadness or longing. He'd barely known her. If her twin sister hadn't come calling, he would never have thought of her again.

"I'm sorry," he said, turning toward Erin and leaning on the stone wall. "It must have been very difficult for you and your family."

Erin nodded. "It was hard on me. Stacey was the only close relative I had."

Wariness joined the other emotions. Wariness and a faint hint of cynicism. He was a wealthy man. He'd sold his software company a few years back for several million dollars. He continued to develop programs that earned him an embarrassingly high income. Erin Ridgeway wouldn't be the first woman to come looking for a free ride.

"While I appreciate the tragedy of the situation, I'm not sure what it has to do with me," he said, wondering how much this was going to cost him. Even if the woman in front of him never got a dime, lawyer fees were expensive.

Erin tried to take a sip of coffee, but her hands were shaking so badly, she could barely hold the mug. She set it down. "I know what you're thinking," she said, not meeting his gaze.

Somehow, he doubted that.

"It's been so long," she continued. "Why am I here now? The truth is, I didn't know who you were until a few weeks ago. Stacey never told me your name. Before she died she said it was her fault and it wasn't fair to bother you with the responsibility. I didn't agree with her. But until I knew your name, I had no choice but to stay silent.'' She looked at him then, her hazel eyes dark with pain.

"I was angry,'' she told him. "At the mysterious man who'd ruined her life. At her for dying. At Christie for messing up my plans.''

"Who's Christie?'' he asked, not sure he understood what Erin was talking about or whether he believed her display of emotions. Were they genuine or was she a good actress?

She reached down and collected her small purse. After opening it, she pulled out a photograph. "My sister never told me anything, Mr. Hamiliton. Nothing about you or what had happened here. We were attending different colleges. I saw her for a few days that last summer when she came home from her internship here, but that was all. We didn't spend Christmas break together. I realized later that she was avoiding me. She didn't want me to know. I didn't have a clue until the hospital called to say there were complications.''

His stomach clenched tight like a fist. Parker stared at her. Foreboding surrounded him and chilled the air. "What complications?''

Erin stood up and started toward him. When she was less than two feet away, she handed him the small picture. He took it without looking at it. He wanted to watch her face as she told him her story.

"What complications?'' he repeated.

"My sister died of complications in childbirth. She was pregnant when she left here. The baby...Christie...is your daughter.''

A daughter? A child? *His* child?

Parker stared at her, hearing the words, absorbing their meaning, but not sure if they had any connection to him. A child. He had a child?

His gaze never left hers. Hazel eyes widened slightly. He watched the emotions race across her face. Confusion, compassion, fear. Why was she afraid? He wondered what she was seeing on his face. Most likely shock. That's what he felt. Stunned shock, as if he'd plunged into an icy river and couldn't catch his breath.

He struggled to remember that night with Stacey. Everything was a blur. Shame and guilt colored all the memories that hadn't been erased by alcohol. He recalled enough to know they'd had sex. He'd taken her again and again, hoping the act would blot out the past, but it hadn't. Instead he'd remembered everything and in doing so, he'd forgotten Stacey.

He hadn't used protection because she'd said she was on the pill. Had she been lying? If so the child could be his.

Or Erin Ridgeway, if that was even her real name, could be trying an age-old scam to make a few dollars for herself.

"How do I know she's mine?" he asked.

He expected her to get defensive and start talking about blood types and DNA as proof. Instead she motioned to the photo he was still holding.

"Just look at her. I always knew she didn't look like Stacey or me. Now I see she gets her features from you. The eyes, the shape of the mouth, although I have to warn you, personality wise, she's just as lively as my sister was."

Still he resisted looking down. Maybe because he didn't want to know. Maybe because, in his gut, he already knew the truth. Erin Ridgeway didn't know how to lie well enough to pull off something like this. Everything she said was true, including the fact that he had a daughter.

He braced himself, tensing all his muscles before looking down. Even so, the picture caught him off guard. It was like taking a sucker punch to the belly. All his air rushed out and he fought against the need to double over.

The photo showed a small girl laughing in a park somewhere. She wasn't looking at the camera, instead the snapshot had caught her in a moment of childish joy. Her arms were in the air, one knee was raised as if she was skipping or jumping. Her hair, in pigtails, flew out behind her. Sunlight illuminated the area, making the trees glow as if lit from within.

He cataloged all that information quickly, almost unconsciously, then he turned his attention to the child's face. Her eyes crinkled with amusement, but he could still see the shape. Her mouth was open wide with laughter, but he knew what she would look like if she smiled. There was something familiar about the way she held her head.

He recognized her.

"How old is she?" he asked, his voice hoarse.

"She turned four in early May." Erin stared at him. "Are you all right?"

He shook his head. "Not really." He continued to stare at the picture, memorizing it.

"I guess this is sort of a shock."

He glanced at her and forced himself to give her a smile. "That's an understatement." He returned his attention to the photo. "I never knew about her." He'd never sensed her presence in the world. That didn't seem possible. His child had existed for over four years, and he hadn't had a clue.

"I'm sorry," Erin said. "I would have come sooner, but as I already told you, Stacey never told me who you were. When she passed away, I asked a friend to pack up her room at home. All these years I never thought to check her personal papers." She shook her head. "I should have. I only found out about you recently because I was packing up to move and I finally went through her things. I found her diary and in it she mentioned your name."

He wondered what else she'd mentioned, then figured it wasn't important. The past was over. All that mattered was the child.

"Where is Christie now?" he asked. Christie. The name was unfamiliar on his tongue, but he liked it. Had Stacey had the chance to name her daughter before she died or had Erin chosen the name.

"At our motel. We're staying in town."

He frowned. "You left her alone?"

"No." Erin smiled. "I drove up with a friend. Joyce is watching her."

He supposed she'd come for money. Child support. A college fund. He opened his mouth to say all that would be arranged. He wouldn't ignore his responsibilities. Instead he blurted out, "I want to meet her."

Erin's hazel eyes darkened with pleasure. The dimple in her cheek deepened. "I'm glad," she said. "I didn't tell her why we were up here. I wasn't sure what you would say or if you would even believe me."

"This kind of proof is difficult to ignore." He shook the picture.

"But I wasn't sure she looked like you. She could have taken after another relative."

"But she didn't." He studied the photograph again, marveling that she really existed. "When can I see her?"

Erin pushed up the sleeve of her cream sweater and glanced at her watch. "It's nearly eleven now. What if I bring her back at two o'clock?"

Three hours. It felt like a lifetime. "Sure."

"Great." Erin started for the small table. She collected her purse, then nodded at the picture. "Would you like to keep that?"

His hold on the photo tightened. "Yes. Thank you." He followed her to the front door. "Do you know how to get to town?"

"I have the map I used to find my way here. I'll be fine."
She glanced up at him. The top of her head was an inch or
so shy of his chin. "I'm glad you want to meet her, Parker.
She's a wonderful little girl. Very outgoing, friendly, she's
almost never shy. Do you want me to explain things to her
before we get here?"

Things? "You mean tell her that I'm her father?"

"I—" She cleared her throat. "She's always wanted one,
a daddy, as she says. I thought it might be easier to try to
answer her questions before she met you, but if you would
prefer to do it yourself—"

"No," he said quickly. "Go ahead and tell her what you
think is best."

"I'll make sure she realizes you didn't know about her
until today."

Now it was his turn to hesitate. "Thank you," he said.
"You're being very understanding about this. I'm still a little stunned."

"Why wouldn't you be? A perfect stranger waltzes into
your home and tells you that you have a child you never
knew existed. I appreciate how well you're handling the situation."

They stared at each other. Parker knew she was wrong
about one thing. She wasn't a perfect stranger. He knew
very little about her personality, but he was familiar with her
looks. It was almost eerie, staring at Stacey's face but
knowing Stacey was gone. He didn't remember her well
enough to be able to pick out the subtle differences in their
features, assuming there were any.

Erin's hair was shorter, barely brushing her shoulders.
Stacey's had fallen nearly to her waist. A tactile memory
flashed through his mind. The feel of silky hair being
crushed between his eager fingers. He pushed it away, along
with the guilt.

He studied her small nose and wide mouth. The latter curled up into a smile and the dimple formed on her right cheek. "We'll see you at two," she said.

"I look forward to it."

He watched her walk to her car. It was a white four-door sedan, probably five years old. Sensible rather than flashy. As soon as she started the engine and drove away, he realized how many questions had gone unasked and unanswered. Was Erin married? He tried to remember if she'd worn a wedding ring. Had she officially adopted Christie after Stacey's death? What was she going to tell the little girl about him?

A faint noise caught his attention. He closed the door and turned around. Kiki was standing in the middle of the foyer. Her blue eyes danced with excitement.

"So, what did she want?" Kiki asked, trying to act as if she didn't already know.

"Don't pretend you weren't listening."

Kiki wrinkled her nose as she battled her desire to protect her dignity by refusing to acknowledge her habit of eavesdropping and her need to share what she'd heard.

She clapped her hands together, then rushed toward him. Before he could step back, she'd grasped his upper arms and squeezed tight.

"This is almost as much fun as having a grandchild of my own living here. This old house needs some life and laughter, and you need something to distract you from those silly old computers."

"Wait a minute." He raised his hands as if to ward off her words. "No one said anything about moving in. I'm going to meet Christie—"

"Christie. Is that her name? I couldn't hear everything you two were saying."

"Next time we'll talk louder," he said dryly.

Kiki ignored him. She released his arms, patted his face, then spun away and began making plans. "I'll make some fresh cookies," she said, and held out her left index finger. "Then lemonade." The second finger went out. "Maybe ice cream. Hmm, I wonder if there's time. Maybe if I start now, it will be finished by the time they come back. What time was that?"

"Two."

She paced in front of him, a fuchsia-colored dynamo. "All those sweets might make her sick. Maybe some finger sandwiches." She glanced up and grinned. The wrinkles around her eyes deepened. Kiki smiled a lot.

"I'll think of something," she said. "Trust me." With that, she hurried toward the kitchen.

Parker watched her go. He glanced down at the picture in his hand. He was going to meet his daughter...the child he never knew he'd had. Stacey hadn't told anyone he was the father. He couldn't blame her, not after the way he'd treated her. No doubt she'd assumed he wouldn't care.

Parker tucked the photo into his shirt pocket, then started for his office. The faint banging of pots and pans drifted through the house. Kiki would be so busy with her preparations, she would probably forget his lunch.

He stepped into his custom-designed workroom. He had three hours until Erin and Christie would arrive. He could work on the program that was giving him so much trouble. Instead he crossed to the wide windows and stared out at the ocean. He had the sensation of free-falling off a cliff. In a matter of moments, his whole life had changed.

For the first time in years, something stirred inside him. Interest, and maybe a little anticipation. He touched his shirt pocket and felt the flat paper of the photo. He had a child and she was coming to meet him.

Chapter Two

"Is he really my daddy?" Christie asked from the passenger seat.

"Yes, honey."

Christie took a deep breath and let it out all at once, curling up her lower lip so the air rushed up her face and lifted her bangs. She giggled as the delicate hairs danced before settling back on her forehead.

"But he didn't know he was my daddy before you told him today."

"Yes."

"Why?"

"Because Stacey didn't tell him about you."

"And you didn't know about him?"

"Right."

"Couldn't he see me when I was in her tummy?"

"Stacey left his house before you were big enough to see."

"How did I get in her tummy?"

Erin gripped the steering wheel tightly and resisted the urge to groan. As if there wasn't enough going on, now Christie wanted to talk about where babies came from.

"Oh, look, you can see the ocean," she said enthusiastically, trying to distract Christie.

It worked. The four-year-old peered over the dashboard and grinned. "It's blue and goes forever. Does the ocean end?"

"The water doesn't stop in one place and start in another, but it gets a new name."

Christie glanced up at her and wrinkled her nose. "The water has a name?"

"Uh-huh. It's the Pacific Ocean."

Christie mulled that over for a minute. Erin gave her a quick look. Her daughter had been asking questions from the moment she learned how to string words together. Her adventurous spirit was pure Stacey. Erin liked to think that Christie had gotten her quick intelligence from their side of the family as well, but after researching Parker Hamilton, she had to admit he probably had something to do with that.

He'd also given his daughter several of her physical characteristics, including the shape of her mouth and her smile. But her dimples were a Ridgeway legacy. Erin thought she and Christie moved the same way, and her daughter had the same habit of tilting her head to one side. Of course those traits could have been learned, not inherited.

The road narrowed and Erin concentrated on her driving. Parker Hamilton lived several miles outside of town. The turnoff for the private road was sudden and not well marked. From there she had a two-mile drive to the house itself. She wouldn't want to try to find it in the dark, or during a storm. At first she'd wondered why anyone would live in such isolation, but after seeing the house, she knew why.

Hawkin's Point was the most beautiful place she'd ever seen. The old-fashioned three-story home rose out of the grass, trees and bright flowers as if it were a magical castle. Peaked roofs topped wide windows and long balconies. The wooden structure blended with the environment, yet had enough fantasy in its design that her first thought had been she could blink and it would be gone.

Stacey had mentioned falling in love with the house in her diary and Erin understood completely. Hawkin's Point was the kind of place the sisters had dreamed of when they'd been young and were shuffled back and forth between relatives.

"Does my daddy have other little girls?" Christie asked.

The question startled Erin. "I don't know. I didn't ask." She thought for a moment. She didn't remember seeing any toys around.

She knew he wasn't married. As soon as she'd found his name in Stacey's diary, she'd started investigating Parker Hamilton. He'd been a big shot in the computer world and the magazine article index in the library had given her a place to begin. She'd read about the start-up of his company while he was still in college. She knew about his rise to the top of his field, that he'd sold his company for a huge but undisclosed sum and that he continued to work on software.

The personal information had been scant, but she'd picked up the essentials. He was a widower and, as of the last article written about three months before, he'd never remarried. But no one had said anything about children.

Up ahead was the turnoff. Erin put on her signal and slowed the car. There wasn't much traffic up here. When she'd checked to make sure the way was clear, she turned onto the private road and started down the long paved driveway. The car windows were already rolled down. She inhaled deeply and caught the scent of salt air.

"Can you smell the ocean?" she asked.

Christie took a breath, then giggled. "What does it smell like?"

"Salt, sunshine."

"You can't smell sunshine."

"Sure you can."

Christie looked skeptical. "It's nice here," she said. "At home it's so hot."

"You're right. It's probably going to be over a hundred back there."

"Two hundred!" Christie said and bounced in her seat. She quieted quickly and smoothed the seat belt over her chest. "My daddy lives far from me."

"Yes, he does."

Erin wondered if Christie was going to ask how they were going to work that out, but then she figured that was a fairly complex thought for a four-year-old. Erin was twenty-seven and *she* didn't know exactly how she was going to handle this difficult situation. She'd come up with a very logical plan, but life had taught her that the most logical solution wasn't always the one chosen.

They wound along the narrow paved road. Tall trees and lush bushes grew on either side. In another couple of minutes, they broke through and could see the house.

"It's big, Mommy," Christie breathed, staring at the three-story mansion.

"I know. And it's very pretty. Can you see the sunlight on the windows? It makes them look like jewels."

"I like that."

Erin glanced at the wood-and-glass structure. Once again her breath caught as she experienced the peculiar sensation of arriving at the one place she'd been searching for all her life. No wonder Stacey had fallen in love with the house and the owner. Erin was far more sensible and even she felt drawn in.

She parked in front of the house and turned off the engine. Christie clicked open her seat belt and bounced impatiently on the seat, but she didn't open the door. She knew she wasn't allowed outside until she was let out.

Erin stepped onto the driveway and inhaled the scent of the ocean. It was stronger here and in the still afternoon, she could hear the crash of the waves. She, her friend Joyce, and Christie had taken the coast route up. The farther north they'd driven, the more the beaches had changed. In Southern California there were long stretches of sand, with the coast highway running alongside. In the north, sandy beaches gave way to rocky shores. Large boulders jutted out of the water, moss-covered sentinels warning off the unwelcome. High cliffs soared over the ocean. Fog was a frequent visitor, adding to the character and mood of the location, if not to the temperature.

Erin walked around the car and let Christie out. Her daughter danced with excitement. "Does my daddy really live here? Does he have the whole house? Can I see every room?"

Erin laughed. "Let's take those one at a time. Yes, your daddy really lives here and he owns the whole house. It's very beautiful. I'm sure if you ask, he'll be happy to show you around."

Before she could continue, the front door opened and Parker Hamilton stepped out. Erin touched Christie's shoulder, then glanced down and gave her a reassuring smile.

"Is that him?" Christie asked softly.

"Yes."

Christie looked at Parker again, then up at her mother. "He looks nice," she said in a stage whisper.

Erin gave her a little nudge. "Why don't we go and say hello?"

Christie took her mother's hand and started across the driveway. Parker waited for them in the doorway. His gaze settled on the child.

Erin wondered what he was thinking. She tried to imagine what *she* would be thinking at a time like this, but her brain wasn't working, even though there was no reason for it not to. Parker might be fairly good-looking with dark hair and dark eyes, but he wasn't stunningly handsome. She tried to figure out what it was about him that made her stomach twitch.

He wore his hair short, barely brushing the collar of his white shirt. The top two buttons were undone and the sleeves had been rolled up to his elbows, but that wasn't especially provocative. Well-worn jeans hugged narrow hips and lean thighs. His legs were long and his white athletic shoes had seen better days. Her research told her he was worth more money than most people could spend in a lifetime, but he looked like an ordinary guy.

So why had her hand tingled when he'd taken it in his? Why had she found it tough to breathe or even think rationally? It must have been nerves. She wasn't the romantic impulsive sister. That had always been Stacey.

As they neared the house, Parker took a step toward them, then hesitated. He looked uncertain. Erin realized he didn't know what to say to his daughter. A little over four years ago, she'd been just as terrified.

Christie pursed her lips. "Are you really my daddy?"

Parker nodded and squatted down so they were at eye level. "Yes, Christie. My name is Parker Hamilton."

"Shouldn't I call you Daddy?"

His dark gaze raised to hers, as if asking her opinion. Erin smiled. "It makes sense to me."

"Okay," Parker said, his voice thick. Emotions chased across his face—confusion, terror, wonder. Erin knew just how he felt. At least when she'd found out about Christie, the girl had been an infant, not a fully formed person with independent ideas and opinions.

"Didn't you know about me, Daddy?"

He shook his head. "Not until today." Slowly he reached out his hand and touched her cheek.

"Are you glad?" Christie asked, cutting to the heart of the matter as usual.

"Oh, yes. I'm very glad."

"Good. Me, too." She gave him her best smile, the one she used to get her way. Erin was immune, but it worked like magic on Parker.

He knelt on the flagstone porch and opened his arms to gather the little girl close. She went willingly, flinging herself at him and holding on tight.

Erin watched them cling to each other. She'd prepared herself for this moment, but even so she felt a twinge of sadness. Nothing was ever going to be the same again. She and Christie were no longer just two against the world.

She studied them, the tall man and the little girl. Sunlight illuminated their heads. Parker's hair was dark brown with no hint of any other colors. Christie's was lighter and showed the reddish tint shared by Erin and Stacey.

Parker's large hands dwarfed the child. He could span her back from shoulders to hip. She'd insisted on wearing her favorite shorts set for the visit—lime green shorts and a T-shirt covered with cartoon fish. Matching green ribbons held her hair in pigtails.

Christie stepped back a little and smiled. "You smell nice. Different from Mommy."

Erin agreed. When she'd first come to the house and spoken with him, she'd noticed the faint fragrance of his spicy after-shave and the musky undertone of pure male.

There was a sound in the foyer of the house. Erin saw the housekeeper hovering in the background. Parker saw her, too, and rose to his feet. "Kiki, this is my daughter. Christie, this is Kiki. She takes care of things here."

"Hi." Christie studied her for a moment. "That's a pretty color," she said, motioning to the brightly colored jogging suit the woman wore. "Are you my daddy's mother?"

Kiki smiled. She looked to be in her mid-fifties, with short blond hair and bright blue eyes. Her smile was warm as she bent toward the child. "I'm the housekeeper, Christie. I'm in charge of the cooking and I look after your father. Do you like cookies?"

"Yes." Christie nodded vigorously.

"I've just taken some from the oven. Would you like to help me bring them to the terrace?" Kiki turned to Erin. "If you don't mind."

Erin glanced at Parker. He looked a little shell-shocked. They both needed a moment to catch their breath. "It's fine. Go on, honey, but you behave."

"Yes, Mommy."

Christie took the hand Kiki held out and skipped next to her as they moved down the hallway. When they had disappeared, Parker shook his head, as if clearing it.

"You okay?" she asked.

"Fine." He glanced at her. "She's amazing."

"Oh, she has her moments. Don't let the charming smile fool you. Christie is a bright, curious and very sweet-natured child, but she also has her share of faults."

Parker stared after the girl for a moment, then seemed to remember his manners. He stepped back and motioned to the house. "Please come inside," he said, then closed the door behind her.

He escorted her to the terrace. His fingers rested on the small of her back. Erin swore she could feel the heat of that light touch clear down to her toes. The accompanying shiver made her nervous, but she was determined to ignore the sensations.

The table they'd sat at before had been covered with a white linen cloth and set with dessert plates, flatware and glasses.

"Kiki is preparing an assortment of treats for Christie," Parker said, holding out a seat for Erin. "She's spent the last three hours in a cooking frenzy."

"I wish she hadn't bothered," Erin said. "Christie isn't a fussy eater. Anything that remotely resembles dessert is fine with her."

He took the seat opposite and leaned forward. One corner of his mouth quirked up in a deprecating half smile. "I don't know where to begin."

"I know this is very sudden," she said. "Why don't you let me tell you about the two of us, and when you think of a question, you can ask?"

"Sounds great."

His dark eyes mesmerized her and she couldn't look away. *You're acting like a fool,* she told herself firmly, mentally using the same tone she used when her daughter was misbehaving. Unfortunately it didn't work nearly as well.

With a conscious act of will, she shifted her gaze to the view beyond the terrace. The sky was a typical brilliant shade of California blue. The Pacific Ocean twinkled, the swaying waves sparkling with light.

"We live in Palmdale," she said. "You couldn't find a place more different from this and still stay in the same state."

"Where is Palmdale? I'm not familiar with the name."

"Most people aren't. It's in the high desert, about ninety miles north of Los Angeles. Remember where they used to land the space shuttle?"

He nodded.

"That's by us. It's cold and windy in the winter and hot and windy in the summer. You know, a hundred and ten, with zero humidity."

He frowned. Well-shaped dark eyebrows drew together. "I think Stacey might have mentioned something about it. I can't remember. But she didn't go to a university there. I recruited most of my interns from Stanford."

"Stacey was at Stanford." Erin bit back a sigh. There hadn't been enough money for both of them to go to an expensive university, so they'd compromised. Stacey had gone to Stanford, while Erin had attended a local state college. When they both graduated, Erin was to have applied for a graduate degree. But that had never happened. Stacey had died and Erin had been responsible for a newborn. There hadn't been time for graduate school.

"She calls you 'Mommy,'" he said.

"Christie knows that Stacey is her birth mother. As much as she can, after all she's only four and the concept of death is difficult to comprehend. She knows that we're twins and look alike. She's seen the photos. But I've raised her from the day she was born. Make no mistake, Christie *is* my daughter."

She made the statement quietly but firmly. She'd wrestled with this for a long time, wondering if she was doing the right thing by letting Christie think of her as her mother. Then she'd realized she didn't have a choice. Stacey was gone forever and Erin was the only mother Christie would ever know.

"I'm not judging you," he said. "I think you made the right decision. I'm still having a hell of a time with this."

There was a noise by the far door. It opened and Christie stepped out, proudly carrying a tray covered with cookies.

Parker stared at her. "Five hours ago I didn't know she existed and now she's here."

Erin glanced at his strong profile and the obvious pride in his expression. She'd wondered what the reclusive man would think and say when he found out about his child. She hadn't expected him to be quite this pleased. Not that his feelings changed anything. She was still going to stick to her original plan. Christie deserved to know her father and Parker had the right to get to know his daughter. As long as a few simple rules were followed, everything should be fine.

Christie made it all the way across the terrace without spilling a single cookie. Kiki followed behind with a pitcher of lemonade.

"I tasted the chocolate chips cookies," Christie said as she handed her mother the tray. "They're 'licious."

"I can tell." Erin set the tray on the table, then leaned forward and wiped a few remaining crumbs from the corner of her daughter's mouth. "How many did you taste?"

"Just one," Kiki said as she poured lemonade into three glasses. She gave Erin a quick wink. "She tried to convince me she was starving."

"We just had lunch," Erin said.

"I *was* starving. For cookies." Christie grinned.

Parker grabbed a handful. "I'm hungry enough to eat anything. Someone here forgot about my lunch."

Kiki turned to him and covered her mouth with her fingers. She shook her head. "Parker, I'm sorry. I was so busy making the cookies and lemonade."

"Yeah, yeah, no problem. Maybe you could make me a sandwich or something."

"Sure." She took two steps, then paused. "Erin, can I get you a sandwich, too?"

"I'm fine."

Kiki returned to the kitchen. Christie scrambled into the seat between Parker and Erin. She picked up her glass of lemonade with both hands and took a drink. Some of the liquid ran down her chin and onto her shirtfront. Erin wiped it away with a napkin.

Christie set the glass down and grinned. "I've never had a mommy *and* a daddy before."

Erin brushed the girl's bangs off her forehead. "You're going to milk this for all it's worth, aren't you?"

"It's not milk, it's lemonade," Christie said, pointing to the pitcher. "Can I have some more, please?"

"I'll get it." Parker reached for the pitcher and filled her glass.

"And cookies."

"Just one," Erin told her.

Parker handed the child the plate. Christie took one, then reached for a second. "I'd like two."

Parker stared at the girl, then looked at Erin. "I—"

"I warned you about her," she said, and took the plate from him. "One," she repeated.

Christie stuck out her lower lip, but didn't say anything. She'd learned that whining usually resulted in her losing the treat she already had.

"I was telling your father about where we live," Erin said. "Why don't you tell him about your preschool?"

Parker broke one of his cookies in half. "You go to school?"

"Every day. I'm very smart. When I grow up I'm going to be smarter than everyone. Except Mommy." She paused and studied him. "Are you smarter than Mommy?"

Parker had popped half the cookie into his mouth and started to chew. He tried to swallow it quickly and only succeeded in choking. As he coughed, Erin handed him his lemonade. He took a sip, coughed again, then said weakly, "What was the question?"

"Are you smarter than Mommy?"

"Think before you answer that," Erin said, then took a small bite of her cookie. It was still warm and the chocolate chips were soft and sweet.

"I probably know more about computers than she does," he said carefully. "But she knows more about other things."

"Nice save," Erin said.

He flashed her a grin.

The cookie turned to tasteless crumbs in her mouth as a bolt of awareness slammed into her chest and roared down to her toes. She blinked, waiting for it to go away, or at least fade. It did neither. Instead she was acutely aware of Parker and a sensation in her chest that felt suspiciously like heat.

So the man was vaguely attractive. So he was nice to Christie. So he had a sense of humor. It was the salt air, or the cookies, or the sunshine. It was the fact that she'd spent the past four years getting her teaching credential, finding a job and being a single mom. She hadn't had the time nor energy to think about having a man in her life. Something long dead was finally coming to life. Nothing more. Really.

Christie munched on her cookie. "Do you have a dog?" she asked, giving her mother a sideways glance.

Christie had been angling for a puppy of her own for nearly a year. Erin understood the girl wanting one, but life was hectic enough without adding more responsibility.

"No, sorry," Parker said.

"Dogs are very nice."

"I'm sure they are." He looked faintly confused. "Do you have a dog?"

Christie raised her shoulders and let go with an exaggerated sigh. "No. Maybe when I'm older." She took a drink. "Do you have any other little girls you don't know you have?"

This time he was drinking instead of chewing when he started to choke. He coughed for a few minutes, then cleared his throat.

"This seems to be a chronic problem for you," Erin said, refilling his glass.

"It's very recent," he said and coughed again. "No, Christie, I don't have any other little girls."

"So I'm your ownliest daughter?"

"Yes."

She wrinkled her nose, then tilted her head so one of her pigtails brushed against her shoulder. "It would be very nice to have someone to play with."

"I don't know of any other children around here. I can ask Kiki."

"If there aren't children, I could play with a puppy."

"Enough about the puppy," Erin said.

"It wouldn't have to be very big."

"Christie!" she said sternly.

"Yes, Mommy. I'll be good." She glanced at Parker out of the corner of her eye. "Sometimes I'm a handful."

"I'll bet."

Father and daughter smiled at each other.

Since finding her sister's diary, Erin had spent several sleepless nights wondering if she was doing the right thing. Everything she'd read about Parker Hamilton had convinced her he was a decent man and that he would want to know about his child. She'd been concerned about his reaction and a little nervous about allowing someone into the special world she'd built with her daughter. But now, staring at the two of them, seeing the similarities and differences, she knew she'd made the right decision.

Everything was going to work out perfectly.

Parker.

Chapter Three

Christie finished her cookie and lemonade without mentioning the puppy again. Parker couldn't help staring at her. She was small, smaller than he'd imagined, but very lively and bright. Her eyes were a few shades lighter than in the photo, but still brown. She glanced at him, then smiled. A dimple appeared on both cheeks. He couldn't help smiling back.

"You're very pretty," he said without thinking.

The dimples deepened as she grinned. "Mommy says so, too. Angela Bedford is beautiful. She's got long blond hair and blue eyes and she's made a 'mercial."

"A what?"

"A commercial," Erin said and reached for her glass. "Mrs. Bedford is hoping to get her daughter into television."

"Why would anyone want to do that?" he asked.

She laughed. "My thoughts exactly."

Her shoulder-length hair brushed against her cream sweater as she tilted her head and glanced around the terrace. Parker felt as if he'd gotten sucked into one of his video games. In the space of a few hours, his whole world had been turned upside down.

Erin was Stacey's twin sister. The longer he was with Erin, the more he remembered about her sister. Yet he had no sense of déjà vu. Despite the physical similarities, he knew Erin was a different personality. They might look alike, but they projected two completely different people. Stacey had been— He frowned trying to remember what she'd been. Intense, driven; she'd been one of the hardest workers on the project. She'd also been underfoot. He remembered the feeling of not being able to escape her.

He didn't know Erin at all, yet even after spending such a short period of time with her he sensed that she was more relaxed and accepting of things. She handled her child easily, without being overbearing.

Her child...his child. He swore silently and wondered what on earth he was going to do with a kid. Not that he didn't like Christie, but he wasn't the paternal type. He hadn't been around children since he *was* one.

Kiki came out onto the terrace and walked to their table. "Does anyone need more cookies or lemonade?" she asked as she placed a sandwich in front of him.

"Christie and I are fine," Erin said.

Parker took a big bite of his sandwich. "Great," he mumbled.

Kiki gave him her "don't talk with your mouth full" look, but fortunately, she didn't say it out loud. Kiki had been with him seven years and was worse than his mother had ever been. He didn't know how he would survive without her, though.

Kiki squatted down next to Christie and touched the girl's shoulder. "I bet you have your own room back home," she said.

Christie nodded. "Uh-huh. I've got a big girl bed and bookshelves."

"You like to read?"

"Yup." She scrunched her nose. "I can read lots of words by myself, but for the extra-long stories, Mommy reads those to me. I want to read big girl books. When I go to school in the fall, I'm going to really learn how to read. And numbers, too."

"Good for you. Do you go to school now?"

"Yes, but it's not real school. Not with the big kids."

Erin leaned forward. "She's in a preschool. Christie can't wait to start elementary school. She wants to learn everything, don't you honey?"

Parker listened to the exchange, all the while eating his sandwich. Kiki didn't have any trouble talking with the girl. She just asked the same sort of questions she would ask anyone visiting. Maybe there wasn't a trick. Maybe he should just talk to Christie as if she were a regular person.

Kiki stood up. "Parker, I'm sure Erin and Christie would like to see the gardens and maybe go down to the beach."

"Good idea," he said, then popped the last bit of sandwich into his mouth. He wiped his hands on a napkin, then glanced at his daughter.

She looked at him. "I love the beach," she said seriously, as if her goal in life was to see his.

Erin laughed. "You've only been to the beach once. How do you know if you like it?"

"It was very nice," Christie said, still serious.

"You're going to love this one," he told her and stood up.

Erin rose gracefully, then helped Christie out of the chair. Parker motioned for them to go through the living room and out the front. They turned left and circled around the house.

''There's no way to get from the terrace to the beach,''
Parker said as he led them to a wrought-iron gate and pulled
it open. ''The stone fence is built into the house itself. This
is the only way down to our private beach. It's not very big,
but it's nice when the tide is out.''

Erin glanced back at him as she walked by. ''What happens when the tide is in?''

''Depending on how high it is, the beach can go under-
water. Not often, though. It's pretty safe.''

''Is there a lock on that gate?''

Parker followed her gaze to Christie. ''Yes. We haven't
been using it, but we can.'' Of course the child was too small
to be trusted down on the beach by herself. He made a
mental note to mention locking the gate to Kiki as soon as
they returned.

Erin reached down and took her daughter's hand. ''It's
very lush here,'' she said. ''I'd expected windswept cliffs and
a couple of redwood trees.''

Parker glanced around at the trees and creeping vines
lining the path. On either side, blooming flowers nestled
against juniper ground cover. ''I have a gardener who wages
a battle against the salt air and bad soil. So far he seems to
be winning.''

She paused to finger a flowering crepe myrtle. ''Very
beautiful.''

Christie stood on her toes and sniffed. ''Smells pretty,
too.''

As Parker followed them to the wooden stairs that hugged
the side of the cliff, he tried to remember the last time he'd
noticed the garden. The house had nearly a quarter acre of
cultivated grounds. He owned everything to the main road,
but left most of it in its natural state. For the past couple of
years he hadn't seen anything past his office.

Up ahead, the path made one last sharp turn before widening into a half circle that ended at the top of the stairs.

Both Erin and Christie stopped to stare. He came up behind them and knew he'd been lucky to find this property when it was for sale.

To the left was the tall three-story house. The path sloped down, so they were below the first floor. To their right was the wild rugged coastline of Northern California. Sea gulls circled overhead. In front of the path, the Pacific Ocean stretched out for miles before disappearing into the horizon.

"Where does it go?" Christie asked.

"Clear around the world," he told her.

She quivered with excitement. "Mommy, Mommy, we could get a boat and sail forever."

Erin gave him a wry glance. "I don't think my stomach's up to it. I was never a very good sailor."

"Me, either," he said. "But cruise ships are fine."

"I've never been on one."

He had the strangest urge to offer to take her on a cruise. Just the three of them. He shook his head to clear it and ignored the impulse. "The stairs are a little steep," he said, then looked at four-year-old Christie. It would take her forever to get down.

"I can carry her," Erin told him.

"You're not any more familiar with the stairs. Besides, Christie looks as if she weighs enough to knock you off balance." He squatted down as he'd seen Kiki do. "How do you feel about a piggyback ride?" he asked Christie.

She beamed at him and clapped her hands. "Yes!"

She wrapped her arms around his neck. He reached behind him for her chubby legs, then stood up. She wasn't that big, at least not to him, but he assumed she was the size of an average four-year-old. Erin watched for a moment to make sure Christie was balanced.

"Look at me, Mommy," the little girl crowed.

"I see." She turned her attention to him. "Do you want me to go first?"

"Sure. Then we can follow slowly."

The sound of the waves crashing on the rocks got louder as they descended. Parker was used to the stairs. Two landings broke up the steep trip. He usually went down at a jog, but not with Christie on his back.

Her small hands clutched his shirt and shoulders. The skin of her bare legs was warm against his hands. She clung to him as if she were a little monkey, and he caught a faint whiff of something unfamiliar over the scent of the salt air. She smelled of chocolate and sweetly of herself. A band tightened in his chest. Not an emotion as much as a reaction. A fierce need to protect her and be there for her.

Erin reached the beach first. She smiled at Christie. "You doing okay?"

"This is fun." She leaned her face closer to his ear. "I want piggyback rides all the time."

"You got it," he told her as he stepped off the last step.

The tide was out, the small half moon of hard-packed sand was still damp. Their athletic shoes didn't make any sound as they left faint imprints. The sun was warm and the sky clear. Erin came up behind him and lifted Christie to the ground. The girl ran to the edge of the water, then raced back.

"There's nobody here but us. And the birds. You can't see the house." She leaned her head back and stared straight up.

Parker followed her gaze. "It's the angle of the cliff. The house is built into the rock so it isn't at risk of sliding during rainstorms."

Christie spun around and faced the water. She flung her arms out and ran in ever widening circles. "I'm a birdie, too."

In her lime green shorts and shirt and her pigtails streaming out behind her, she was an exotic creature. At least in his world.

"She's got a lot of energy," he said.

"More than usual." Erin tucked her hands in her jeans front pockets. The action emphasized the swell of her breasts under her sweater. "We took two days to drive up from Palmdale. We took a lot of breaks, but that's a long time for a child to sit still in a car. Besides, I'm all in favor of you tiring her out so she goes to bed early tonight."

"You mentioned you drove up with a friend?"

"Joyce. Her fiancé is waiting for her in San Francisco. He's on a business trip, then they're going to spend some time together in the city." Erin glanced at him out of the corner of her eye. He noticed her eyelashes were thick and dark.

"Having her along has been great," she continued. "Not only did we get to split the driving, but she looked after Christie this morning and has given me moral support."

"What does she have to say about all of this?"

"She thinks I'm crazy for dropping in on your life. She warned me you wouldn't be interested."

"In my own daughter?"

Erin turned as if to check that Christie was out of earshot. The girl was digging for crabs. "She thought you wouldn't want to be reminded of a four-year-old mistake."

The bright sun heated the air and danced on the top of the waves. Christie looked up at him and smiled. He smiled back. "Is that how you thought I'd think of her? As a mistake?" He kept his voice low.

"I was willing to give you the benefit of the doubt."

"I'm glad."

He still didn't know anything about Erin Ridgeway. This could be a scam to get money out of him. But he didn't give a damn. He knew Christie was his and that's all that mattered.

The girl stood up and raced toward them. She stopped about a foot in front of him and stared up. Her eyebrows pulled together in a frown. "Angela Bedford's daddy is a policeman. What do you do?"

"I design programs for computers."

"We have computers at school. I like them." She shrugged casually. "I like puppies better, though."

Erin burst out laughing. She swooped down and pulled her daughter close. "I'm going to tickle you into behaving."

"I'll behave! I'll behave!" Christie shrieked, but didn't try to pull away. She wiggled close and threw her arms around Erin's waist.

Parker watched them, feeling like the odd one out. The relationships between children and parents were unfamiliar to him. His family had never been affectionate. He didn't remember either of his parents playing, tickling or even teasing him.

"She's a monster," Erin said, looking up at him and smiling. "Should we throw her to the other sea monsters?"

"Nah, they'd just spit her back."

"Spit?" Christie repeated, sounding outraged. "They would not spit me back. They would make me their princess and I would have a castle under the sea and you would miss me very much."

"I think I might at that," Erin said, then dropped a kiss on the top of her head. "We better head back up. I still have to talk to your father about a few things."

"Okay." Christie ran to the stairs and started to climb.

Parker brought up the rear. He walked slowly marveling over how easily Erin referred to him as Christie's father. Of course he was, but the word was unfamiliar. He reminded himself that she'd had longer to come to terms with that.

She'd known for weeks. He'd only found out a few hours ago.

Questions spun through his mind. What did Erin want from him? What was his place in Christie's life? Did he have one and did he want one? Underlining it all was a thin thread of fear that came from the knowledge of how easily all this could be destroyed. He'd done it before.

When they reached the pathway, Christie raced ahead of them. She paused every few feet to bat at the crepe myrtle, laugh, then run again.

Erin placed her hand on her chest and drew in a deep breath. "I need to exercise more," she said between breaths. "Those stairs are a killer."

He pushed a branch out of the way so she could duck under it. "Do you have a job?" he asked as he caught up with her.

She laughed. "Of course. What did you think? I'm an elementary school teacher."

"I thought there might be insurance money, or something."

Erin shook her head. Her hazel eyes darkened with emotion. "There was a little when Stacey died, but not much. I stayed home with Christie that first summer. Having an infant thrust upon me with no warning was a shock."

"I can relate to that."

She smiled, exposing the dimple in her right cheek. "I'll bet you can. I didn't know how else to tell you."

"You did fine." He touched his hand to the small of her back. She jumped a little, so he dropped his arm to his side. "Had you always planned on becoming a teacher?"

"No, but with a child to raise, it seemed the most sensible plan. I could get off work at a decent time and have summers with her. I used the last of the insurance money getting my credentials and went to work when Christie was a year old."

They'd reached the gate. Parker opened it and Christie raced across the lawn. She started spinning around, then collapsed on the smooth grass and stared up at the sky.

"I wish I'd known," he said.

"Do you?" She shrugged. "I don't mean to sound surprised, but I tried to get in touch with you after Christie was born. I didn't think you were her father, but I thought you might know who was. All my letters were sent back unopened."

Guilt flooded him. "I'm sorry. I'd sold the company and told them not to forward any mail. I didn't think anyone would be trying to get in touch with me."

And he hadn't wanted to have any contact with the world. After Stacey had left, he'd fallen apart. Pain and guilt had overwhelmed him until getting through the day had been more than he could manage. He'd betrayed his wife's memory—traded in their special love for one night of passion. One night of trying to feel alive. It was as if Robin's death had killed him, too. God, he'd missed her. He still did. Sometimes missing her was all that kept him going.

"We all survived," Erin said as she headed for the front door. "Now, we start over."

Christie bounced to her feet and skipped toward her. Parker stared at the child and battled regret over the first four years he'd lost.

Kiki was waiting in the foyer. "Did you enjoy the beach?" she asked.

Christie nodded vigorously. "It's beautiful. We saw birds and I got a piggyback ride. I almost caught a crab, but it kept digging and digging and I can't dig that fast."

Kiki ruffled the girl's bangs. "You can catch it next time." She glanced at him. "Why don't you show them around the house? It's very unusual."

"If you'd like," Parker said, looking at Erin for her approval.

She nodded as they walked into the living room. "It's a great old place. When was it built?"

"In the 1920s by an eccentric millionaire who made his money in railroads, lumber and oil. Much of this room is original," he said. The open-beamed ceiling soared nearly twenty feet high. Dark wood broke up the plain white walls. There were huge windows that looked out onto the terrace and the ocean beyond. Opposite, smaller windows gave a view of the front yard. Dark blue leather sofas and chairs were grouped together in conversational areas. Bold paintings, some modern, some old, added color to the room.

Erin walked over to the one above the fireplace. It showed a wild storm raging against an island. "Did you pick these out yourself?"

"Some I have because I like them, others are investments. That one I bought because of how it made me feel." He still remembered how the anger and power of the painting had called him from across the gallery. He'd accepted an invitation to a showing on impulse. That had been about a year or so after Robin had died, when he was trying to put his life back together. The threads had remained unraveled, but the painting had allowed him to believe he wasn't the only person dealing with powerful and unexplained emotions.

"Very raw," she said.

Kiki walked across the hardwood floor. She pointed to the right hand wall. "This buffet and those two chairs are original pieces from the house. The former owner had much of the furniture custom-made."

From there they walked into the dining room. Again Kiki pointed out the original dining room set. Here the windows were smaller, but the view no less impressive. In fact, it was better than the living room because the room butted right up to the cliff.

He hung back as Kiki took Erin and Christie through the kitchen, then back through the living room to the other side. Parker wondered how this house must appear to Erin. She lived on a teacher's salary, which couldn't be a lot. There hadn't been much in the way of insurance money, and she hadn't mentioned receiving help from any relatives. Was she doing it on her own?

"There's another fireplace," Christie said loudly, when they walked into the study.

Parker followed more slowly. This was one of his favorite rooms. There weren't any windows, in fact part of the ceiling sloped because the room was partially tucked under the stairs. Bookshelves lined two walls and flanked the fireplace on a third. The fourth wall contained a built-in entertainment system complete with laser disc and four-way speakers.

As he entered the study, Christie was staring reverently at the big screen television.

"I don't think I have anything you would like," he said, motioning to his library of laser discs. "But maybe you can tell me what you enjoy and I'll get it."

Her brown eyes widened. Her mouth opened. Before she could speak, Erin touched her shoulder. "You can give Parker your list later," she said. "For now just say thank you."

"Thank you," Christie breathed, practically quivering with excitement. Her gaze darted around the room, then settled on something. "Ooh, who's the pretty lady?"

Parker knew before he turned that Christie had spotted the portrait of Robin. The eleven-by-sixteen print fit into an oversize frame on one of the bookshelves. A small light illuminated the picture.

Parker took the little girl's hand and led her to the photograph. He lifted it down so Christie could see it more easily. "That's my wife, Robin."

Christie frowned. "If you have a wife, how can you be my daddy?"

He heard someone take a sharp breath of air and assumed it was Erin. "No matter what, I'm still your father, Christie. Robin died a long time ago." He looked at the girl's solemn eyes. "Do you know what that means?"

"She's gone, like my other mommy, Stacey." Christie touched the glass protecting the photograph. "She's pretty. I like her hair. It's all wavy." She touched the pigtails that barely brushed her shoulders. "My hair's not that long and it doesn't wave like that."

"You're still pretty, too," he said.

Christie grinned.

He set the picture back in its place. He studied it for a minute. It was a beautiful shot taken by a skilled photographer. He kept it out because it was Robin's favorite picture of herself. She was dressed in period costume, something from the 1920s, when the house had been built. Her white lace dress fell straight to her ankles. A large hat shaded her face. She stood with her head turned slightly away from the camera.

The black-and-white film dulled the color of her red hair and the shadows muted her freckles. She was stunningly beautiful in this picture, but in his mind, she was a stranger. He preferred Robin in real life with her too-bright hair and glasses falling down her nose. He liked the freckles she despised and her slightly awkward way of moving through a room.

"I'd forgotten about her," Erin said, almost under her breath.

When he turned toward her, she flushed and held her hands palm up in a gesture of surrender.

"Your late wife was mentioned in a couple of articles I read in the library, but I'd forgotten that you lost her. I'm sorry, Parker."

Her words were an uncomfortable reminder that he was the sort of person people read about in magazines. He'd hated that part of his success. He preferred to remain out of the public eye. What else had Erin learned? What exactly did she want from him?

"Maybe it's time we talked," he said, motioning to the red-brown leather sofa across from the entertainment unit.

"This is going to be boring grown-up talk," Kiki said quickly. "Christie, why don't you come with me and I'll show you the upstairs? There are a couple of secret rooms."

"Really?" She glanced at her mother.

"Go ahead, honey," Erin told her. "Be good and don't touch anything."

"Yes, Mommy."

Kiki led the child out of the room. Parker waited until Erin was seated before taking a wing chair for himself. The lighting was such that he could see her face clearly, but knew he was in shadow. He hadn't liked his time in the business world, but he'd learned from it.

"Let's cut right to the heart of the matter, Ms. Ridgeway," he said calmly. "I'm convinced Christie is my daughter. I assume you want to enter into negotiations about her support."

Erin stared at him for several moments, then started to laugh. The bright sound filled the dark room, sweeping away the emotional dust. She placed her hands on her thighs and leaned toward him. Her mouth curved up slightly, her dimple playing hide-and-seek on her cheek.

"It's Erin, Parker. We'd already agreed on that." She studied him for a moment and the smile faded. "I had thought it might be nice to be rich, but I see I was mistaken. How many people come here looking only for money?"

"More than you can imagine."

"I'm sorry. I know you don't believe that, but I am. Christie and I are doing fine. We don't want financial assistance. As far as that's concerned, all I care about is a college trust fund for her."

Her fingers were long and lean. They rested on her jeans. She'd pulled up the sleeves of her sweater. He could see her finely boned wrists and the inexpensive watch she wore. He raised his gaze past the tempting curve of her breasts—ignoring the faint stirring of interest that started deep inside—to the small gold hoops at her ears. She wasn't flashy. If she really wasn't interested in his money, then she was unlike any woman he'd met since Robin died.

"Frankly I'm more interested in what you can give Christie emotionally rather than financially," she said.

He braced his arms on the chair. "What does that mean?"

"Christie needs a father in her life. If you want to take on that role, then it's a real commitment. She would need regular contact with you. Before you agree to anything, you have to think this through. I'd rather know now if you're not interested, because I don't want her heart broken."

"I would never hurt her," he said quietly, then wondered why he spoke the lie. Of course he would hurt her. He hurt every woman who had ever cared about him. Eventually he let them down.

He pushed the past away and concentrated on Erin. "Assuming I want to be involved with Christie, what are you suggesting? You sound as if you have a plan."

She nodded. "The distance is a problem. Also, Christie has friends and school. She can't be taken away from that just because it's convenient for you. My suggestion is that you fly down and visit her every third weekend. It will be easier for you to travel than for her. She's too young to go on a plane by herself, and I can't drive her up here for the weekend."

"Agreed," he said, wondering what on earth he was getting himself into. He was going to take Christie for a weekend? Down there? He wouldn't even have Kiki to help, unless he brought her, but he doubted his housekeeper would be willing to give up her social life to travel with him.

"During the summer Christie can come up for two weeks at the beginning and two weeks at the end. Also, you can have the week after Christmas."

Dates and times whirled through his head. "You've thought this through."

"I figured I'd better. After all I've known about this longer than you have. If it's agreeable, Christie and I will stay in town for the next couple of weeks so the two of you can get to know each other. I'll be around to help you over the rough spots." She smiled. "I know how hard it is to suddenly be responsible for a child, especially without warning."

He didn't know what to say. Erin's plan was sensible, although there was something about it he didn't like. However, he couldn't come up with anything specific so he let it go. Of course he wanted to spend time with his daughter. He'd just found her and he wasn't going to lose her again.

Then he realized what was wrong. Erin's sensible plan placed limitations on his time and involvement. What if he wanted to be a full-time father instead of a part-time one? There wasn't room in her equation for that.

Before he could mention it, Christie burst into the room followed by Kiki. The girl had an armful of flowers cut from the garden.

Erin looked at her. "Those are beautiful."

"Kiki said I could pick them for you." She crossed the room and placed the flowers in her mother's lap. "They smell nice, too."

"Thank you." Erin's smile included the housekeeper as well.

"You know what else?" Christie asked, dancing from foot to foot.

"No. What?"

"Well, you said we would stay in town for a while so I could get to know my daddy." Christie smiled winningly. "But we don't have to stay so far away. We could stay right here. I found the perfectest room all for myself."

Chapter Four

Erin stared at her daughter, sure she must have misunderstood what she was saying. One look at Parker's stunned expression told her she had not. Christie wanted to stay here—with her father.

It wasn't possible, of course. The complications. The awkwardness alone boggled the mind. Besides, Erin had a feeling she was going to need some breathing room away from Parker. For some reason her hormones had decided to start line-dancing whenever he was in the vicinity.

She caught a quick movement out of the corner of her eye. Kiki was inching toward the door.

"It's all the way at the top of the house," Christie said, her voice bright with excitement. She was completely oblivious to any tension in the room. "I can see the ocean and the whole sky. There's a rocking horse and playhouse and a big bed to sleep in all by myself." Her smile was winning. "Across the hall is a grown-up room just for you. There's a window with a seat. There's even a little wooden box by the bed," Christie went on, grinning widely. "You know, for a puppy."

Erin dropped her head to her chest and fought back a groan. When had everything gotten so out of hand?

"Kiki," Parker said sternly. "What have you been telling Christie?"

The housekeeper had almost made it to the hallway. At the question, she paused, then slowly walked back into the room. "I didn't say anything."

Parker raised his eyebrows and waited.

"Well, I didn't," Kiki said defiantly. "Christie mentioned that she and her mother were planning on staying in town for a couple of weeks. This place is large enough to house a regiment. It seems silly for them to be paying a hotel bill when all this space is available."

"So you thought you'd tell her that?"

"It may have slipped out," she confessed. "But you must admit having them stay here isn't a bad idea."

Parker glanced at Erin and shook his head. "She's been with me too long to fire, but sometimes she tries my patience."

"Don't talk about me as if I weren't in the room," Kiki said.

"Would you rather I said what I was thinking?"

Kiki sighed. "Not really."

Erin looked at Parker and was pleased that he didn't seem truly annoyed by the conversation. At least he had a sense of humor. The real question was did he have a solution? Kiki and Christie stared at her with matching hopeful expressions. She didn't know what to say. For one thing, Parker hadn't invited them. For another, it wasn't a good idea. She could feel it in her bones, and in her stomach.

"I don't think—" she began.

"If Christie stays here, Parker has a better chance to get to know his daughter," Kiki interrupted. "After all, he has a lot of time to make up for."

That one hurt, Erin thought, as the blow fell squarely below her belt.

"Kiki, I appreciate what you're doing," Parker said. "But it isn't necessary."

Erin touched the cool leather of the sofa and wondered what she should do. While she was still trying to figure that out, Christie cut to the heart of the matter. She crossed the study and stood directly in front of her father.

After placing one small hand on his knee she said, "Daddy, do you want Mommy and me to stay with you?"

Erin rose to her feet. "Christie, that's enough. You can't put your father on the spot like that. This morning he didn't even know about us. We're here to get to know each other and that's what we're going to do. We don't have to live in the same house to become acquainted."

Christie turned toward her. Her lower lip trembled slightly. "But, Mommy, we're 'posed to live together. Mommy and Daddy and me. You read that to me. 'member?"

Unfortunately, Erin did *'member*. She'd checked out a couple of books on different kinds of families from the library. She'd thought they would help Christie understand that she wasn't the only one being raised by a single parent. Some of the chapters had talked about extended families. A new mommy or daddy joined the family, then he or she came to live with them. It was perfectly normal. Common even. Only it wasn't going to happen this time. She and Parker might be Mommy and Daddy, but they *weren't* going to live together.

Erin walked over to her daughter and knelt down on the area rug. Parker was a scant foot away, but she did her best to ignore him. She took her daughter's hands in hers, marveling as she always did at how small her palms and fingers were; small, yet perfectly formed.

"Christie, it doesn't matter if Parker and I live together or never see each other again. You're the important one. You need to get to know your father. That's why we're here. You're going to get a chance to do that, but it will be easier if we're staying at the hotel."

Easier for the adults, at least, Erin thought. Aside from the privacy, she was going to need the downtime.

She glanced at Parker who was staring at her intently. "I'm sorry," she said. "You've had a lot of shocks today. Why don't I take Christie back to the hotel and we can pick this up in the morning?"

He didn't respond. Instead he frowned slightly. "I'm not sure what's best," he said, then turned to Christie. "Do you want to stay here?"

She nodded until her pigtails flapped like two flags in a stiff breeze.

He leaned forward in his chair and placed his elbows on his knees. His face was close enough to hers that she could see the individual whiskers that would soon darken his jawline. His dark irises were a mixture of colors. Brown, dark blue, hints of green and gold.

"It's not a bad idea," he finally said.

Erin blinked at him. Not a bad idea? Was he insane? It was a hideous idea. It was the worst idea she'd ever heard. Unfortunately she couldn't say any of that. The air had fled her lungs and she couldn't speak. She didn't know if it was the force of his gaze or the scent of his body, but either way, she was immobilized.

"I would like the time to get to know Christie," he continued. "There's plenty of room for both of you."

"Please, Mommy," Christie begged.

"Don't forget, I live here," Kiki said from her place by the door. "I'll be the chaperon."

Parker straightened immediately. His face hardened, and his expression became unreadable. Erin felt as if she'd been slapped. Obviously even the thought of anything happening between them was so repugnant, he could barely stay seated. Well, that was just fine with her. She wasn't interested in him, either. Pray God he hadn't been able to tell what she was thinking earlier when just the lightest touch of his fingers on the small of her back had sent heat spiraling through her body. Something was very wrong with her and as soon as she figured out what it was, she was going to get it fixed.

She stood up and glanced from Parker to Kiki to Christie. She didn't know what to do. Staying would probably be best for Christie and Parker. They would need time to get to know each other before they could bond.

"Say yes," Christie whispered.

"Say yes," Kiki said.

Finally Parker glanced up at her. "I would like the two of you to stay."

She drew in a deep breath. "All right."

Christie whooped loudly and flung herself at Erin. "You're the bestest mommy ever."

Erin placed her hand on her daughter's head. "I'll remind you of that when you're fighting your bedtime."

Christie giggled, then spun around and grinned at Parker. "Can I have that room upstairs? The one with all the windows so I can see the whole sky? And the rocking horse and the playhouse?"

"Of course." Parker also rose to his feet. He towered over Erin by a good seven or eight inches and she was five feet seven inches. "Kiki will make up the room across the hall for you, Erin. That way you can be close by. I'm down on the second floor."

His tone told her he was reassuring her that she would be safe from him. She'd already figured that out.

"I've paid for the motel room for today," she said. "I think Christie and I should stay there tonight. My friend Joyce will be leaving in the morning, then Christie and I will check out and come here. Say ten or eleven?"

"That sounds perfect," Kiki said, before Parker could comment. She moved forward and took Christie by the hand. "You're going to have to tell me everything you like to eat. I can cook anything. Would you like a cake for dessert after lunch tomorrow?"

Christie's answer was lost as Kiki led the girl out of the room. Erin watched them go, then turned her attention to Parker. Some of the tension seemed to have left his body, but his expression was still unreadable.

"You can change your mind," she said quietly. "It's not too late. Christie would understand."

His dark gaze met hers. "That's not an option. I want to get to know my daughter. After all, she'll be spending time here." His mouth eased into a smile. "I'll admit to being a little overwhelmed."

"Only a little?" she teased.

"Okay. A lot overwhelmed. But this is important to me. Now that I've found her, I want to be a part of her life."

"I'm glad," Erin said and was pleased that she really meant it. "Christie is a great kid. She deserves a father who cares about her."

Something very much like pain flashed through Parker's eyes. Before Erin could figure out what it was, he'd placed his hand on the small of her back and was urging her toward the door. Her out-of-control hormones took over and all she could do was endure the heat the contact produced and concentrate on not making a fool out of herself.

"I think you're insane," Joyce said the next morning as she pulled the shoulder strap of her purse up her arm and settled it in place. "Coming up here to meet the guy is one thing, but living with him is another. What if he's an ax murderer?''

"I've met the man. He seems very nice. He has a live-in housekeeper. I've read magazine articles about him and even seen his credit report. None of them mentioned anything about being an ax murderer."

Joyce brushed her long blond hair out of her face. "You think serial killers can't get a credit card?"

"I think serial killers aren't millionaires who set up foundations to help poor children get a good education."

"He did that?"

Erin nodded, then rose to her feet. The bathtub was almost half full of water. She checked the temperature, then turned off the faucet. Christie was already pulling off her nightgown and stepping into the water.

"I have to be pretty when I see my daddy again," she said and she sat in the tub.

It was the first time the girl had ever requested a bath, so Erin wasn't about to discourage her. "Do you want your toys?" she asked.

Christie rolled her eyes. "Of course."

Erin grinned, then handed her the net bag containing all her bathtub entertainment. She left the bathroom door open and stepped into the bedroom. The sound of splashing followed her.

Joyce glanced at her watch. "I should be going."

"I wish you hadn't rented a car. I would have been happy to drive you to San Francisco."

"No, it's too far. Christie was cooped up in the car enough on the way up here. I'll be fine." Joyce smiled. "Besides, I rented a convertible. A far cry from my sensible import back home, but it is just for the day."

"You'll be okay?"

Joyce touched her oversize handbag. "I've got maps and the number of Dan's hotel. I'll be fine."

Erin looked at her friend. Joyce was a stereotypical California girl with blond hair and blue eyes, and a petite figure that made her the envy of most of her friends. If she hadn't been a genuinely nice person, someone would have done her in years ago. She taught at the same school with Erin. When Erin had first mentioned driving up to meet Christie's father, Joyce had offered to tag along to spell the driving and to baby-sit if needed. Then she would hop down to San Francisco and spend a week with her fiancé who was there on business.

"You're sure about this guy?" Joyce asked, obviously reluctant to leave.

Erin crossed the room and gave her friend a hug. "I would never put Christie in danger. Parker Hamilton is a very nice man. A little reclusive, but that's not a horrible fault. He seems genuinely excited to meet his daughter. Christie needs this."

Joyce hugged her back, then stared at her. "You always worry about what Christie needs, but who worries about what you need?"

"Me? I'm fine."

"You're twenty-seven years old, and you're living like a nun."

"I happen to like living like a nun."

Joyce laughed. "Don't lie to me. You hate it. You have to. It's not easy being responsible for everything yourself. I just wish—"

Erin returned to the double bed by the door and sank onto the mattress. "You wish what?"

"I wish it had turned out differently."

Erin shook her head. Off-key singing floated out of the bathroom. Christie was mangling a song she learned at her preschool.

"I don't want to change anything," Erin said. "I know you have trouble believing me, but it's true. Christie is the best part of my life."

"She's a wonderful little girl, but you need more."

"Agreed. When there's time."

"You have to make time." Joyce glanced at her watch again. "Speaking of which, I've got to get going. You have the name of the hotel?"

"Yes. And if there's any problem, I'll be on the phone instantly." She made an *X* over her heart. "I swear."

"Have fun," Joyce admonished.

"That, too."

Her friend waved, then stepped out of the motel room and shut the door behind her.

"Are you doing okay?" Erin called.

"Yes, Mommy," Christie answered.

Erin stood up and crossed to the open suitcase on the dresser. Most of her daughter's things had already been packed. Her suitcase was on the bed. She walked over to it and dug under a couple of sweaters for her sister's diary, then sat back on the mattress.

Erin knew she hadn't been completely honest with Joyce. If she could, she would change one thing about her past. She would change Stacey's death. Even five years later, she still missed her twin. They'd spent four years going to different colleges, but Erin had always felt connected. Now she could never shake the feeling that a piece of her was gone. After twenty-two years of being half of a pair of identical twins, she'd been left alone.

The leather-bound diary was cool to the touch. When she'd found the journal she hadn't been able to read more than a few entries. The familiar handwriting made her miss Stacey more than ever. Now reading the words brought her sister back to life. Erin flipped it open, randomly turning pages until Parker's name caught her eye. She began to read.

Parker gave us an introductory session this afternoon. There are five other interns, four guys and one really mousy-looking nineteen-year-old in thick glasses. I don't think he'll notice her.

Erin skipped the paragraphs about the programs Stacey had been so excited to work on. There were details about schedules, then she found Parker's name again.

I sat next to him at dinner. I know Erin would laugh if I told her, but I was too excited to eat. He's very handsome, yet it's more than that. It's the sadness in his eyes. It calls to me. I want to hold him and heal him until he smiles again. My blood races whenever I'm near him. It's as if he's my destiny and I am his.

The next sentence had been obliterated by thick strokes of black pen. No matter how Erin held the page up to the light, she couldn't make out the words.

I've fallen for him. Love has made me a giddy fool. I'm trying hard to be sensible, but part of me doesn't want to be. I want to feel the romance and the magic. I want my blood to race and my heart to pound. I want to feel the heat of his hand against my skin.

Erin slammed the diary shut. She was feeling some heat of her own, but it came from the flush of embarrassment on her cheeks.

"How you doing?" she called.

"I'm fine." Christie's voice was patient. They went through this ritual every time she bathed. The four-year-old liked to have her playtime with her tub toys. Erin didn't mind, but she needed to hear splashing and singsong conversation to know that her daughter was doing all right in the water.

She placed the diary on the bed and covered her face with her hands. Why was this happening? She wasn't the young romantic innocent Stacey had been. She was a mature woman, a single parent, a respected teacher. She was stronger than this. Falling apart when she was around Parker Hamilton wasn't an option.

Easier said than done, she thought, remembering the heat she, too, had felt when Parker had touched her. What was going on? Why did Stacey's diary make sense? Why was she experiencing the same reaction around the same man? She wasn't the emotional sister. She wasn't the romantic one. She'd always been practical and logical. After all, when the girls had realized there wasn't enough money for both of them to go to the college of their choice, Erin had been the one to figure out if they left some of the money in for an additional four years, then one could go away to college and one could go away to graduate school.

She knew she had a brain, so why wasn't it working now? *You're living like a nun.*

Joyce's words came back to haunt her. For the most part Erin didn't miss having a man in her life. She never met anyone special enough to make her heart race or her blood...

Don't think about it, she ordered herself. It wasn't important. She wasn't really caught up in some situation that forced her to re-live her sister's life. The point was, she just hadn't had time to date. Obviously that was the problem. Parker was the first good-looking, single guy she'd been around since college. Of course she had a reaction to him. It didn't mean anything except that maybe it was time to dump the nun act and start behaving like a woman. Not around him, but around someone safer.

"You all right?" she called, listening to the splashing.

"Yes, Mommy." Christie's voice was slightly less patient.

She would get her feelings under control, she told herself firmly. She would stop reacting like...like...like *Stacey* and start acting more like herself. Otherwise she was going to say or do something foolish. That would only make an awkward situation worse. After all, Parker hadn't once hinted he found her attractive.

He'd been attracted to Stacey, a voice in her head whispered, and you look just like her. But had he been attracted to Stacey? Stacey's diary was full of romance and melodrama, but nothing very substantive. How much of their relationship had been in her sister's head?

However they *had* been lovers.

Erin opened the diary to the last page and stared at the photograph there. She'd tucked it next to the half-finished letter she'd found in the diary. She wasn't sure why. She didn't usually travel with pictures of her sister in her luggage, but it had seemed important to bring one of Stacey on this trip.

She smiled at the silliness of that thought. If she wanted to remember Stacey all she had to do was look in the mirror.

Even so, she picked up the photo and stared at her twin. Stacey wore her hair long, she always had. Erin preferred it short. They had the same features, the same smile, the same dimple. Erin had a tiny scar on her forehead from a run-in with a coffee table when she was about Christie's age. The sisters had always weighed the same and although they shared clothes, they hadn't dressed alike if they could avoid it.

"I'm fine, Mommy," Christie yelled from the bathroom.

"Thank you."

Erin stretched out on the bed next to the suitcase and wondered what had happened.

"Why did you do this?" she whispered to the photo.

As her fingers clutched the small picture, she knew the answer. There was no voice from the great beyond or psychic connection. She didn't need that. She'd known her sister as well as she'd known herself. She could read between the lines.

Stacey had wanted to fall in love with Parker from the first moment she saw him. The handsome, brooding stranger was her fantasy come to life. The fact that his house was a stunning mansion fit for a modern-day princess and the knowledge that he mourned the loss of his wife would only have added to Stacey's desire to make it real.

The twins had lost their parents at an early age. Going from relative to relative had left them with an emptiness that could only be filled by having a place to belong. Erin assumed she would find a man and fall in love one day, but in the meantime, the emptiness would have to be filled with friends, activities and self-confidence. Stacey had wanted to be rescued. Like a damsel in distress, she waited for the handsome prince on a white horse. Parker had fit her dream perfectly.

"Oh, Stacey," Erin murmured, aching for her sister, knowing the pain she must have felt.

She sat up and studied the photo for a moment, then tucked it into the diary. The letter fell out. Erin picked it up and unfolded the single page.

Dear Parker,
I don't know where to begin, so I'll just say I'm sorry. I'm so ashamed of myself. Of what I did and how I acted. I see now that you were right about everything. I don't know what love is. I hope someday I'll find what you had with Robin.

In the meantime, I regret to tell you that I'm pregnant. That night, well, I lied about being on the pill. I was so afraid you would stop if I told you the truth. The problem is, I don't know what to do now.

Please forgive me, Parker. I'm going to have our baby. I'm sure that makes you angry. Maybe I won't do anything today. Maybe I'll wait and tell you after the child is born. Then you can decide what you want to do.

Erin folded the letter and placed it in the diary next to the photo. Stacey hadn't lived long enough to do anything about telling Parker the truth.

"I hope I'm doing the right thing," Erin whispered as she listened to Christie play in the tub. "I hope I'm doing what you would have wanted me to do."

Chapter Five

"**Y**ou weren't kidding about the room being on the top floor," Erin said as she paused on the landing to catch her breath and stared up at the last flight of stairs.

Parker was right behind her. He set the suitcases down and frowned. "There are plenty of bedrooms on the second floor. Why don't you look through them and see if there's something you like?"

She gave him a quick smile, then shook her head. "Christie has her heart set on staying up here, and I don't want to disappoint her."

"You could leave her up here and take a different room for yourself." Kiki was right. He did have enough bedrooms to sleep a regiment. He supposed keeping the house was a mistake but he couldn't imagine living anywhere else.

"Your room is on the second floor, right?" Erin asked.

"Yes, but—"

She cut him off before he could explain there was no reason for her to be concerned about them sleeping on the same floor. Then he reminded himself that all she had to go on was what had happened with her sister. No wonder Erin was wary of him.

"This is a strange house to Christie," Erin said. "She's having a great adventure and enjoying everything, especially meeting you. But later, when she's sleepy and tired, she might get scared or have a bad dream. It's better if I'm across the hall and can hear her call out."

"I hadn't thought of that," he admitted, following her as she climbed the last flight of stairs. Raising a child was a daunting task full of potential pitfalls he couldn't begin to see.

She reached the third floor and paused. "It's so beautiful," she whispered.

He looked down the corridor. All the bedroom doors stood open. Sunlight spilled onto the hallway's polished wooden floor. It bounced out of each of the bedrooms and beamed through the large window in the far end wall. There were abstract paintings between the doors, and a small deacon's bench by the landing.

"I didn't realize how large this place was," she said, her voice laced with awe.

"Some bedrooms up here are smaller," he said. "But much of the construction follows the roof line, so they have more character. The one Christie chose is down at the end."

They walked slowly. Erin stopped and stuck her head into each room as they passed it. "There aren't any bathrooms," she said, then glanced at him over her shoulder. "I'm sorry but I don't do the chamber pot thing."

"No problem. The bathrooms are between bedrooms. See that door on the right?"

She leaned in the room further, then nodded. "So every two rooms share."

"That's right. With you and Christie on opposite sides of the hall, you'll each have your own."

Kiki came out of the room at the very end. She paused when she saw Erin. "I've changed the linens and there are plenty of fresh towels in the bathroom." She reached into the pocket of her jogging suit pants and pulled out a small plastic box. "I gave Christie a night-light in her bedroom and bath; yours is just in the bath. If you want an extra let me know. I'm going to put one here by your door then another at the end of the hall. It gets dark here at night." She paused to draw a breath.

"Thank you," Erin said. "You're being very generous. We'll be fine."

"Well if you need anything, just let me know."

Kiki was still offering to be of assistance as Parker moved past her. He walked to the room Christie had chosen and paused in the doorway.

The room was oddly shaped, an *L* with a bulbous end. Windows allowed light in on two walls. There were built-in seats with puffy cushions and small bookcases. A bed had been pushed up against the wall nearest the door. To the left was the closet and the entrance to the tiled bathroom. Around to the right was the reason Christie had chosen the room in the first place.

Parker supposed this had once been the schoolroom and the adjoining area had been for play. He set both suitcases down and walked toward the octagonally shaped alcove.

Small paned windows ran from floor to ceiling. In between them, built-in shelves and cubbyholes filled the walls. There was an old-fashioned rocking horse and a playhouse big enough for Christie to live in.

When he and Robin had bought this house, they'd talked about the babies they wanted and how much fun those children would have in this room. After she was gone, Parker had almost gutted the floor and started over. But he'd never had the time. Now he was glad. He wanted Christie to enjoy staying with him. He was only going to have her for a small part of her life so he had to make every minute count.

She was staring out the windows at the ocean.

"At night the stars come out," he said. "They are bright and clear but there are too many to count."

She spun toward him, a small ragged teddy bear clutched in her arms. Big eyes got bigger. "Daddy, this is the bestest room in the whole world. I'll love it forever."

She rushed toward him. Parker barely had time to brace himself before she plowed into his legs and held on firmly. An uncomfortable and unfamiliar tightness wrapped around his chest.

"I'm glad you're here, too," he said, his voice a little thick. "I want you to be happy here."

"I will be." She looked up and smiled. "And I'll be very good."

He touched the tip of her nose. "I'm sure you will be."

"Parker, this is amazing," Erin said.

Christie released him and raced to her mother. She grabbed her hand and tugged her around the bed toward the play area. "Mommy, look at this. You can see the ocean and at night Daddy says there's stars. There's a rocking horse and a playhouse and a place for all my toys." Her whole body vibrated with joy.

Erin looked around, then raised her gaze to him. "I'm stunned. I knew the house was fabulous, but I wasn't expecting anything like this."

"These were all here when we bought the place," he said, motioning to the wooden playhouse. "Most of the upstairs furniture is original."

"But it's in such good shape." She moved closer to the rocking horse and touched its flowing mane.

Parker suspected the toy had been carved by hand. The craftsmanship alone made it functional art. The paint used to highlight the eyes and saddle had muted with time, but it wasn't flaking.

"The house had been unoccupied but well cared for when we bought it. It must have been standing empty for nearly twenty years. Everything had been covered up or stored. Every sheet we pulled off exposed a new treasure. It was like Christmas."

She tilted her head the same way Christie had the previous day. Her reddish brown hair brushed against her shoulder. "We?" she asked, obviously confused.

"I—" The sharp pain was familiar. He welcomed the connection to the past. "My late wife and I."

"Oh. Of course. I should have realized." She started back toward the door. "It's very lovely here. You've been quite generous with your home. Christie and I appreciate it."

He knew he'd upset her, but he wasn't sure why. "Erin, please don't think you have to watch what you say. It's been over five years since Robin died. You're not going to accidentally touch a nerve."

"I'm glad," she said and paused by her daughter.

Christie had opened the smaller of the two suitcases and was pulling out her clothing. Small T-shirts and sweaters, jeans, socks and a couple of dresses were piled on the bed.

"This is Millie," Christie said removing a soft doll with an oversize head and brown yarn pigtails. She sat the doll on the bed, propping her up on the pile of clothing. "She's my favoritest, next to my teddy. I've got books, too." She slapped them down next to the doll.

Parker perched on the edge of the mattress. "There's a library here."

"I know." Christie gave him a wide smile. "It's in the same room with the picture of the pretty lady."

"No, there's another one. On the next floor down. When we bought the house, we got the library, too. These are old books. I never went through them but I wouldn't be surprised if there are some for children."

"Really?" Christie stood up. "Let's go look."

He laughed. "The books aren't going anywhere. Why don't you finish unpacking?"

"You think I should?"

"Yes, I do."

"Okay." She dropped to her knees and continued flinging things out of her suitcase. A nightgown sailed across the bed and settled next to him. He stared at the small bit of cotton. It was pink with a picture of a kitten on the front. He touched the ruffle on the edge of the sleeve.

Her clothing was so small, but then so was she. Four years old. He tried to imagine how tiny she must have been when she was born, but the thought terrified him. He shuddered. She was fragile enough now.

She tossed up more toys. Other dolls were introduced. The rules of a board game explained. He noticed Erin had left, but he couldn't say when. He appreciated all she was doing for him. Not many women would have given him the chance to get to know his child. Watching Christie laugh and talk he decided it didn't matter what this cost him financially. It would be worth it.

"Where's the dresser?" Christie asked when the suitcase was empty.

"Over there," he said, pointing behind the door.

"Okay, I'll put these away and you can hang my dresses." She thrust three at him.

He took them and walked to the closet. There were several empty hangers. He took one and slid it into the first dress. His hands were large, his fingers awkward, yet he relished the simple task. Christie continued to chatter away, talking to him and to her dolls, including everyone in the conversation.

When he was done, he moved back to the bed and touched the top of her head. "I'm going to check on your mom."

"Okay. I'm going to read." She waved one of her books at him, then climbed on the bed. Most of her clothing was still scattered in a pile. Toys were everywhere. In less than ten minutes, the room had gone from perfect order to chaos. He couldn't have been happier.

He crossed the hall and knocked on the open door. This room was larger and faced the ocean. Christie's only view of the sea was from the play area. A large four-poster bed stood in the center of the room. The mattress was new, but everything else was original furniture. The sensual lines and rounded corners were in keeping with the time period.

A large vanity stood against the far wall. The fabric of the rich burgundy brocade-covered stool matched the bedspread and curtains. The walls were white, the starkness broken by small cameo portraits hanging from ribbons, and a window seat under a picture window.

Erin came in from the bathroom and saw him. "It's lovely," she said. "I adore the view."

"If you're lucky, we'll have a storm while you're here. They can be pretty impressive this close to the ocean."

She glanced out the window. "I would like to see that."

"Do you have all that you need?" he asked.

"Yes. You and Kiki have thought of everything."

He leaned against the doorjamb and folded his arms over his chest. "I had nothing to do with it. I think Kiki was a general in her previous life. She's always prepared and always has a plan. Sometimes it makes me nervous."

She smiled at him. Sunlight poured through the windows illuminating her. The rays turned her hair to the color of flame and outlined her feminine shape. She wore a hip-length red sweater over stone-washed jeans. He caught a hint of curves at her hips and her breasts. A flicker of awareness sparked to life inside of him. By force of habit, he quickly snuffed it out. He hadn't allowed himself to be interested in a woman since Robin had died.

"Is Christie unpacked?" she asked.

"Everything is out of her suitcase, which isn't exactly the same thing."

"I can imagine. She is only four, so she doesn't have too much of an attention span. I'll go over in a minute and put the rest of her clothes away."

Erin moved to the bed and picked up a couple of books. She set them on the nightstand.

"Christie showed me all *her* toys," he said. "Did you bring anything interesting?"

He'd meant the remark to be teasing, something to ease the tension he felt between them. But instead of laughing, she flushed. The awareness he'd squashed just a minute before returned, this time hotter and brighter.

"I don't have much time to play," she said.

"Maybe you should change that. You're on vacation for the next couple of weeks. There's plenty to do around here. Hiking, bike riding. There's even a movie theater in town. I'd be happy to watch Christie if you want to go sometime."

She looked at him oddly. "Please don't think you have to entertain me. I know I'm here because of Christie and not because you want the pleasure of my company."

He winced. "I didn't mean it like that."

"But it is the truth."

Sometimes the truth wasn't pleasant. He watched her graceful movements as she took out a couple of sweaters and carried them to the dresser. He found himself concentrating on the sway of her hips as she walked.

What the hell was wrong with him? He'd never had a problem resisting a woman before. Of course he worked at home and didn't come into contact with many. Was it because he had been alone five years and Erin was simply here? Or was it something else? Was it about Stacey and the fact that Erin was her twin? Had he secretly been attracted to Stacey that summer, yet had tried to hide the truth from himself?

It didn't matter, he reminded himself. He'd learned his lesson and he wasn't going to ever forget it. Getting close to someone was too risky. He destroyed those who got close to him, so for the safety of others, he'd learned to keep his distance.

He pushed off the door frame. "Please ask Kiki or me for anything you need," he said.

"Thanks." She opened a small black case and pulled out an expensive looking camera. "I'm sure we'll be fine."

"I didn't know you were a photographer," he said.

"Oh, I'm not. I just take snapshots of Christie. If you don't mind, I'd like to take a few of the house."

"Feel free." His gaze settled on the camera. "That's fancy equipment for snapshots."

"I suppose it is."

He lingered for a moment but when it became obvious that she wasn't going to say anything else, he left and started down the hallway. The camera was just a symbol of their problem, he thought. There was so much he didn't know about Erin Ridgeway. Who was this woman who had given up her life to raise someone else's child?

Parker nervously followed Erin down the hall. The sun hadn't quite set yet, so it was still light. In Christie's room, someone had drawn the drapes, giving the illusion of darkness. A small night-light glowed by the open door as he stepped inside.

Christie was on her side in bed and she smiled when she saw him. "I'm not very tired," she said.

Erin had already warned him that Christie would try to get out of going to bed at her regular time. He sat on the edge of the mattress and stared at the girl.

"I'm tired," he said. "This was an exciting day. You moved here and unpacked your things. We played on the beach." Her hair was loose. He'd never seen it out of pigtails. He touched the silky strands marveling at the perfection that was his child. "Millie is already asleep." He motioned to the doll nestled in her arms.

"Dolls don't sleep," she said with the authority of an expert.

"Of course they do. Everything sleeps, even flowers."

"Flowers?" She rolled on her back and looked up at him. "When do they sleep?"

"In the winter."

Her gaze was trusting, as if she knew he would never hurt her or lie to her. He vowed he would rather die than let her down.

"Now go to sleep," he said. "The quicker you do, the quicker tomorrow will get here. We'll do something fun together."

"Okay." The word was punctuated by a yawn. "'Night, Daddy," she murmured, her eyelids drifting closed.

"Good night." He sat there for a moment, then bent over and kissed her cheek. His heart thudded painfully as the band across his chest tightened.

He wanted to sit here and watch her sleep, but he knew Erin was waiting for him in the hall. He rose to his feet and silently crossed the room.

"She's already out," he said.

"I knew she would be. She protests going to bed then falls asleep in about a minute. Sometimes I'm surprised it takes that long. She uses so much energy in her day."

They walked to the end of the hall and started down the stairs. "She looks so small in bed," he said.

Erin chuckled. "I think you're right. While she's running and doing, she's seems almost grown-up. But at night, sometimes I think she shrinks."

They were still laughing when they reached the bottom of the stairs. Kiki came out of the dining room and walked toward him. Parker noticed she'd changed out of her jogging suit and was wearing a frilly cotton dress. Her tanned legs were bare, and instead of athletic shoes, she had on high-heel sandals.

"Another big night?" he asked.

Kiki ignored him. "Erin, I'll be back later. Let Parker know if you need anything. What time do you usually have breakfast?"

"You don't need to cook for us."

"Honey, that's my job. I would guess Christie probably wakes up around seven?"

"Usually."

"Then I'll have something ready for seven-thirty. Bye." She wiggled her fingers at them, then walked to the front door. A few minutes later a car drove off.

"Kiki often goes out at night," Parker said, then motioned to the terrace. "You want to sit outside and watch the sunset?"

"Ah, sure."

She sounded a little nervous. Parker wondered if it was because they were alone together, or if she was waiting for him to stick his foot in his mouth again.

He led her to one of the chaise lounges pushed off to the side.

"How about some wine?" he said. "There's some white already chilled."

"Okay." Her hazel eyes were dark with confusion.

He went into the kitchen and got a bottle out of the refrigerator. After pulling out the cork, he grabbed two glasses and returned to the terrace. Erin had perched uneasily on the edge of the lounge.

She'd changed for dinner. If he'd known she was going to he would have told her not to bother. Neither he nor Kiki was interested in being formal. Erin wore a soft silky white shirt tucked into beige tailored trousers. A thin belt emphasized her narrow waist.

He poured the wine and handed her a glass, then sat in the chaise lounge across from hers. After setting the wine bottle between them, he leaned over and touched the rim of his glass to hers.

"To Christie," he said.

"Christie," she repeated softly, but did not drink.

He leaned back in his chair. "Are you settled in your room?"

"Yes."

He studied the horizon, the last sliver of sun still visible and the golden glow on the restless ocean. "Why are you nervous?"

"Is it that obvious?"

"I don't consider myself very observant, so if I noticed, it must be."

She laughed. "Oh, that made me feel better. Thanks."

He looked at her. "At least you don't look so scared anymore."

The humor faded from her face. She stared at the glass of wine. "The situation is a little awkward. I thought I'd planned everything when I decided to bring Christie to meet you. I was wrong. I didn't realize all the details to be worked out, or the logistics of two strangers dealing with a child."

"I'd like you to be comfortable here, Erin. Tell me anything you want, even if you just want to be left alone. I'd like us to be friends."

She raised her gaze to his. Emotions flickered through her hazel irises. Was she remembering what he'd done to her sister? Did those actions five years ago mean that she would never trust him?

"I'd like that, too," she said softly.

A last glimmer of sunlight touched her face and high-lighted the curve of her cheek. For that moment, her skin was iridescent and she looked like a beautiful creature from another world.

She set her glass on the stone terrace and folded her hands in her lap. "Maybe we should talk and get to know each other. You must have some questions about Christie."

What he wanted to ask was if there was a man in Erin's life. He swore silently. No, he didn't want to know that, because it wasn't important. Concentrate on the child. She was all that mattered.

"Who named her?" he asked instead.

"Stacey."

"She had—" He hesitated. "She had time to do that?"

Erin nodded. "Those couple of days are a blur. I remember getting a call from the hospital. I'd just finished my last final exam and was starting to pack to come home. The nurse told me that the baby was doing fine, but Stacey wasn't. Could I come right away? I was stunned. I didn't even know Stacey was pregnant."

"You don't have to tell me this," he said.

"Don't you want to know what happened?"

He didn't. Hearing the words made the images clear. For now he would just listen, but later he would feel the guilt. Still, there was no way to stop her.

"Tell me everything," he said, knowing he would pay for that.

Erin drew in a deep breath. She laced her fingers to-gether and stared at him intently. "When I got to the hos-pital, she was dying. Thank goodness she came home to have the baby, or I would never have arrived in time. I re-member how pale she was and all the tubes they had hooked up to her. There had been some problems. They tried to save her, of course, but . . .''

Her gaze never left his. He wanted to look away, but he couldn't. He wondered what she read on his face. Did she know how he blamed himself? Did she know he wasn't surprised about any of this?

"Stacey whispered that she'd seen the baby for a minute and named her Christie. She—'' Erin swallowed hard and looked away. "She said she was sorry for doing this to me, but there was no one else. I asked her to tell me about the father. She wouldn't say anything except it would be wrong to bother him. You, I mean. Then she died.''

Parker's gut clenched as the guilt washed over him like an acid bath. It burned him clear down to his soul. He'd known he was responsible for Robin's death and now he'd killed Stacey, too. How much longer would this go on? Who else would he inadvertently destroy?

"It's not your fault,'' Erin said.

He stared at her.

"It's not,'' she repeated. "Stacey didn't blame you, and you mustn't blame yourself. It wasn't anyone's fault, it just happened.''

"How can you be so sure?'' he asked, standing up and walking to the edge of the terrace. "You weren't here that summer. You don't know what happened between us.''

"I know it wasn't your fault,'' she said a third time.

"Yeah, right.'' If only that were true. If only the ghosts of the dead would leave him be. He clutched the edge of the balcony.

She followed him, then reached into her trouser pocket and pulled out a folded sheet of paper. "Stacey wrote this to you, but she never got a chance to mail it. I think she'd want you to have it now.''

He stared at the paper a long time before he finally took it and turned it over in his hands. He wasn't sure he wanted to know what she'd written, but he didn't think he had a choice in the matter.

When he'd unfolded the note, he quickly scanned the contents. In his mind he heard her voice speaking the words and realized she sounded different than Erin. Stacey's voice was higher and faster. More intense, like the woman herself.

She wrote that she was sorry for what she did to him. He wished he could tell her he was sorry, too. For the harsh words he'd hurled at her that morning. If he could he would tell her that he'd been angry with himself, not with her. But it had been easier to direct his rage at someone else.

I regret to tell you that I'm pregnant. He swore silently. That was his fault, too. Not just the baby, but the regret.

He started to hand the letter back to Erin, but she shook her head. "You keep it."

"For what it's worth," he said. "I didn't mean to be such a bastard."

"Don't blame yourself, Parker. We used to laugh together at the odd personality quirk that made her gifted with computers and so completely illogical in her personal life. We lost our parents when we were young and we were shuttled between different relatives. We never had a real home, but we used to dream about one. Oddly enough, your house is pretty close to what we'd imagined. Stacey was intrigued from the moment she arrived."

"How do you know?"

"Her diary. After she died, I was so busy with Christie I asked one of our friends to pack up Stacey's things. It wasn't until a few months ago when I was packing to move that I finally went through the boxes. I found her diary and your name."

What else had she said aside from his name? He wanted to know but didn't think he had the right to ask.

The sun had finally set and the sky was that murky color of twilight blue. The first stars glinted in the heavens. Surf pounded against the shore in an age-old rhythm.

"She saw you as the dark prince of her fantasies," Erin said. "Please don't be angry with her."

"Stacey was the innocent in all this, Erin. The only person I'm angry with is myself." Dark prince. Hell, he didn't belong in anyone's fantasy.

"Stop blaming yourself."

"There's no one else. Did Stacey ever stop to consider how dangerous a dark prince could be? After all he's first cousin to the devil."

"Stacey would have liked that."

Then Stacey was a fool. But he didn't say that aloud. Stacey had been foolish and young and inexperienced. He'd been in too much pain to notice. Surviving had taken everything he'd had. Otherwise he could have taken care of the situation before it became a problem.

Erin touched his arm. "Don't you see? This isn't about you, it's about her. She expected something very specific from you. She would have taken your words and twisted them around until they had the meaning she wanted."

He looked at her. The few lights from the house didn't reach this far on the terrace and they were both in shadow. He couldn't see her clearly, but he could feel her heat and inhale the floral scent of her perfume. Her hand was warm and sure on his forearm.

"Why are you defending me?" he asked. "You don't even know me. You weren't here. You don't know what happened."

"I've read her diary. I know what she wanted, and I know my sister. I'm not absolving you of blame. Of course some of this is your fault. It takes two to—" She paused and her hand fell to her side. "I think it's time to put the past behind you. You feel badly for what you did, but Stacey wanted a relationship with you and she wasn't going to let anything stand in the way. Not even reality."

He wanted to believe her. Maybe one day he would. Just not tonight.

"If you don't mind, I'm going to go up to my office. Help yourself to the television in the study or the books," he said.

"I'll be fine." He heard the smile in her voice.

"Let me know if you need anything."

"I will."

He took a single step away, then turned back to her. "I know you didn't have to bring Christie here. I'm glad you did."

Without stopping to consider it wasn't a smart idea, he bent forward to kiss her cheek. At the last second, he tilted his head and brushed his mouth against hers.

She jumped, obviously startled, but didn't pull away. Neither did he. He couldn't. The fire that leapt between them consumed his will and his ability to think. He could only feel. Passion swept through him. Passion and desire and need. The parts of him he'd thought long dead boiled painfully to life.

Finally he raised his head and stared at her. In the darkness he could see little more than the shape of her head. He didn't know what she was thinking. Dammit, he didn't want to know. He only wanted to erase what he'd just done.

Without a word, he turned and walked away. But even as he climbed the stairs to his office, the fire continued to burn low in his belly. As if it were a slumbering beast who had accidentally been awakened, the need demanded attention and release. He sensed with a growing certainty that this time it would not be ignored.

Chapter Six

Erin gave up pretending to sleep at about five-thirty in the morning. She'd done fine when she'd first gone to bed, drifting off with a dopey smile on her lips. Then about midnight she'd awakened suddenly, jerked into consciousness by a frantic dream she couldn't remember.

Since then she'd tossed and turned. Trying to think soothing thoughts didn't help. Trying to think about Parker had only made matters worse, because once she'd started recalling the previous evening she hadn't been able to think about anything else.

Maybe it was the terrace, Erin thought as she stood up and stretched. The worn stones, the vines climbing the side of the house, the scent of the ocean and the sound of the surf on the shore. It was a living, breathing romantic post-card and she was stuck in the center of the picture. So much for being the more logical of the twins.

Maybe it was the man himself, but Erin didn't want that to be true. If only they'd kept the conversation on Stacey and Christie where it belonged. If only she could stop thinking about him. If only he hadn't kissed her.

That kiss. That damn kiss. It had been so unexpected. One minute they'd been calmly talking and the next he'd excused himself to go work in his office. On the way out, he'd kissed her. As if it were a common occurrence.

Had he meant to? Did it mean anything?

Yes, it means something, she told herself. *It means you're losing your mind.*

She crossed to the bathroom and quickly washed her face. After brushing her teeth and combing her hair into sleek order, she returned to the bedroom and dressed. A quick peek out the curtained window showed her that the sky was still dark. There was no hint of the sunrise so she couldn't tell what kind of day it was going to be. She walked into the closet and grabbed a pair of jeans. Mornings were usually cool at the beach.

Five minutes later she poked her head in to check on her daughter. Christie was sound asleep, her worn teddy bear tucked under her arm. Erin adjusted the covers, then started along the hallway. The old house seemed to creak with her every step. She crept down the stairs, holding her breath and keeping to the side by the wall. As she passed the second floor, she wondered which room was Parker's. She hadn't been with Christie during the tour of the upstairs of the house.

She tried not to think of him sleeping, but trying wasn't enough. Pictures of him in bed—what did he wear, if anything at all?—flashed through her mind. Her lips tingled as if he'd just repeated the brief kiss.

"Forget it," she said softly as she reached the first floor and walked toward the kitchen. Three lights on the terrace shone through the living room windows and illuminated her way.

"He's not interested in you," she went on, trying to talk some sense into herself. "He's made that clear. It was just a thank-you sort of kiss. Meaningless." Except in her suddenly unruly mind.

It *was* the terrace, she decided as she entered the kitchen, flipped on the light switch and started looking for the coffeemaker. There was no other explanation. She wasn't melodramatic or romantic. That had been Stacey's problem. She loved her sister dearly but had never understood her need for drama. Life had a certain rhythm. People took turns. It was balanced and orderly.

She found the coffeepot and the coffee, then poured in the water and sat on a stool to wait. The kitchen was large and bright with big windows overlooking the side garden. Unlike the rest of the house, this room had been completely modernized. Oak cabinets and new appliances lined three walls. The huge center island had a cook top and a sink as well as an eating area running along one side. The cobalt blue bar stool seat cushions matched the tile splash guard along the stretch of wall between the counters and the cabinets.

The smell of coffee revived her. Erin leaned on the counter and wondered why this was happening to her. What was it about the situation that made her act so out of character? She'd always been so calm about everything, taking things as they came, waiting until the time was right, until it was appropriate to respond. Waiting for her turn. Unlike Stacey, she'd never grabbed at life with both hands.

The coffee finished dripping. She slid off the stool to get a cup at the same moment the back door opened. Kiki stepped inside and the two women stared at each other.

Erin registered several facts at once. First, Kiki wasn't wearing the dress she'd had on the previous night although she recognized it as the garment slung over the housekeeper's arm. Second, the pink jogging suit was the exact color of the blush climbing the other woman's cheeks. Third, there was the distinctive sound of a car driving away.

Kiki recovered first. "The coffee smells great."

"Help yourself."

"Don't mind if I do." She set the dress and her purse on the small table in front of the window, then walked over to the cupboard above the pot and pulled down a cup.

Erin stared at her. "Are you just now getting in?"

"Why, yes."

"But it's nearly six in the morning."

"I know, dear." Kiki held out the pot. "Do you want some?"

"What? Oh, thank you." She waited while the housekeeper poured coffee then added cream into the steaming liquid, and glanced at the other woman. Kiki was getting home at six in the morning? She'd been out all night?

"I'm always available to baby-sit," Kiki said, "but in the past, if Parker didn't need me in the evening, I went out." She took a sip of her coffee, then smiled. "Don't look so shocked."

"Do I?" Erin resumed her seat on the stool. "I don't mean to be. It's great that you have a . . . life."

Kiki settled next to her. She grinned. "What you mean is that it's nice that I have a man. It's true what they say, you know. Life does begin at forty. I've been living mine for nearly fourteen years."

"You've been dating the same man for fourteen years?"

Kiki laughed. "Honey, no. Not the same man. Several men. I go out, I enjoy myself. Sometimes I don't come home before dawn."

Great, the housekeeper had a more interesting life than she did, Erin thought glumly. Joyce had been right. She was living like a nun.

"What's his name?" Erin asked.

Kiki leaned one elbow on the counter and looked at her. Bright blond hair fell over the housekeeper's forehead. Lines crinkled around her blue eyes as she smiled. "Which one?"

"How many are there?"

"Three."

Three? "Three different men?"

"You're looking shocked again. It's not all that uncommon."

"It is to me."

"You young people are so conservative. You should live a little. Play the field. I recommend it highly."

Erin thought about that for a minute. She hadn't had a date since Christie was born, and Kiki was keeping company with three different men. "Do they know about each other?"

"Of course." Kiki raised her hand and began ticking off fingers. "Dan is nearly sixty. His wife died a couple of years ago. He likes living by himself and doesn't plan to remarry. Still, a man has needs, so I see him once a week. Next is Roger. He's my age and he's divorced."

Erin made the mistake of taking a sip of her coffee while Kiki was talking. She swallowed it the wrong way and started choking. Kiki pounded her on the back, then waited politely until she was done.

"Better?" she asked when Erin finally caught her breath.

"Sure," Erin croaked. "Go on."

"I also see Roger once a week. Now Skip is my boy toy."

Erin had learned her lesson. This time the cup was only partway to her mouth. Coffee sloshed over the side, but she managed to keep it off her sweatshirt.

"You have a boy toy?"

"That's what I call him. Skip is younger, barely forty, I think, although he's never said. He's also divorced and not ready for a relationship. But he's a man, and a man has—"

"Needs. Yes, I've figured that part out."

"I see Skip at least twice a week." Kiki leaned forward and lowered her voice. "Younger men have more powers of recovery, if you know what I mean."

Erin felt a flush climb her cheeks. She cleared her throat. "Who were you with last night?"

Kiki sighed dramatically. "Skip. A few hours with him and I feel like a new woman."

"They know about each other and don't mind?"

"I'm very honest with them. Everyone is getting what he or she wants, so why would anyone mind? I'm discreet and careful. Skip and I even use condoms. Imagine, a woman of my age."

"Secretly you're nineteen," Erin muttered.

Kiki laughed. "I know."

"I've never known anyone like you."

Kiki's laughter faded. She slid off the stool and walked over to the cupboards. While she pulled out flour, spices and an open box of raisins she said, "Oh, I'm not so different from everyone else. I was thinking of cinnamon rolls for breakfast. Would you and Christie like that?"

Erin's stomach growled. "Sounds wonderful."

Kiki brought the ingredients to the opposite side of the center island. "Christie is a sweet girl. I'm sure she brings you a lot of joy."

"She does."

Kiki glanced up at her. Sadness filled her eyes. "I had a child once. A little boy. He died when he was twelve. A car hit him while he was riding his bike."

Erin's breath caught in her throat. "I'm so sorry," she whispered.

"It was a long time ago." Kiki began measuring out ingredients. "My marriage failed. Many do, you know, after the death of a child. There's so much suffering and need. I was clinically depressed for nearly three years. Then one day

I began to get better.'' She wiped her hands on a towel by the island sink. "One of the things that wore me down was the regrets. The things I should have said to my boy. All the places we could have gone.''

The animation fled her face leaving her looking old and tired. Erin ached for her. "Kiki, I—''

"No. Don't you worry about me. When I left that hospital, I swore to myself I wouldn't ever have regrets again, and I haven't.'' She smiled then, the skin by her eyes crinkling and her generous mouth turning up. "I live my life the way I want and there's not many who can say that.''

Kiki finished mixing the dough, then sprinkled flour on the counter and dug through the drawers for a rolling pin. Erin sipped coffee and watched her. She admired Kiki's spirit and willingness to go on despite the tragedy in her life. She remembered how immobilized she'd been after Stacey died. If it hadn't been for Christie, she didn't know what might have happened.

Did she have regrets? Erin wasn't sure. She couldn't regret Christie. The bright young child was so much a part of her life, she couldn't imagine a world without her. She was sorry she, Erin, hadn't gone on to graduate school. She'd had dreams of studying photography, of taking pictures that made people feel something. Stacey used to tease her about wanting to find her work in coffee table books across the country. Erin had been pleased by the idea. But after Christie entered her life there had been neither time nor money to pursue her dream.

Sometimes she regretted that she was so alone. She didn't miss any specific man, but it would be nice to have someone to share things with. Instantly her mind conjured up an image of Parker. Her lips tingled as she remembered their kiss.

It wasn't a kiss, she reminded herself. It was a brief peck, the kind one might give a distant relative. At least it was to him, and that's what mattered. It was one thing to have fantasies in the privacy of her own mind. It was quite another to try to force someone into making those fantasies come true.

Kiki sprinkled cinnamon and raisins on the dough, then rolled it up. "Sounds like someone else is up," she said.

Erin tilted her head. She could hear creaking from the stairs and the faint sound of laughter. She glanced at the clock and was surprised to find it was nearly seven.

"I hope Christie didn't wake up Parker," she said as she slid off the stool.

"Don't worry if she did. That man needs a little shaking up, and I think she's just the person to do it."

Erin gave her a quick grin, then left the kitchen and headed for the living room. As she crossed the hardwood floor, she glanced up. The sun had moved past the horizon and faint fingers of light filtered into the room. She could see the groupings of furniture and the stairs beyond.

Parker came into view, his long, lean legs moving easily. Christie sat on his shoulders. She clung to his head and squealed with delight.

"Mommy, Mommy, look at me!"

"I see you."

Parker and his daughter were laughing. Erin noticed their identical smiles and felt a faint twinge of discomfort. She'd known coming here and introducing Parker to his child would change everything. It had been the right decision, but nothing would ever be the same again. She would always be Christie's mother although now that precious love would be shared.

"You're up early," Parker said when he reached the bottom stair. "Couldn't you sleep?"

No, and it was his fault. She'd hoped that the hours of darkness would have given her a little perspective on the situation, but they didn't seem to have helped. He was just

as good-looking as he'd been yesterday. Worn jeans posses-
sively hugged his thighs. His flannel shirt had been washed
to the point of fading. It caressed his broad strength with the
clinging attention of a lover.

"I often have trouble sleeping in a new place," she said.

"I slept the whole night," Christie said.

He reached up and grabbed her under her arms.
"Ready?" he asked.

"Yes."

He lifted her over his head and lowered her to the floor.
Christie landed on her feet, then raced to give her mother a
hug. "I got dressed my own self," she said proudly.

Erin glanced at the red shorts and mismatched pink-and-
blue shirt. "I see that. You did a fine job."

"I even brushed my teeth." She opened her mouth to
show proof. Her dark hair stood up in little tufts, so she'd
forgotten that, but it was pretty good grooming for a four-
year-old.

"I checked your room, but you were gone," Christie
continued. "So I came downstairs. That's where I found
Daddy."

Parker gazed at her fondly. "I was already working when
I heard these very quiet footsteps."

"I can guess how quiet," Erin said. Parker didn't have a
problem meeting her eyes so apparently he wasn't spending
every other minute reliving their kiss. Forget it, she ordered
herself. Forget it before you make a fool of yourself.

Parker sniffed the air. "Ah, I see Kiki is making cinnamon rolls." He glanced at his watch. "I've got some work
to do this morning. What do you think about a picnic lunch
on the beach around noon?"

"I want to go to the beach *now,*" Christie said and
stomped her foot.

"But I have to work now."

"Why?"

He bent over and touched her head. "So I can pay for this house and the beach and our picnic lunch."

Christie looked up at him and wrinkled her nose. "Okay."

"Would you like that, Erin?" he asked.

"The picnic sounds great. I'll keep Christie quiet this morning."

"This might be a good time to check out the library on the second floor," he told her.

"We'll go investigate."

"Intestivate," Christie repeated.

"Almost," Erin told her. "Let's go eat breakfast."

She held out her hand and Christie took it. She tilted her head. "Are you coming, Daddy, or are you going to work now?"

"I'm going to work. Kiki will bring me some breakfast later."

"Okay, bye." She waved with her free hand, then turned and headed for the kitchen. "I didn't know my daddy was going to be this nice. I'm glad we found him."

Erin glanced over her shoulder and saw Parker staring after them. He must have heard Christie's comment. The masculine planes of his face were harsh with longing. Erin knew what his regret was—he regretted all the time he'd lost with this precious child.

The remains of their picnic lay scattered on the blanket. Kiki had prepared sandwiches and two different kinds of salad. The cookies had disappeared quickly. She'd even provided juice for Christie and wine for the adults.

Erin sat cross-legged on the blanket. A warm breeze ruffled her hair. The temperature was close to seventy-five, the sun was bright, the ocean a brilliant shade of blue.

"Ooh, it's so cold!" Christie screamed as the white foamy fingers of a wave tickled her bare feet. The ocean surged away from the shore, and she raced after it, only to shriek and run back when it flowed in again.

Parker had stretched out on his back, one hand under his head. His wineglass rested on his flat belly. He turned toward Christie. "If you see little bubbles in the sand, that means there are crabs hiding there."

"Really?" She bent over and checked for the narrow holes. "But I can't dig very fast." Her smile turned sly. "If I had a puppy I bet *he* could dig faster than any old crab."

"Nice try," Erin said. "It's not going to work, but it's a very nice try."

Christie raced toward them, swooped down and picked up the inflatable beach ball Kiki had unearthed from somewhere. It was bright yellow and nearly too big for Christie to hold. She flung it in the air and raced after it.

Parker continued to watch her for several minutes. "If you and Stacey are identical twins and Stacey is Christie's mother, what does that make you?"

"Her aunt and her legal guardian."

He turned his head until he was looking at her. "I know that. I was thinking about the biology. Genetically, aren't you more her mother than her aunt?"

"I'm not sure." She frowned. "I suppose I am. Identical twins share DNA. In theory I guess I could be her genetic mother."

Which raised another interesting theory. If she and Parker had a child together, they could have one exactly like Christie. Of course the odds were against it, but next time she couldn't sleep, she would mull it over in her mind. It sounded more interesting than counting sheep.

She reached for her wine.

"Did you legally adopt Christie?" he asked.

Her hand froze in midair as a shiver raced down her spine. "Why do you want to know?"

His mouth softened with concern. He stretched out his arm and grabbed her hand. "I didn't mean to upset you. I was curious not probing. I swear I have no plans to kidnap Christie or sue for custody."

His fingers squeezed hers. Awareness coursed through her easing away the fear. She liked the feel of him holding her hand. Foolishly it made her feel safe. She settled her gaze on his chest, watching the rise and fall from his breathing.

"I overreacted," she said. "I think it's this situation. Even though I tried to plan for everything, it's still very strange to be here with you, to watch you with Christie."

He gave her fingers a final squeeze, then released her. "She loves you. Nothing can change that."

"I know. Christie has a big heart. She could love the world." In the distance the little girl laughed and tossed her beach ball in the air.

"Robin and I talked about having children. We met in high school. We were both computer nerds back before it was popular." One corner of his mouth lifted in a smile. "Everyone thought she was kind of goofy looking, but I thought she was pretty."

A lock of dark hair fell across his forehead. She itched to push it in place. Instead she curled her fingers toward her palm and willed herself to pay attention to his story. Maybe if he talked about his late wife enough, she, Erin, would stop being so attracted to him.

"We went to the same college. She was brilliant."

"What were you?"

His half smile turned into a grin. "Merely smart."

"I doubt that."

"It's true. Robin thought like a computer. We started the company and were wildly successful. Then one day she didn't feel well." His eyes fluttered closed.

Erin wondered what he was remembering, then figured it was better that she didn't know. She stared across the sand to where Christie was digging for crabs. The waves rushed in and filled her handiwork. She sat back on her heels and laughed.

"It took the doctor a while to figure out what was wrong. Finally they diagnosed amyotrophic lateral sclerosis. Lou Gehrig's disease," he added, before she could ask.

"How horrible. For both of you. But—" She frowned. She knew Robin had been dead for several years. "It's ultimately fatal, but I thought it moved slowly."

"You mean it shouldn't have killed her yet?" His voice was harsh.

"Yes," she said softly.

"You're right. It shouldn't have. Robin got the flu. It turned into pneumonia and she died of that."

He still hadn't opened his eyes. She couldn't read his expression, but she felt his pain. And his guilt. But why would he feel guilty? He couldn't have prevented her from dying. He wasn't a medical expert.

"How long has it been?" she asked, vaguely remembering he'd mentioned it yesterday but not recalling the exact amount of time that had passed.

"Just over five years. She died in April. It was the same year your sister was here as a programming intern." He raised his hand to his face and rubbed his forehead. "I should have canceled the program. I wasn't in any shape to help those kids. But I knew they'd given up lucrative summer jobs to come here and work with me. In a way, I thought it might help me recover. I was wrong."

Erin sucked in a breath. "You loved her very much."

He opened his eyes and stared at her. "Yes." *I still do.* He didn't say the words but she heard them.

The last confusing pieces of the puzzle fell into place. Stacey had fallen for the emotionally tragic Parker. He had been her dark prince personified. With her need to create the most drama in a situation, Stacey could have inflated all kinds of half-truths into what she wanted to believe. She had been ripe for romance and Parker had fulfilled her every fantasy. Except one. He had never even known she was alive.

Her throat tightened painfully. The situation had been a disaster waiting to happen. If only Stacey had told her what was going on. She might have been able to help her. Erin sighed. She was wishing for the moon. Stacey wouldn't have wanted to hear the truth. She was more interested in her romantic fantasies.

But if she *had* contacted Erin, maybe Stacey wouldn't have died.

"I'm sorry," Parker said.

Erin blinked at him, trying to figure out what he was apologizing for. Surely he couldn't read her mind. He set his wineglass on the blanket, then sat up.

"I didn't mean to dump all that on you," he said.

"It's okay."

"For some reason you're easy to talk to."

The compliment made her want to smile. "Maybe because we're strangers," she said. "I'm safe."

"Possibly. And I've been hiding out here too long. Maybe I have become a recluse."

No problem, Erin thought. He was a recluse, and she was turning into her sister. She'd wanted to grin like a fool because he told her she was easy to talk to. Now she was crushed because he practically told her it was because she was convenient. Anyone would have done. *Get a grip!*

He rose to his feet. "I'll try not to be a self-centered bore," he promised.

"Gee, what kind of bore will you be?"

He grinned. Her heart shifted into overdrive.

"An entertaining bore." With that he sprinted down the beach toward Christie.

Erin watched him go. Sunlight gleamed on his dark hair and he moved with the loose-hipped grace of a natural athlete. He was far too handsome for her peace of mind. Thank goodness she was the sensible Ridgeway twin. If she wasn't, she might be in danger of falling for him, and the last thing she needed was a broken heart.

Chapter Seven

Parker pulled his Mercedes into the spacious garage that had originally been built to store both automobiles and carriages. He grabbed his bulging briefcase and headed for the main house. By the time he hit the grass-lined path, he'd already loosened his tie and was in the process of pulling it off. There was a time when dabbling in the corporate world had been interesting and new but today the meetings had interfered with his limited time with Christie.

He jogged the last couple of feet, then stepped into the kitchen. Kiki was simmering chili for dinner. The spicy fragrance tempted him, but he hurried past without stopping to taste.

It had been a week since Erin had shown up on his doorstep with her wild tales about a child that belonged to him. A week since he'd first met Christie and she came into his life. A week of seeing in color, instead of in black-and-white.

"I'm back," he called when he stepped into the empty living room.

"We're on the terrace," Kiki said.

He followed her voice and found his housekeeper and Erin sitting on chaise lounges and talking.

After a couple of weeks of summerlike weather, the temperature had dropped fifteen degrees and the fog had rolled in. For the past three days the mornings had been gray and misty, and the afternoons not much above sixty-five degrees. Erin wore a fuzzy blue sweater and black jeans. He ignored the curve of her breasts and long lines of her legs. Since that first night when he'd kissed her and experienced a reaction that had left him stunned and the next day when he'd squeezed her hand and had to fight painful arousal, he'd avoided any physical contact with her. He'd been pleasant and accommodating, but he'd refused to touch her. If he didn't look or touch he wouldn't do something stupid, such as get interested. So far the plan was working.

"How was your meeting?" Kiki asked. She was in one of her jogging suits. This one was white with a trail of butterflies up one leg and across the jacket. What amazed him the most was the tiny butterflies on her athletic shoes.

"The meeting was too long," he said. "But we got everything accomplished. I shouldn't have to go back for about a month." He glanced around the terrace. "Where's Christie?"

Kiki raised her pale eyebrows. "Come join us, Parker. We were talking about vacations. You haven't had one in a long time. Sit. You might learn something."

"Yeah, maybe next time." He glanced around the terrace one more time, then stepped toward the living room. "Christie?"

Erin took pity on him. "She's upstairs playing."

"Thanks."

"You're quite smitten, Parker," Kiki said.

"She's my kid. I'm supposed to be."

He met Erin's gaze. A flash of understanding connected them. Her mouth curved in a smile, exposing the dimple in her right cheek. Without the bright sunlight to highlight the red in her shoulder-length hair, the color was a dull brown. He supposed she wasn't especially beautiful, but he didn't mind. She was generous with his daughter's time, allowing him to be with Christie as much as he wanted, and he was grateful for that. She was a nice person. Her only request was that he treat her daughter well. An easy enough task.

"When's dinner?" he asked.

"Six o'clock." Kiki glanced at her watch. "You've got an hour and a half."

He was in the living room before she finished speaking. He left his briefcase and tie on the floor and started up the stairs, taking them two at a time.

"Christie? I'm home."

"Daddy!" Christie barreled out of his office. They met on the second-floor landing.

He caught her before she crashed into his legs. With a quick lift, he had her up in the air and circling around like an airplane.

"Can you fly?" he asked.

She laughed loudly. "I'm a birdie."

One arm supported her chest, the other her hips. "I thought you'd want to be a jet."

She shook her head. "Birdies are pretty. Planes smell bad."

Interesting logic. "What have you been doing while I was gone?" He drew her to him. She wrapped her legs around his waist and put her hand on his shoulder. The trust inherent in the gesture made his knees weak. He'd only known this child for a week, yet she believed in him and knew that he would never hurt her. She'd accepted him with the innocence of one who has never been betrayed. Every time he was with her, he swore he would die before causing her a moment's pain.

"Mommy and Kiki took me to the store today," she said. "We had lunch out, too." She grinned. "I had an ice cream for dessert."

He touched the stains on her red T-shirt. "Chocolate, I'll bet."

Her soft giggle made him smile. "You're so funny, Daddy."

"What else have you been doing?"

"I'll show you." She wiggled to get down.

He lowered her to the floor and she headed for his office. Once in the doorway she turned back and motioned for him to follow. "Come on, Daddy. Come see."

His office was long with his computer work station at one end and a good-size library of technical manuals at the other. In between was a small sitting area. The far wall was windows. Christie had pulled most of the cushions off the furniture to create a private world. She knelt down on the floor and pointed to the jumble of cushions.

"This is the castle," she said. She picked up her doll Millie, whose everyday dress had been replaced by something fancy and long. "This is Princess Amdromada."

"Amdromada?" He squatted beside her.

"Uh-huh. She's very beautiful, and she has a handsome prince, only he's busy right now. There's a terrible dragon who wants Princess Amdromada for himself." She pointed to a floor lamp she'd dragged over from the far corner. "He's very dangerous. The princess has to be careful."

"Why is the prince busy?"

Christie considered that for a moment. "He just is. Sometimes princes have a lot to do."

How much of this was pretend and how much from her life? She and her mother lived alone. According to Erin,

Christie had wanted a father for a long time. "Do you think the prince has forgotten about her?"

She stared at him, her brown eyes wide and troubled. "Princes don't forget."

"Does the prince know about his princess?"

"He should," she said firmly. "Princes should know everything."

Parker wondered if daddies were supposed to know everything, too. "Will the princess forgive the prince when he finally comes back?"

Christie thought for a moment. "If he promises to never go away again, she will."

But he wasn't going to be able to make that promise, Parker thought grimly. In seven days, Erin would take Christie back to Palmdale and he wouldn't see his child again for weeks. He couldn't imagine what his life would be without her.

He rose to his feet and held out his hand. "Would you like to see a different castle with a prince and a dragon?"

"Sure." She clutched his fingers.

He led her to his computer, then sat in the chair and booted the system. Christie trustingly climbed into his lap. "It's a program!"

"Yes. Something new. The recommended age is seven to ten, but you're very smart so we'll give it a try."

Christie beamed at him. "You're very smart, too."

"Thank you."

She leaned against his chest and stared at the screen. "Oh, it's beautiful," she said as the colorful shimmering castle appeared.

"The princess has been stolen by the evil dragon who takes her all over the world. The prince has clues and has to use them to find his princess. He must ask questions, battle against wizards and do good deeds for points."

"I like it," she said.

"It still has a few problems to be worked out," he said. "But it's a pretty good program." A business associate had asked Parker to look the software over. The company had been forced to do some reworking when he'd pointed out having the prince rescue the princess was a little sexist for the nineties. They should let the princess do the rescuing every now and then.

He rolled the chair closer, then grabbed the mouse and slid it along the pad until the arrow pointed to the word *Begin*.

"First the dragon crossed an ocean," he read. "We have to pick an ocean." A map of the world appeared.

"Pacific Ocean!" she said loudly. "'Coz it's so pretty."

"Pacific it is." He moved the mouse and clicked. The screen changed.

Slowly he and Christie worked their way toward saving the princess. Her bright chatter made him smile and her silly jokes allowed light in the darkness of his soul. Once again he realized their time together was half over. What was going to become of him when she was gone?

Sometimes when he was with her, he wondered what it would have been like if he and Robin had had children. Would a child have given her the will to survive? Would a child have given *him* a reason to go on or would he have destroyed that innocent being the same way he'd destroyed his wife?

At least Christie was safe from him. Erin was strong. She would protect her daughter, keeping her safe from all that threatened Christie, even if that meant keeping her away from him. He admired that about Erin. She had done what she had to do for Christie. She didn't complain, she just got the job done.

It was as if his thoughts conjured her from thin air. Suddenly she was standing in the doorway to the office.

"Christie, it's time to wash up for dinner."

"We're rescuing the princess. She needs me."

"The princess will still be here after dinner, or even to-morrow," he said. "Look, I can save the game in prog-ress." He showed her how to move the arrow, then click the command. When the screen had returned to the main menu, he swiveled the chair around and let Christie slide off his lap.

"I want to play again," Christie said as she skipped to-ward her mother.

"I'm sure you will." Erin gave him a weary smile. "I did warn you she was a handful."

"She's worth it," he said.

"You're right." She touched her daughter's shoulder. "Did you say thank you?"

Christie smiled shyly. "Thank you for playing with me."

"You're welcome. I enjoyed it, too."

The little girl dashed toward the stairs. Erin glanced after her, then returned her attention to him. "You were worried about getting along with her, but it's not so hard."

"You're right. I've enjoyed having her here."

"She's had a great time, too. See you at dinner." She followed Christie to the stairs.

Parker watched her go. He found himself studying the gentle swaying of her hips. By now he'd grown used to the low level awareness he felt whenever she was around. If he didn't touch her or get too close, he could keep it under control.

What surprised him was the more he was around Erin, the more he remembered Stacey. Or maybe it wasn't all that startling. After all, they were twins. But he didn't see their similarities as much as he saw their differences.

He remembered Stacey being intense and emotional. Erin was as bright as her sister, although in a different way. She didn't converse knowledgeably about computer program-ming, but she was well-read. Her quirky humor often made him laugh in spite of himself. If not for that damn awareness, he would be perfectly comfortable around her.

He turned his chair until he was facing his computer screen again. He could go back to work on that program that was giving him so much trouble. He reached for the mouse, then pushed it away. He still didn't have the solution so there was no point in wasting time. What he needed was a flash of brilliance. What he needed was Robin.

The thought propelled him from his chair. He crossed the office and headed for his bedroom. The master suite was close to the stairs. As he entered the large room, he glanced at the sleigh bed, and antique nightstand and dresser he'd found in the attic. Old and new blended well. He had Kiki to thank for that. When he'd redone his bedroom, she'd helped him pick out fabric and decide which pieces to use. He'd made the change in an effort to forget. It hadn't helped much.

He crossed to the closet and quickly shrugged out of his dress shirt and trousers. After pulling on jeans, he buttoned the fly then returned to the dresser in the bedroom for a sweatshirt.

He slipped his arms into the soft fleece, then paused to look at the picture on top of the dresser. It showed Robin working at her computer. She hadn't known she was being photographed. Oversize glasses slipped down her nose as she leaned back and stared at the screen. Her jeans were torn, her boots scuffed, her sweater slipping off one shoulder. The photo captured her at a moment of inspiration. Her wide mouth turned up in a smile while her arms were extended, palms up, in a gesture of victory.

He'd seen her that way dozens of times. For a while he hadn't been able to look at the pictures without feeling pain. Now it gave him a bittersweet connection to the past.

He looked around the room and wondered if he'd been hasty in moving. The original master suite had been down the hall. He'd gutted two bedrooms and a bathroom, then converted them into the new master. The old suite had been divided into the second-floor library and storage. He'd sold the furniture he and Robin had used. It had been his way of trying to get on with his life. It hadn't helped much.

He pulled the sweatshirt over his head then grabbed a pair of socks and his athletic shoes. He knew he would always love Robin and he would always miss her, yet the past week had taught him an important lesson. Having Christie in his life had shown him that five years after the fact he might finally be ready to let go of Robin. Maybe it was time to stop living in black-and-white.

When he got downstairs, Kiki was alone in the kitchen. She'd changed from her jogging suit into wool slacks and a sweater.

"I see you have a date tonight," he said. "Which one is it?"

She raised her eyebrows and smiled. "Skip."

"Ah, so I won't expect you before dawn."

"Maybe not even then. The chili is done. It can simmer until you're ready to eat. I mixed up corn bread. Pop it into the oven for thirty minutes." She leaned against the counter and stared at him. "You know it wouldn't hurt you to try it once and a while. If you still remember how."

He pulled a bottle of beer out of the refrigerator and opened the top. "The corn bread? I'll have some tonight."

"Not food, Parker. A woman."

Dammit, why did people insist on saying things like that when he was drinking? He swallowed, then choked. After coughing for a couple of minutes, he could finally breathe again.

"Kiki," he said warningly.

She ignored him. "I'm serious."

"So am I."

She walked to the island and braced her hands on the counter. Blue eyes met and held his gaze. "It's been five years, Parker. That's a long time to miss someone."

He turned away and stared out the window. "It doesn't matter how long it's been, I still love Robin. I'll always love her."

"And I'll always love my son, but that doesn't mean I'm going to forget I'm alive. That's what you've been doing all these years. You're a walking corpse."

"Thanks for the compliment."

"I'm only saying this because I care about you. You have needs."

He groaned silently. "My needs and I are just fine, thank you."

"Are you? Really? What about the difference Christie has made in your life?"

He couldn't deny that. "I like having her here."

"Being alive isn't so bad, is it?"

He glanced at his housekeeper. "Leave it alone, Kiki. It's none of your business."

"Bull." She moved in front of him and tilted her head back as she stared at him. The fact that he was nearly a foot taller didn't seem to intimidate her in the least. "I've seen how you look at her."

What was she talking about? "Christie?"

"Erin."

For one horribly uncomfortable moment he was afraid she'd been able to read his mind. He was willing to admit he might have felt the odd moment of desire, but so what? "She's Christie's mother."

"So? That only makes it more convenient."

"I'm not interested in convenient."

"You're not interested in anything."

He took another sip of beer. "Maybe I should be like you and have several lovers."

She smiled. She made a fist and gave him a mock punch in the upper arm. "You're not the type, Hamilton. You couldn't handle the pressure to perform."

"I'm flattered," he said dryly as she crossed to the small table in front of the window and collected her purse.

"Don't take it so personally." She headed for the door. "I'll see you in the morning."

He stared after her. "Kiki?"

"Yes?" She paused.

"I've been thinking of asking Erin to extend the visit. Would you mind?"

Her smile was blinding. "Finally. Of course I don't mind. It would be terrific to have Christie here. Plus you'd have more time to work on her mother."

"Erin is off limits."

"Where did that rule come from?"

"I just made it up. I don't want to complicate my relationship with Christie by getting involved with Erin."

"Sure." Kiki nodded. "Falling in love with Erin, marrying her and living with the two of them forever would be a real complication. I can see why you're determined to avoid it."

He let her sarcasm wash over him. It didn't matter what she said, he couldn't change his mind. After Robin, he'd sworn never to risk love again. The price was too high for everyone involved.

"I hear them coming this way," Kiki said, then opened the door. "Ask her. I'll be expecting good news in the morning."

Ask Erin now? "I was thinking of mentioning it later in the week."

"Figures. Just like I said, Parker, you can't perform under pressure. Bye."

The door slammed behind her just as Erin walked into the room. "Was that Kiki?" she asked.

"Yeah. She's got one of her dates."

"Oh, which one?"

"Skip."

Erin grinned. "She won't be back until morning."

Her humor was contagious. "I wouldn't count on it. You want a beer?"

"Sure, I'll get it." Erin opened the refrigerator. "She mixed up some corn bread and left it in here. If you tell me what time you want to eat, I'll heat it up."

"Say a half hour?"

"That will make Christie happy. She's in your study watching a cartoon program that ends in—" she glanced at her watch "—twenty-seven minutes."

After slipping the corn bread into the oven, she sat on one of the stools by the center island. Parker took the one next to her. Erin uncapped her beer and took a sip, then glanced at him.

"I have to admit I admire Kiki. She knows what she wants, and she does it."

"Is this specifically about her having three lovers or are you talking in generalities?"

Erin ducked her head but not before he saw a faint blush stain her cheeks. "Oh, I just meant her philosophy about life. Not having regrets."

"What regrets do you have?"

She thought for a moment. "None where Christie is concerned. I don't regret what I had to give up to keep her or be a good mother. But sometimes I wonder if I needed to give up everything I did. Maybe I could have made a few compromises." She shrugged. "It's hard to say now."

She turned back and forth on her stool. Her blue sweater twisted with her, alternately tightening, then releasing around her torso. When it tightened, he could see the shape of her breasts and the slender line of her rib cage. He tried to convince himself his interest was simply male appreciation of the female form, but he knew it was more. The heat slowly licking up his body felt suspiciously like desire.

"You could make some changes," he said.

"I've been thinking that, too." She tilted her head and her hair brushed across her shoulders. "I've really enjoyed spending time here. I've been able to relax and think. You've been a very gracious host, Parker."

He picked up the beer and downed a large gulp. *Ask her,* a voice in his head insisted. It was the perfect opening. But what if she didn't want to stay? What if he'd been a lousy father and she couldn't wait to get Christie away from him? What if...

Oh, hell. "Erin, I'd like you and Christie to stay with me for the rest of the summer."

"What?" She spun the stool toward him and stared. "Stay here?"

He nodded. "You don't go back to work until September. That's nearly eight weeks away. There's plenty of room. I think Christie likes it here, and I enjoy having her. You, too, of course."

"Of course," she murmured, her delicate eyebrows drawing together. "Stay here for the rest of the summer? I had no idea."

He put the beer bottle on the counter and resisted the urge to wipe his suddenly sweaty palms on his jeans. "I like being with my daughter. I want to have more time with her before she has to go back to school."

She stared at him and he stared back. Her hazel eyes were wide like Christie's, and fringed with dark lashes. Her skin was smooth and soft looking. They were close enough for him to smell the sweet scent of her perfume.

He wanted to hope she would say yes. He wanted to beg. He wanted to promise he would never hurt her or Christie. Instead he waited.

"Christie would like it," she said at last. "She loves this house and being with you. I wasn't sure what kind of father you would be, but I'm very impressed."

"Thank you," he said quietly, the anticipation building. "I don't have a clue what I'm doing, so I'm winging it."

"You have good instincts." She tilted her head again, then smiled. "I don't really have anything to go home to. Summer in Palmdale is hot and windy. Staying here is like being at a vacation resort. You must promise to let me know if either Christie or I get in the way."

"Is that a yes?"

"Yes."

"Yeah?" He stood up and grinned. "Great. Thanks."

Without thinking, he pulled her to her feet. She came willingly, and then she was standing very close to him. She was smiling, too, and her hands rested on his chest.

He could feel the heat from each of her fingers. His heart rate increased. The need and the relief got tangled up together, feeding each other until they both exploded into a raging fire. His humor faded and he wanted to kiss her.

He placed his hands on her shoulders. Her sweater was as touchably soft as he had imagined it would be. He could feel her shoulders and the thin strap of her bra.

"Erin," he breathed as he lowered his head to hers.

The kitchen door popped open.

"I *have* seen this cartoon before," Christie announced as she raced into the room. Her shoes skidded as she came to a sudden stop.

Parker released Erin and took a step back. Christie was staring at him. "Are you going to kiss Mommy?"

He didn't know what to say.

Erin solved the problem by going to her daughter and taking her hand. "Don't be silly. We were just talking." As she led the girl out of the room, she gave him a quick glance over her shoulder.

He wasn't sure what she saw on his face. After all, he wasn't sure what he was feeling at this moment. He was glad they were staying and he *had* wanted to kiss her. Even though he knew it was wrong.

But as Erin looked at him, he knew exactly what emotion she was experiencing. Regret.

What he didn't know was why. Was she sorry they hadn't kissed or sorry that he'd tried at all?

Chapter Eight

Lightning cut through the night, followed by the rumble of thunder. Erin crossed her bedroom and went into the hall. The small night-lights glowed. She bent her wrist toward the illumination and checked the time. Eight-twenty.

When a second clap of thunder shook the house, she pushed open the door to Christie's room and stepped inside.

"Are you doing okay, sweetie?" she asked quietly.

"Mommy?" Her daughter sounded sleepy. "I can see the lightning with my eyes closed."

"I know." Erin sat on the edge of the bed and stared at the little girl. Her hair was dark against the white pillowcase. She looked small and fragile in bed, with only her teddy to protect her from harm. "Are you frightened by the storm?"

"It's just the clouds," Christie said. "They're talkin' to each other. They can't help it if their voices are really loud."

Erin had never figured out where Christie had found this theory on thunderstorms, but as long as it kept her from being scared, it really didn't matter.

"And the lightning?" she asked.

Christie yawned. "They're passin' notes."

"Hmm, that's what I thought." She bent over and kissed her cheek. "I'm going to read in my room or watch TV downstairs. If you get frightened, you come get me. Promise?"

"Promise," Christie murmured as her eyes drifted shut. She sighed softly, then fell back to sleep.

The storm raged around them but the innocent child was oblivious to its fury. Erin left the room and returned to her own. Once there she paced the length, then tried to find a book that sounded interesting.

She was restless. Maybe it was being cooped up in this house so much. Erin grimaced. Living in this huge mansion was hardly being "cooped up" anywhere, so it wasn't that. But how else could she explain dull buzzing in the back of her mind and the urge to keep moving?

She crossed to the window and pulled open the heavy drapes. Rain battered against the windows. A flash of lightning arced through the night. She waited for the accompanying roar, and when it came, the panes rattled.

There shouldn't be a problem, she told herself. Everything was settled. Last week she had agreed to stay for the summer so Parker could get to know Christie. Her daughter had been thrilled at the prospect. Erin had wondered if Christie might miss her friends, but apparently a few four-year-olds couldn't compete with the excitement of a new house, a housekeeper who went out of her way to bake delicious things and a new father. Christie loved it here. Erin's only regret about staying was how hard it was going to be to go home in September.

Leaving the drapes open, she went back to her dresser and studied the stack of books there. She and Kiki had made a trip to the local library. While Parker had an impressive selection of reading material, it didn't include the latest mysteries and romances that Erin preferred. She ran her finger down the spines of the books, but none of them caught her fancy. Without wanting to—even as she told herself she shouldn't—she opened the top drawer and pulled out Stacey's diary.

Erin turned on the bedside lamp, then settled on the mattress. She flipped through the pages all the while wondering why she was torturing herself. Reading the diary made her feel foolish and inadequate. It brought up feelings that she didn't like. Yet she felt compelled to read it, as if the pages somehow held a treasure she had yet to discover.

A sentence about a summer storm caught her attention. The passage was dated about three weeks after Stacey had moved in to the house.

The old house practically dances in the thunder. Oh, I'm laughing as I write this. Dances in the thunder? Gee, next I'll take up writing depressing literary novels and go live in France. No, I won't be going anywhere. If I had my way, I would stay here always. With Parker.

How he broods. Apparently his wife died a short time ago. He loved her and loves her still. I want to tell him that I can heal him. In my arms he can find... whatever he's looking for.

Several sentences were scratched out, then the entry continued. *I want to put on something sexy and feminine, go downstairs and find him. I want to dance with him and hold him. I want to make love to him. I want to belong to him. I think I love him.*

Erin slammed the diary shut. Irritation warred with sadness. Stacey couldn't help what she was feeling, but if she were here, Erin would shake some sense into her. Couldn't her sister see that Parker truly mourned his wife? No amount of holding or dancing would make that kind of pain go away. It took time. But Stacey wouldn't have been interested in reality. She only saw what she wanted to.

Poor Stacey. The relationship—if that's what it could be called—had been doomed from the start. She'd taken a few truths and created an unreal world. She'd acted on it and had expected Parker to do the same.

Parker. Erin felt for him, too. He must have been in so much pain. His wife's unexpected death had been recent. He'd needed a friend, not an overgrown adolescent throwing herself at him. If only he'd been able to tell Stacey the truth.

Erin set down the diary. Stacey wouldn't have heard anything except what she wanted to hear.

She stood up and crossed to the mirror. The lights in the room illuminated her features. She studied them, seeing Stacey instead of herself. In her mind's eye, her hair was longer, the scar on her forehead gone. She wondered if other people had this ability to step out of themselves and see someone else, or if it only happened to twins. Probably it was unique to twins. Other people rarely looked exactly like someone else. She blinked and the memory was gone. She was just herself again.

"You always leapt into things without thinking," Erin said aloud, then smiled. She was in more trouble than she thought if she stood here waiting for an answer.

But she knew her sister well, and in her head she heard what Stacey would have said if she'd been there. Stacey would have rolled her eyes, planted her hands on her hips and said, "I might plunge forward, but you're going to *die* waiting for the right moment. Quit waiting and do something. Act. Everything isn't always perfect, so you have to take what you can get."

Erin turned away from the mirror. Was Stacey right? Had she spent her life waiting for the right moment?

"I didn't have much choice," she said defensively. "I had Christie to think of."

Or was that just an excuse?

Her thoughts made her uncomfortable. Erin turned off the lamp on the nightstand, then left the bedroom. She walked down the hallway to the stairs. The storm had lessened some, but according to the weather report, it would return later.

On the second story landing, she paused, trying to listen. Was Parker still in his office? He often worked after Christie went to bed. With Kiki usually gone, the evenings could get lonely. Sometimes Erin got tired of her own company. But she never went looking for Parker. She didn't want to disturb him. Besides, what was she going to say? Entertain me? She shook her head and continued down the stairs.

There weren't many lights on the first floor. A lamp in the corner of the huge living room cast a small glow on the hardwood floor, but it didn't reach to the French doors leading out to the terrace. Erin stood in front of them and watched the storm. Rain flung itself against the glass. She wondered what the ocean looked like. Would the white, foamy waves crash high on the rocks, the spray exploding into the night? She licked her lips, as if she could taste the salt. The sense of restlessness returned and with it the need to do *something*.

"How's Christie?" Parker asked from behind her.

She jumped and spun around. "You startled me," she said, placing a hand on her chest. "I thought you were upstairs working."

"Not tonight. I don't want to risk losing power while I'm in the middle of something. I'm in the study, if you'd care to join me."

He blended well with the darkness. His hair, his eyes, even his black jeans and boots. His white shirt was pale against his tanned skin. The shadows in the living room transformed his familiar features into something mysterious. Something otherworldly.

A shiver of anticipation raced through her. "Thank you," she murmured, then followed him into the study.

She settled on a corner of the burgundy sofa, then nodded when he held up a decanter of brandy. A fire burned in the fireplace. Here the storm was far away. There weren't even any windows. They could have been anywhere. They could have been the last two people in the world.

As he handed her the glass, their fingers touched. Erin felt the spark clear down to her toes. She didn't know whether to swoon or break out into hysterical laughter. Both thoughts were equally unpleasant.

I'm not Stacey, and I refuse to act like her, she reminded herself. Bits of the diary floated through her brain. Phrases about desire and the storm, the night and the man.

Erin stared at Parker as he sat at the other end of the sofa. She was going insane. There was no other explanation for her reaction. Okay, there might be a couple. He was good-looking and charming. He turned her on in a big way. He reminded her that she hadn't been with a man in years.

All of this would have been easier if Stacey hadn't been here first. Erin didn't want to relive her sister's life at Hawkin's Point. She didn't want to have a crush and act like a fool. If Stacey hadn't written all those things about Parker, Erin would have felt more comfortable experiencing her emotions without judging them. It wasn't as if she was going to act on them.

But Stacey *had* been here first. She had written those things. Erin knew she was the sensible one and it made her uncomfortable to act like her impulsive twin.

Ignore it and it will go away, she told herself. Excellent advice that she was going to take, starting now.

"Does the storm frighten Christie?" he asked, placing his glass on the oak table in front of them.

"I checked on her a little bit ago. She's fine. She thinks that the thunder is just the clouds talking to each other."

He smiled. "She's very creative."

"I agree." She took a sip of brandy. The liquid was warm and smooth as it slipped down her throat. "Is Kiki gone?" she asked.

"Of course. I don't remember who she's seeing tonight."

"Your housekeeper is amazing."

Parker leaned back in the corner of his sofa and stretched his arms along the back and side. The action pulled his shirt tight across his shoulders. She tried not to notice how masculine he looked sitting there, or how much she wanted to lean closer. She wished she could explain her reaction away as the result of too much brandy, but she'd only had the one sip.

"Kiki is her own person," he said.

"How did you come to hire her?"

He grinned. "She brought brownies to the interview. Robin and I had already spoken with three or four women. They'd shown up in conservative dresses with sensible shoes. Kiki walked in wearing one of her bright jogging suits and carrying a plate of the brownies. After one bite we were hooked." His smile faded. "She has her reasons for what she does."

"The men you mean?"

He nodded.

Erin took another sip of her brandy. "I don't judge her, Parker. Even if I didn't know about the loss of her child, I wouldn't be put off by what she does. If it makes her happy and doesn't hurt anyone, then she should be free to do as she pleases."

"Not everyone would be so open-minded."

She shrugged. "They're wrong."

He leaned forward and picked up his glass. "You were an unmarried single parent. Did you ever have to do any explaining?"

"Not really. Once people knew that Christie was my sister's child it was never an issue. Palmdale isn't all that small but even if it were, it wouldn't matter. The weather might not be my favorite, but the people are friendly."

"Do you miss it?"

She met his gaze. His dark eyes held her captive. Maybe it was the night. Maybe it was the man. Maybe it was her ridiculous fantasies about him.

"No. Not really," she said as the house shook and the lights flickered.

"Looks like we might lose power," he said and stood up. He crossed to the mantel. There were several candles sitting beside some framed pictures of Robin and himself. He moved the candles to the coffee table, lit them, then returned to the sofa. "The night-lights upstairs have battery power if the electricity goes out. Christie won't be in total darkness."

"Good."

He leaned forward and picked up his glass, then cradled it in his large hands. She stared at his fingers. Her mind was filled with erotic pictures. She tried to shake them off but it didn't work. To distract herself, she imagined what Stacey would think of this evening and how she would romanticize their quiet time in the study.

Then Erin realized she didn't want to think about her sister or what she'd felt for Parker. That was the past. She might be experiencing what Stacey had written about in her diary, but her emotions came from her own dealings with him. At least she was pretty sure they did. Everything was so confusing.

"What are you thinking about?" Parker asked. "You're frowning."

"Am I? I was just wondering..." She drew in a breath, then decided to tell him the truth. At least part of it. "Do you think of Stacey when you look at me?"

He was obviously startled by the question. He stiffened slightly, then stared at her face as if seeing her features for the first time.

"I did at first," he said. "Being around you made me remember her more. But now I don't really think about her when I see you. You've become two separate people. Does that make sense?"

"Yes. What do you remember about her?"

"Not a lot." He took a drink of brandy. One corner of his mouth twisted down. "Obviously we were lovers, Christie is proof of that, but that doesn't mean I knew her. I was drunk and she— Damn. Sorry, Erin. This isn't what you want to hear."

"I do if it's the truth." She set her glass on the table and leaned toward him. "I have her version of what happened. I'd like to know yours."

"It's not a great story." He rubbed his right temple. "That summer is a blur for me. All the students blended together for the first few weeks. I missed Robin more than I could have believed possible."

His confession tore at her heart. Parker had suffered greatly when he'd lost his wife. Erin wondered if she would ever have the courage to risk that kind of love and loss. She loved Christie more than life but she hadn't had a choice in the matter. The moment she'd held the infant in her arms, her fate had been sealed. But loving a man required a conscious choice. At least that was her understanding. One didn't just fall in love unexpectedly, without wanting to.

"That must have been a difficult summer for you," she said.

"Yeah. It was. The first thing I noticed about Stacey was that she was there. Always there, in the background. I resented the students." He grimaced. "Makes me quite the bastard, doesn't it? I hated their laughter and jokes. I wanted everyone to feel as sad as I did." He met her gaze. "I was very angry with your sister. I resented the fact that she was alive and Robin was dead."

He'd stretched his left arm across the back of the sofa. His hand rested about a foot from her shoulder. She reached up and touched the back of his fingers. She ignored the sparks that singed her skin and the fact that he didn't pull away. "You say that as if you now expect me to be angry with you."

"Aren't you? It wasn't Stacey's fault that she was alive."

"It wasn't your fault Robin was dead."

He pulled his hand free, turned and faced the fire. After setting his glass on the coffee table he rested his elbows on his thighs and laced his fingers together between his knees. "Wasn't it?"

"What are you saying?"

"Nothing. The past gets ugly sometimes. I've always regretted what happened with Stacey. At first I was angry and blamed her. She was just a kid, an inexperienced young woman who thought she saw something where there was nothing. I was cruel to her the morning...the morning after. I'm sorry for what I said."

Erin wanted to ask for details. What *had* he said to Stacey? Her sister had hinted at some of it in her letter of apology. Something about Stacey not knowing what real love was. Had Stacey declared her feelings and then been rejected?

"I feel guilty, too," she said.

Parker glanced at her. "You? What do you have to feel guilty about?"

"Not knowing. We were twins. We were supposed to have a connection that went beyond words. I knew something had happened while she was here, but when she didn't want to talk about it, I didn't press her. I never knew she was pregnant. How could my twin sister have hidden that from me? Why didn't I sense what was wrong?" She folded her arms over her chest and sighed. "I have always felt badly that Stacey went through it alone."

"That's not your fault, it's mine."

"So we're going to argue over blame?"

"This conversation is too quiet to be an argument."

She smiled slightly at his words. "I'm not the screaming type."

"Me, either." Some of the sadness faded from his gaze. "But I'd still change the past if I could."

"What would you do differently?"

"I wouldn't sleep with Stacey."

"Oh, don't say that," she told him. "Please, don't even wish that."

"Why?"

"Because then Christie would never have been born."

"You're right. She's a great kid."

Erin scooted a little closer to him, then reached out to touch him. At the last minute, she pulled her hand away and rested it on her lap. He stared at the ground. She could see the muscles in his back and feel the heat of him.

"When we were growing up, Stacey was always the wild one," she said. "She jumped into whatever we were doing. She wanted to experience everything and she didn't worry about the consequences."

"You're more cautious," he said.

"A little. I like to test the water first, figure out what I want. Wait for my turn." *You're going to die waiting for your turn,* a voice in her head whispered. It wasn't true, she told herself. Caution wasn't a bad thing. Not everyone had to seize what they wanted. There was more to life than being greedy and myopic.

"What if you don't get your turn?" he asked.

"I don't know."

The restlessness that had plagued her earlier returned. When was it going to be her time? When did she get to follow her dreams? She only had questions, not answers.

She grabbed her glass of brandy and finished it in a single swallow. The warmth flowed through her stomach and up her chest. The edges of her mind blurred a little and she knew the alcohol was starting to take effect. She'd never been much of a drinker.

"Another one?" he asked.

"No, thanks," she said. "I'm fine."

But she wasn't fine. She wasn't a lot of things, including Stacey.

She stood up suddenly and left the room. The storm still raged over the sea. The lightning had returned, plunging across the sky, leaving an earthshaking roar in its wake.

The night and the liquor worked together to leave her feeling confused. Longing filled her. Longing for what she'd given up and for what she'd never had. Forgotten needs swirled through her, stirring to life, reminding her that she was a woman, with a woman's desires.

She closed her eyes, trying to force the images away, but they only intensified. She could see Parker as clearly as if he were standing in front of her. She could feel his dark gaze and the touch of his hands on her body. She ached for him.

It wasn't real, she told herself. It was about the diary, or the night or something else. This couldn't be happening. Nothing made sense.

"Erin, are you all right?" Parker asked as he came up behind her.

"I'm fine." Her voice didn't sound fine. In fact, it was shaking. Her whole body trembled.

"I didn't mean to upset you earlier."

She continued to stare out the window. She refused to turn and look at him. Lord knew what he would see on her face. If he knew how much she wanted him— The mortification would be more than she could stand.

Think logically, she told herself. If she hadn't read the diary and known about Stacey's unrequited crush would she be so concerned about her own attraction to Parker?

No.

Erin touched the cool glass in front of her. The trembling lessened and she was able to draw in a deep breath.

"You didn't upset me," she said quietly, her voice stronger.

"I did. I shouldn't have said those things about your sister."

Now that she had herself under control, she felt safer turning around to look at him. She pressed her back against the door so the chill would chase the heat from her body. They were both in shadows and she couldn't make out his individual features. He was less than a foot in front of her.

"I know the truth about Stacey better than anyone," she said. "The whole situation is a little confusing for both of us, so there are bound to be awkward moments. We're going to have to learn to muddle through."

"That's my fault, too," he said, then shoved his hands into his jeans pockets. "Damn."

"What?" His fault? She was the one with the psychotic hormones.

"I've made you uncomfortable."

"What?"

"I have no excuse except that I like you. And it's not about Stacey," he added hastily. "She and I never talked the way you and I do. I didn't know her, despite what happened. This is different. I'd tell you it's because I haven't seen an attractive woman in a while, but that's not true. Kiki's been parading them in front of me for years.''

''What?''

His dark gaze bore into hers. ''So it must just be you. The problem is, I don't know why. Worse, now it's upsetting you.''

''What?'' She was beginning to sound like a parrot, repeating the same word over and over.

''My attraction to you,'' he said. ''You sense it and it makes you uncomfortable.''

''Your what?'' At least she was leaning against the glass doors. As her knees gave out, she had a way to support herself so she didn't go sliding into a heap on the floor.

''Dammit, Erin, don't you feel it, too?'' he asked, then jerked his hands out of his pockets and grabbed her upper arms. His grip was firm but not punishing.

Her head spun as she tried to make sense of what he was saying. He was attracted to her? To her?

''Parker, I—''

She never got a chance to say what she was thinking. Not that it mattered. The moment his mouth touched hers, all rational thoughts fled her brain, leaving a void that filled with sensation.

This was not like that brief kiss before. The one that had left her breathless. Although this time she still couldn't breathe, this was anything but brief.

His lips pressed against hers in an act of possession. Desire consumed her and she felt his flames, as well. The point of contact was combustion and the resulting explosion would blow them both away.

She didn't remember reaching for him, but suddenly her hands were on his back and she could touch the muscles she'd admired. His lean strength rippled under her questing fingers. His shirt was smooth, his skin hot, his body pressed against hers from shoulder to knees.

His hands still held on to her arms, but instead of pushing her away, he drew her closer. Her breasts flattened against his chest. His mouth explored hers, learning the curve of her lips, tasting her, caressing her into mindlessness. His tongue probed gently. She parted for him, angling her head to admit him fully.

He was hot and sweet as he swept the delicate skin of her lower lip. When his tongue brushed hers, she felt the jolt ripple through her to the heat flaring between her thighs.

A painful ache began there and in her breasts. She tried to remember the last time she'd kissed, really kissed, a man. She tried to remember the last time she'd been aroused. A lifetime ago. Before Christie had come into her life.

He wrapped his arms around her waist and drew her closer still. She could feel his arousal pressing against her belly. Her panties were damp, her nipples hard.

She slipped her hands up to his shoulders and clung to him. He cupped her face, holding her still as he plunged inside her mouth. He imitated the act of love. The power she felt in his quivering muscles made her weak with desire. He pressed kisses to her cheeks, her chin, her jaw. He bit her left earlobe, then rested his face against her neck and breathed her name.

Every part of her was ready for him. Every cell in her body ached for his touch, for the release that would follow. His arousal flexed once against her belly. She moaned and pressed closer.

Parker straightened. He tucked her hair behind her ears. She searched his face but it was too dark to see what he was thinking. The occasional flashes of lightning didn't provide enough light and the glow of the lamp didn't reach this far.

"I'm shaking," he said huskily.

"Me, too."

"I can't do this."

"I know." She'd always known. He wasn't for her. He wasn't the one. He still loved Robin. Stacey confused things. Erin wasn't ready to claim her turn.

He pressed a quick kiss on her forehead, then left her. She listened to the sound of his footsteps on the stairs. When she was alone, she touched her fingers to her throbbing mouth and told herself it was for the best. Getting involved with him would be silly. This was a temporary situation. At the end of the summer, she would return to her own life. It was enough to know, at least for tonight, he'd wanted her. Because wanting was so much safer than doing.

That's what Stacey had never learned. Erin knew better. She wasn't going to be Stacey all over again. *She* wasn't going to make the mistake of falling in love with Parker Hamilton.

Chapter Nine

Parker quickly climbed the stairs to the second floor and headed for his room. He didn't want to think about what had just happened. He couldn't not.

He'd kissed her. More than that, he'd devoured her as if he were a man facing sustenance for the first time in years. Perhaps that *is* what had happened. It had been years...at least for him.

He walked to his window and stared out at the storm. Lightning continued to flash, but it had moved away. Now the glimmering bolts came from a distance. He raised his hand to press it against the pane of glass, then noticed his fingers trembling. His whole body was shaking. Still. The desire threatened to overwhelm him. He wanted to go back downstairs, haul her into his arms and pick up where they'd left off. He wanted to love every inch of her body, starting at the bottom, working his way up, only to start over when he reached the top.

His need frightened him as much as the vivid images of what Erin would look like in his bed. And it was Erin he wanted there, not Stacey. God forgive him, not even Robin.

He closed his eyes against the storm and the night, against the tactile sensations still lingering in the memory of his body. Why now? Why with her? In the past five years he'd avoided any kind of emotional relationship. It hadn't been difficult. After the first year, he'd felt a stirring of some physical need. He'd dated a couple of women, had even had sex with them. But that had been about finding release, not making love. It had been about being naked, not being intimate.

With Erin, he could imagine being both.

Self-loathing and guilt rose in his throat like bile. How could he have done that? How could he have confessed his attraction to her? Of course she had to have known, but she'd been polite and had pretended not to notice. He had to bring it out in the open. She must think he was the biggest jerk she'd ever met. Some role model for Christie.

He ignored the voice that whispered she hadn't kissed him like a woman who was appalled or disgusted by his confession. She'd gone willingly into his arms. He just wasn't sure why.

He swore under his breath. The desire had stunned him with its intensity. He hadn't expected to ever feel it again. He'd wanted to take Erin right there, on the floor. He hadn't cared about anything but being with her.

He pushed off the windows and walked to the dresser. Robin's picture was there. He picked it up, moved to the bed and sat down. He stared at the likeness, at the familiar lines of her face, at the shape of her mouth. He forced himself to remember what it had been like when they were together. Then he waited for the pain.

He braced himself against the inevitable longing, against the memories that would crash in around him. He knew that while he had that, he had her.

He closed his eyes, sucked in a breath ... and felt only bittersweet sadness. The love was there, the memories. He could recall a thousand different moments with her. He could imagine her smile, the sound of her voice, even a silly joke she'd told. The corner of his mouth turned up as he recalled how she'd insisted he turn his back if he was in the bathroom when she got out of the shower. They could spend an afternoon in bed together, but she wouldn't let him watch her step out of the shower stall naked.

The memories were good. Intellectually he knew they might even be better than the marriage had been. He didn't recall the fights or her stubbornness. He almost never remembered the times she'd turned away from his touch because she was tired or not in the mood. Held in his memories, their marriage was forever perfect.

He wasn't sure how long he sat there staring at the photograph. He touched his fingertip to her face, as if he could trace her cheek. Instead of warm skin, he felt only glass. She was gone, and with her, the pain.

Instead of relief, he felt empty, as if a familiar companion had moved on without him. Now what? How did he remember? The sharp edges of hurt had kept him close to her. He loved her; he would always love her. Was that going to be enough? What would become of her if he let her go?

He lay back on the bed and rested the photograph facedown on his chest. Perhaps this is what Robin had wanted all along. After all it was his fault that she was gone. She'd died because of him.

Stacey had died because of him. Because of what he'd said to her. Because he'd let her go without a thought. Did Erin ever think of that? In the blackness of night, did she rail at him for what he'd stolen. Not only her sister, a twin so much like herself that they were nearly halves of the same whole, but he had also stolen her dreams. Whatever Erin had wanted after college had been snatched away by the day-to-day grind of looking after an infant.

He was dangerous to anyone who loved him. That put Christie in danger. He closed his eyes and swore he would die before he would let anything happen to his child. Somehow he would break the curse.

He also couldn't take a chance on Erin. He couldn't let her know that she was the first one to get through the barricade he'd built around himself. He couldn't let her know that she was slowly bringing him back to the land of the feeling. He would have to resist the life she offered and the passion he felt. If he didn't, she would be at risk, too.

The storm continued to rage for another thirty-six hours. When it was finally done, the sun made a watery appearance over the ocean.

Parker was at his computer when he first noticed a finger of light creeping across his desk. He glanced out the window and saw that the clouds had broken up and nearly blown away. Erin and Christie were in the second-floor library, going through books. Without stopping to consider that it might be best for everyone if he tried harder to stay away from Erin, he saved what he was working on, then left his office and started down the hall.

He paused in the doorway of the library. Books were in tall, teetering piles. Erin sat cross-legged on the floor with Christie curled up next to her.

"What's that one about, Mommy?" Christie asked, pointing at the book Erin had just picked up from a stack next to her.

"I'm not sure. Let's see. Hmm, it seems to be about elephants."

"Lelephants?"

"You've seen them in the zoo and on television."

"I *know* what they are," Christie informed her, her tone indicating everyone knew what "lelephants" were.

Erin leaned over and tickled her daughter one-handed. "Don't act so high and mighty with me, miss. You are only four years old, and I'm still your mother."

Christie wiggled closer and giggled. Their heads bent together. Erin put the book down and gathered the girl in her arms.

"You're my best girl," she said, then hugged her close.

"I love you, Mommy."

"And I love you."

Their affection was tangible. Parker could have watched them for hours. He felt the residual warmth of their caring and it helped heal him a little.

Suddenly Christie noticed him standing in the doorway. "Daddy!" she crowed, then grinned. "You've got a book on lelephants."

"So I heard," he said and stepped into the room.

Erin released Christie who scrambled to her feet and raced to him. He picked her up and swung her around the room. "What are you doing in here?" he asked.

"We're helpin'."

He settled her against his side. She slipped her legs around his waist and rested one arm on his shoulder. He leaned forward and they rubbed noses, a ritual she'd started a few days before.

"Looks like you're making a mess," he said.

Erin stood up and glanced around. "I can see why you'd think that, but trust me, the original plan was about helping. I thought we could get the library in order. Sort the books by type, then alphabetize them."

"You don't have to do that."

"I want to."

He risked looking at her. In jeans and pink T-shirt she looked more like Christie's baby-sitter than her mother. She met his gaze easily, as she had yesterday. He was the one who was nervous. Every time he looked at her, he relived their kiss and fought against the urge to do it again. Obviously she wasn't having the same kind of trouble. Or maybe it had only been good for him.

He dismissed that thought as soon as it appeared. He might not have been with a woman in a long time, and before that he might not have slept with a long list of women, but he knew a sensual response when he felt one. Erin had clung to him with unmistakable desire.

He supposed he should be grateful she was acting so normal. Life would be difficult if she were mooning after him, or worse, angry. But he couldn't quite make himself feel anything but annoyed that she was so calm.

"Parker, I have to do something with my time," she said as she dusted off her behind. "I'm not used to playing the lady of the manor. Besides, I like looking at all the different books. This is an amazing collection."

"I can't take credit for it. Some were here when I bought the house and I picked up the rest at estate sales."

"There's even some books for me," Christie said, plucking at his shirt to reclaim his attention. "You can read me one tonight."

"I can't wait."

She gave him her best smile.

"I have a surprise for you," he said, bouncing her in his arms.

"What?" she asked.

"It's sunny outside. I thought we could walk along the beach and look at what the storm blew in."

"That would be fun," Christie said and clapped her hands together. "Can we, Mommy?"

"Sure." Erin started out of the room. "I'll go grab our sweaters then meet you two in the foyer."

There were a few leaves and branches on the stairs down to the water. Parker went first and tested the way. Christie had insisted on climbing down on her own, although it took her nearly twice as long. Erin brought up the rear.

The breeze was stiff and cool. Sea gulls and some of the shore birds circled over the violent surf.

"We can't stay too long," Parker said, waving at the foamy water thundering onto the sand. "High tide today will cover the beach." He glanced at his watch. "We've got about an hour and a half."

Erin zipped up her blue sweatshirt, then adjusted the camera she'd hung around her neck. "That should be enough time to tire this one out." She bent over and buttoned Christie's jacket.

"I'm not tired," the little girl said.

"With any luck, you're going to be," Erin said, then smiled at him. "It's horrible when we get a couple of weeks of solid rain back home. She can't go outside and she practically jumps off the wall. Kids have so much energy. Sometimes I get worn out just watching her."

"Then we're going to have to run it out of her," Parker said. He pointed to a large twisted piece of wood that had washed on shore. It was about twenty-five feet away. "I'll race you, Christie."

"Okay, but I go first 'coz you got longer legs."

"All right, go!" he shouted.

She took off running. Her short legs pumped for all they were worth.

"You don't have to do this," Erin said, her hazel eyes bright with amusement.

"Why not? I've been cooped up, too." He started jogging. "I'm going to catch you," he called.

"No, you're not!"

Christie reached the driftwood three steps ahead of him.

"I won, I won, I won," she squealed, punctuating each "I won" with a little jump. Her small pink athletic shoes crunched on the sand but didn't make an imprint. Her pigtails flapped up and down.

He picked her up, turned her around in midair and set her on his shoulders. She grabbed hold of his sweater.

"Go fast!" she ordered.

"Yes, ma'am." He took off down the beach.

"Faster! Faster than anybody!"

He raced to the cliff, then back along the shore. Erin sat on the bottom step and loaded film into her camera.

"The wrong person is getting tired out," she told him as he ran by for the third time.

"I know," he said, his breathing heavy. He grabbed Christie and set her down. "Now it's your turn to carry me."

His daughter giggled at him. "Daddy, you're silly." She gave him a playful pat on the thigh, then turned and saw a small crab racing across the sand. "Come back, little crab. Come play with me." She hurried after her new playmate.

He leaned against the stair railing and glanced after her. "Sometimes it's hard for me to remember how small she is. She's so bright and articulate, I expect her to be bigger."

"And older," Erin agreed. "Sometimes I think she's secretly thirty-five and just her body is four. Other times, she's a real baby and I wonder if she'll ever grow up."

"But most of the time you know you were lucky when you got her."

Erin tilted her head and glanced up at him. "That's very perceptive, Parker."

"You think I don't feel the same way?"

"I suppose you must. I'm glad you appreciate her."

He placed one arm on the top of the railing and leaned toward her. "You took a big chance when you came to find me. I could have been a real jerk." Not to say he wasn't, but he was talking about his relationship with Christie, not Erin.

"I was worried at first," she admitted. "Then I found this article tucked away in the back of a business magazine. It was on successful entrepreneurs who gave back. Some of them were very flashy about it, but a lot weren't. There was a sidebar about some of the silent givers, I think they called them. You were listed there. I was impressed. I figured anyone who gave that much money to help kids get a decent education couldn't be all bad."

"Yeah, well." He shifted uncomfortably. "It's a tax write-off."

"Sure, Parker. Sell that somewhere else. I know the truth."

"What's that?"

She finished loading the film, then shut the back of the case. "You're just a softy at heart."

"Tell that to my competition."

"Maybe I will. They're trying to pry industrial secrets out of me. We chat nightly."

When she smiled, both her dimples appeared. He decided he liked looking at her. She wasn't conventionally beautiful. Some men might not think she was even pretty, but he disagreed. She had an honest and open face. He knew he could trust her. And she had a warm and giving heart. That was more important than model-perfect beauty any day.

"Look what I found," Christie said, racing toward them. She held a shell in her hand. It was small and circular, pale cream on the outside and the softest pink within.

"I wonder how it survived the storm," Erin murmured as she raised the camera to her left eye. "Honey, hold your hand up by your chin, but flat. That's right. Don't you think I'm being silly?"

"Yes," Christie said as she did what her mother asked. "Very silly."

"I want you to make a face and show me how silly."

Christie wrinkled her nose, then grinned. "You're funny, too, Mommy."

"I know." The camera clicked several times, then Erin lowered it to her lap. "Do you want me to keep your shell for you?"

"You're busy," Christie said. "Here, Daddy. You keep it." She carefully handed him her treasure, then returned to search the shoreline for more."

Along with shells and battered pieces of wood there were bottles, a couple of cans, bits of clothing and twisted chunks of metal and plastic that could have come from anywhere. The tide would take most of it back tonight and in a few days the sand would be clean again.

"A dinghy washed up here once," he said.

"Had it come loose from a larger boat?" Erin asked as she stood up.

"Probably. It wasn't marked, though, so I had no way to find the owners. I ended up donating it to a kids' club in town."

"I'm sure they appreciated that."

He shrugged.

"Why do you do these nice things, then act all weird when I mention them?" she asked.

"I don't do them to get noticed. It's just right."

Hazel eyes studied him. Her mouth pulled into a straight line. "Sometimes you're a confusing man, Parker Hamilton."

She was close enough to touch, close enough for him to feel her heat and want to pull her into his arms. "Is that good or bad?"

"I'm not sure," she admitted, then started toward Christie.

Christie had found a small plastic bucket, no doubt left over from a child's afternoon at the beach. She filled it with sand and water. "In case I catch a crab," she said. "I can take it home."

"Fortunately the crabs are faster than you," Erin said, then kissed the top of her daughter's head. "You're a wild one."

As Christie raced around, finding treasures and chasing sand crabs, Erin took her picture. A couple of times she took him, although he wasn't sure why she would want to.

At one point she had him put Christie on his shoulders, then seated them on the large piece of wood. She took her pictures slowly, thinking out what she wanted rather than just snapping randomly. He liked watching her try different angles and turn them so the sun hit just right.

"You take your photography seriously," he said when he set Christie on the sand.

Erin shrugged. "I've always liked it. There was a time when I'd hoped to become a professional photographer."

"What got in the way?"

"Life in the form of an unexpected child."

He glanced at Christie. Her pigtails bounced in time with her skipping steps. She swung her bucket back and forth as she danced to the far end of the cove.

"I'm not saying she wasn't worth it," Erin added quickly as she followed his gaze. "I love her more than I ever thought it possible to love anyone. And I wouldn't give her up for the world. But she wasn't part of the original plan."

"What was the plan?" he asked.

Erin opened the back of the camera and pulled out the full roll of film. She stuffed it into her front right pocket. She transferred the camera to her opposite hand, then removed a new roll of film from her front left pocket.

"I was going to study photojournalism in college."

"But you went to college."

"I was going to study it in grad school. For my bachelor's, I got my degree in English, with an emphasis on history. I wanted something to fall back on. I thought if I couldn't make a living as a photographer, I would be able to get my teaching credentials."

"Which you did because of Christie."

"Right." She dropped the film into the back of the camera and set it in place. She clicked the cover closed and advanced the roll. "I guess I lost my turn."

"What does that mean?"

"Oh, nothing really. Just something Stacey and I used to talk about. Usually there wasn't enough money for both of us to do something, so we took turns. She was more intense than I was, so she usually went first. I've gotten very good at waiting my turn."

He thought about her plans. "But this time Fate intervened."

"Something like that."

He stared out at the ocean. Despite the growing strength of the sun, the water remained a cold muddy gray. The storm had churned up the bottom and it would take a few days for everything to settle back down and for the water to turn blue again.

Like the ocean, Erin's world had been turned upside down, but she hadn't had a chance to return to what she used to be. She wouldn't get her turn because of him. Yet another of his sins. All because of a single night. If only he'd refused what Stacey had offered. If only he hadn't felt so damn empty inside.

"I wish things could have been different for you," he said.

Her gaze darkened. "Parker, it just happened. You didn't plan on—" She paused and blushed. "On doing that with Stacey, and you certainly didn't know that she was going to get pregnant."

"And why aren't you taking pictures instead of teaching school?"

"Because it's not my turn yet," she said. "I don't mind waiting."

She'd waited her whole life, he thought. He wondered if she ever wanted to just seize her turn and be done with it.

"You don't need a degree to take pictures," he told her. "You're doing it now."

"I know." She glanced at the camera. "I like to take the odd photo or two. Most of Christie. But it's not the same. I have a good eye, but I need some training in composition, light, that kind of thing."

"You sure that's not an excuse to let fear get in the way of what you want to do?" he asked without thinking.

"An interesting question from a man who lives like a hermit," she said, then turned away and started toward Christie.

He felt her anger and the faint whisper of hurt. "Erin, I didn't mean anything by that." He hurried to catch up with her. "Erin?"

She stopped and looked at him. "I know. I guess you touched a nerve." Her gaze intensified. "Maybe I did, too. It's okay that you live like a hermit."

He touched her cheek. She didn't pull away. "It's okay that you're scared to take pictures," he said.

Once again he wanted to kiss her. He wanted to take her in his arms and make love to her until they both forgot their pain and their pasts. But they weren't alone. This was neither the time nor the place. If he were very careful, he could avoid ever finding the right time and place. Then maybe, just maybe, they would both get out of this in one piece.

"Race you to the end of the cove," he said, sprinting in that direction.

"No fair," she called after him. "You got a head start."

As they laughed, the tension between them faded.

* * *

"A family is very imp...imp... Daddy, what's that word?" Christie asked, holding up her book.

Parker leaned over the side of his chair. Christie was on the floor next to him, reading in front of the fire. Erin sat on the sofa deeply engrossed in a book of her own. They'd just finished dinner and Kiki had already left for one of her rendezvous.

"Important," he said. "See, you can sound it out. *Im-por-tant*."

"What's a 'tant'?"

"It's not a real word. It's just a sound."

She wrinkled her nose. "I like real words better than sounds. Sounds are hard."

She rolled onto her back, pulled the book with her and continued to read. "A family is very important. We all have a family. A family can be big or little. A family is more than just a mommy or a daddy." She dropped the book to her chest. "Is Kiki part of my family?"

Parker didn't know how to answer that. "I defer to the resident expert. Erin?"

"Hmm?" She glanced up from her book. "What?"

"Is Kiki part of my family?" Christie asked.

"Sure."

"Is Millie?"

Millie, Parker remembered, was Christie's favorite doll.

"Yes," Erin said. "Family is anyone we care about a great deal. Pets can be part of a family."

Christie sat up and grinned. "So if I had a puppy, he would be part of the family."

Erin groaned and leaned her head back on the sofa. "I can't believe I said that."

"You brought it on yourself," Parker told her.

"I know."

"A puppy would be very nice," Christie said. "Just a little one. He would be very quiet."

"Somehow I doubt that." Erin looked at her daughter. "You're not going to get a puppy tonight. Nor are you going to convince me to get you a puppy. Why don't you go get Millie and bring her downstairs and I'll read you both a story?"

"Okay." Christie scrambled to her feet and raced out of the room.

"You handled that very well," Parker said. "This parent thing is harder than I thought."

"It has its rewards."

He nodded. "I see that." The lamplight caught her hair and turned the red highlights to the color of fire. "I'm glad you agreed to stay. I appreciate the time to get to know Christie so it will be more comfortable when she's here on her own."

"Oh, I thought I'd break you in gently. Maybe give you a practice session or two. You know, leave you two alone for an afternoon."

"When?" he asked, suppressing his uneasiness at the prospect. God knows what horrible mistakes he could make in a few hours. Thinking about being alone with Christie was fine as long as the reality of it was in the future.

Erin laughed. "Parker, you look as if I just threatened to murder nuns. It's going to be fine. You and Christie get along great."

"Sure, while you're around. What if she starts to cry? What if she falls down and hurts herself? What will we talk about? What will we do?"

"You'll figure it all out. I promise."

He didn't believe that. Maybe he could convince Erin to join her daughter when Christie visited here. Not just because the thought of being alone with Christie made him nervous but also because he liked having Erin around. She was funny and bright. She considered herself on equal footing with him. He knew she often forgot he was a millionaire several times over. He liked that. He hadn't grown up around money so he wasn't used to people treating him differently.

She set her book down and leaned forward on the sofa. Her feet were tucked under her. "Kiki will be here," she reminded him. "I'm sure if you ask her, she'll forgo her nocturnal visiting. At least for the first couple of nights."

"Very funny," he muttered.

She laughed. The sweet sound found an answering chord deep in his chest. Sometimes he thought her laughter was the most healing sound he'd ever heard. She complicated the hell out of his world. He wanted her. He liked her. He refused to screw things up by acting on his desire.

Life was damn hard sometimes, but he knew how to make it easy. He wasn't going to let her know she got to him. He was going to be her friend, nothing more. He was going to be polite and pleasant and never let on that he'd once had the insane thought of asking her and Christie to stay. Permanently.

Chapter Ten

Erin opened the large manila envelope and dumped the contents onto the small desk in the corner of her room. She sorted through her forwarded mail, picking out the bills, tossing junk mail disguised as real correspondence. There wasn't much here. Her rent was due, as were the utilities and the phone bill. Four bills. She got her checkbook from her purse and started to write.

Ten minutes later, she had finished. She leaned back in her chair, then glanced out the open window to her right. A perfect starry night winked back at her. If someone had told her she was going away for the summer she would have thought it would take weeks to prepare. But the reality was very different. Joyce picked up her mail and forwarded it once a week. The landlord's gardener took care of the small yard. There were no pets, no other commitments. She and Christie had simply disappeared into Northern California and no one noticed.

That wasn't completely true, Erin reminded herself. Joyce noticed. She'd called a couple of times to make sure Erin knew what she was doing. Erin always told her yes, even though she wasn't sure. She'd been here a month. In that time, she, Parker and Christie had settled into a routine. They were living like a family. She enjoyed the situation, even if it wasn't real.

Joyce warned her that Parker could still be an ax murderer in disguise. Erin had reassured her friend on that point. Parker was a complex man, but he wasn't a sociopath. They were both a little confused about their relationship. It was complicated by Christie, the fact they were strangers trying to parent together, and by the past. And by her attraction to him.

As she sealed the envelopes and wrote the return address, she fought the memories of that night they'd had the storm. The night he'd said he was attracted to her and then had kissed her.

She'd relived that night a thousand times in her mind. Every time she was just as confused and just as aroused. What had really happened between them? Why had he walked away from her? Not that she wasn't grateful, because she was. She hadn't been with a man in years and she and Parker had barely known each other a few days. It was too soon, although her hormones didn't agree.

But why had he kissed her? Should she believe what he said? Logically it made no sense to lie to her. She'd already agreed to let Christie spend the summer, so there wasn't anything to be gained by seducing her or pretending a physical attraction that didn't really exist. In fact, a physical relationship would only complicate matters between them.

Was it just straight sexual awareness? Was she trying to make it more complicated than it needed to be? Erin smiled. What a concept! It was possible he really wanted her, she supposed. Although she'd gotten so used to thinking of herself as a sexless single mother, a man finding her attractive was startling to say the least.

After four weeks, Parker still had the power to make her knees tremble. She hated the weakness and loss of control. Fortunately he hadn't done anything about it. Since that last kiss, he'd been a perfect gentleman. They'd spent long afternoons together with Christie. Once Christie was in bed, she and Parker often talked in the evenings. She'd even shared some details about her past. And through it all, he'd barely touched her. She was relieved.

Erin brushed the tip of her nose to see if it was growing. She didn't usually lie to herself. Especially not about something so obvious. She wasn't relieved. She was confused and aroused and frustrated. She wanted to grab Parker by his shirtfront and kiss him until they forgot the "supposed tos" and simply reacted. She wanted to run home to Palmdale and pretend this summer had never happened. She wanted to follow Kiki on her next date and ask if the guy had a friend.

Instead of doing any of that, she collected her mail and left the bedroom. Before heading downstairs, she stuck her head in Christie's room. The little girl was sound asleep in her bed. Erin moved back into the hall and headed for the stairs.

She paused on the second-floor landing and glanced out the window. It was one of those perfect summer nights that usually only happen in the movies. The stars were a glinting backdrop for the brilliant half moon. Below, the ocean reached endlessly for the shore. The temperature was still pleasant.

She continued down the stairs. The house was quiet. It usually was once Christie was in bed and Kiki had left for her evening out. Erin envied the other woman's life-style. Not that she, Erin, wanted to be having sex with three different men. She envied Kiki's freedom and her willingness to do exactly what she wanted. Kiki was happy and content. Erin was only mildly frustrated to admit that Kiki had had more sex in the past month than Erin had had in her whole life.

When she reached the main floor, she dropped her bills on the table by the front door. Kiki would take them out to the mail tomorrow. As she turned toward the stairs, Erin noticed the terrace doors were open. She could see Parker standing by the waist-high stone wall.

She walked toward him. "Is this a private party or can anyone come?" she asked.

He settled one hip on the stone wall and beckoned her closer. "You're welcome if you don't mind sharing the dance floor with a few ghosts."

"Don't tell me this place is haunted. I haven't heard a peep since I arrived."

His dark hair drifted onto his forehead. He brushed it back with a smooth, easy gesture. "No ghosts in residence. The only ones here tonight are mine."

She moved closer and studied him. "Are you all right?"

His dark gaze met hers. "Never better."

She saw the pain etched in his face and knew the ghosts he talked about were from his past. "Liar," she said softly. "There *is* something wrong."

"Yeah, I knew you were going to say that. I thought maybe I could fool you."

"I know you pretend to be a tough guy, but the act is wasted on me. I saw you reading a bedtime story to your daughter tonight. Hardly a macho act."

Instead of teasing her back, as he usually did, Parker stared out at the ocean. "That damn book," he muttered.

The day had been warm. He wore a red polo shirt tucked into tailored shorts. She'd tried not to notice his long, lean, tanned legs as he'd walked around the house. Thank goodness it was too dark to see them clearly now. But she could see the sadness twisting his mouth and the restless stirring of his hands as he first gripped the railing, then folded his arms over his chest. His brooding emotions doused her heat as effectively as a cold shower.

She moved closer still, this time spurred by compassion rather than desire. "What book?"

"Christie's book on families. That's what I was reading to her tonight."

"I don't understand."

He shrugged. "It's about what makes up a family and explains how families can be different, so long as they work. It made me think about—"

"Robin?" she asked quietly.

"I wish. That would be easy. It made me think about my folks."

"What about them? Do you want them to meet Christie? I wouldn't mind. They must be very proud of you and all you've accomplished."

He laughed harshly. "You'd think so, but they don't give a damn."

"Parker, I'm sorry." She leaned against the railing and stared up at him. She and Stacey had lost their parents at a young age. She would have given anything to have been able to change that. All she and Stacey had cared about was being part of a family again. Why couldn't people realize how lucky they were before they lost everything?

"I tell myself they're unhappy people," he said. "When I was growing up they never talked. I would go to friends' houses for dinner and their parents actually talked to each other. Not my folks. The television always played at dinner, no one ever spoke."

"How did you get into computers?" she asked.

"A science project in junior high. I had a weird teacher who encouraged exploring different things. I wanted to learn what made a computer work so he gave me a broken one to take apart. The first time I looked inside and saw all the components, then sat down with a working system, I thought it was magic. Then I figured out how to make that magic work for me.''

He continued to stare out at the ocean. "I tried to tell my dad about it that night, but he didn't want to listen. He drove a cement truck, worked hard all day and just wanted to come home and sit in front of the television. I never did figure out what my mother did with her life. She didn't work, but she was always too busy for me. Eventually I gave up trying to get their attention. I buried myself in computers and never looked up until college.''

He'd told her this part. "When Robin was your lab partner.''

"Yeah. We were nerds together.''

It was funny, but over the past week or so, his talking about Robin had ceased to bother her. Erin wasn't sure why. His voice changed when he mentioned his late wife. She knew he loved her and would always love her. But Robin was gone and she'd figured out that because Parker was faithful enough to continue to mourn her, he was the kind of person she wanted to know.

"I can't picture you being a nerd," she said. "You're too good-looking.''

He glanced at her and raised his eyebrows. "You think I'm good-looking?''

She rolled her eyes, then realized that's where Christie had picked up the habit. "Stop fishing for a compliment." She leaned close to him and gently bumped him with her shoulder. "You've done great. If your parents don't want to acknowledge that, it's their loss.''

"I tell myself that. When we first hit it big, I sent them a check for fifty thousand dollars. I thought they could fix up the house, or sell it and move somewhere else. Maybe buy a car. I was willing to give them anything they wanted.''

"What happened?"

"Nothing. They didn't move, they didn't even get new carpeting. My mother barely mentioned receiving the check. I know they got it because it cleared the bank, but the last time I visited them, everything was the same, right down to the peeling linoleum in the kitchen."

"How sad for them and you," she murmured.

He placed his hand on the back of her head and drew her close to him. She rested her forehead against his chest. The contact wasn't sexual. She sensed he wanted comfort and connection. She was pleased to offer both.

"Some people are afraid of living," he said. "There's nothing I can do about that."

His words echoed in her brain. *Some people are afraid of living. You're going to die before you get your turn.* Different voices, different sentences, same sentiment. Parker's parents hid from life. Is that what she was doing? Was she like them, living an empty existence, so mired in unhappiness that the thought of moving on was more than she could imagine?

She didn't want to believe that. She wasn't unhappy. She had her job. It wasn't her dream or even close to perfect, but it wasn't horrible. Then there was Christie. The little girl was the most precious gift she'd ever received. Christie was alive. But was she the only one?

"What are you thinking?" Parker asked. He placed his finger under her chin and forced her to look at him. "Did I say something to upset you?"

"Why do you ask?"

"You've gone all stiff."

She sighed. "I was just thinking about what you said and wondering if I'm like your parents."

He smiled. "Trust me, you're nothing like them."

"Don't be so quick to say that." She placed her hands on his waist. His presence warmed and comforted her. "Do you remember when we went down to the beach a couple of weeks ago? It was right after the storm.''

''Yes.''

''I brought my camera and told you about my dream of being a professional photographer. You asked me why I wasn't doing what I wanted to do.''

''You told me it was because you didn't get to study in graduate school.''

She nodded. ''And you pointed out that I didn't need a degree to take pictures.''

''I had no right to say that.''

''Didn't you? I'm not so sure. You made an excellent point. I've been thinking about it ever since. Why do I need a degree to take pictures? I own a camera. I can afford film.''

He placed his hands on her shoulders. ''You'll take pictures when you're ready.''

''When I quit being afraid, you mean. I know that's what this is about.''

She started to turn away, but he held her in place. ''Erin, you're the bravest person I know. You've raised Christie on your own and you've done a damn fine job.''

''Thanks. But that wasn't about being brave.''

''Weren't you scared doing it on your own?''

''Sure. I was terrified. But I didn't have a choice.''

''You could have given her up for adoption.''

''No. Never. I loved her from the moment I knew she was alive.''

''So you were scared, but you did it anyway. That's what being brave means.''

''It makes sense when you say it,'' she mumbled, turning away in embarrassment. This time he let her go. She walked to the small table and pulled out one of the chairs. Parker followed her and took the one opposite. They sat in the darkness and gazed up at the stars.

"It's a beautiful night," she said. "And warm. That's a nice change." She rubbed her bare arms. Like Parker, she was wearing a shirt and shorts.

"Do you ever think about Stacey?" he asked.

She glanced at him. He was still looking at the sky. "Yes."

"Often?"

"I think of her more now than I used to. Probably because I'm here with you. At first I missed her terribly. We'd been attending separate colleges, but I still felt connected to her. I suppose it's a twin thing. I just knew she was there and that I could count on her. Then when she was gone, it was as if someone had ripped out a piece of heart." She paused. "That sounds so melodramatic."

"It sounds honest," he said. He placed his hands flat on the table between them. "I'm sorry she's gone, Erin, and about what you had to go through. I know it doesn't change the past, but I want you to know that I take full responsibility for what happened that summer. I accept the blame for Stacey's death."

She stared at him. What was he talking about? "You had nothing to do with it."

"You weren't here that morning, Erin. You don't know what I said to her."

"Words don't kill someone."

"They can take away a reason for living."

He was telling the truth as he saw it, she realized, stunned that he blamed himself for Stacey's death. Why? "Even if you had destroyed her emotionally, it's not as if she left here and drove her car off a cliff. She lived for several more months."

"Nine," he said grimly. "Nine months carrying a child she knew I wouldn't want. Nine months of keeping secrets from the one person she loved in the world. You."

His pain swept over and around her. She ached for him, and for Stacey.

He drew in a deep breath. "I was drunk the night she came to me. Several students had taken a break and headed into town, but Stacey stayed here."

Erin realized he was going to tell her what had happened that night. She wasn't sure she wanted to hear the details, but she couldn't think of a way to stop him from talking.

"I knew she had a crush on me, but I couldn't get past the grief enough to figure out what to do. I should have sent her away. Or turned her down." He leaned forward. "I swear, Erin, I didn't plan to be with her that night. Then she was here offering herself, and I figured I could use her to forget the pain." He laughed harshly and without humor.

Erin moved her hands to her lap so he couldn't see she was shaking. Emotion built up inside her. Concern for Parker, regret and empathy for Stacey, confusion for herself. His story made her ache for what had happened. It also made her think about loving Parker and the forbidden fantasy was powerful in its intensity.

"I used her," he said. "But it didn't help. The next morning I knew I'd betrayed Robin's memory and that some connection between us had been severed. I was enraged, both at myself for my weakness and at Stacey for daring to be alive."

He leaned back in his chair and closed his eyes. "She tried to hold me and tell me she loved me. I told her she was a child. She didn't know what real love was. While she lay there, naked in my bed, I stripped her soul bare and ridiculed her. I told her about how Robin and I had met and what we'd meant to each other. I deliberately made Stacy feel foolish and used."

He pushed the chair away abruptly and walked to the edge of the terrace. Erin watched him go. She thought about the letter of apology Stacey had written to Parker. She remembered the haunted sadness in her sister's eyes when she'd come home at the end of that summer. Parker's truth came from self-loathing. Stacey's truth came from her infatuation. Erin suspected the real truth about what had really happened that morning lay somewhere in the middle.

She stood up and moved toward him. She could feel his tension. Cautiously she put her hand on his back. He stiffened but didn't pull away.

"I've read my sister's diary," she said. "I know what you did was wrong, but she was wrong, too. From the moment she saw you, she was determined to see you the way she wanted to."

"The dark prince," he muttered. "Some prince."

"She created a dream based on her past and what she'd always wanted. You had nothing to do with that. You have to see she manipulated the situation so she could get what she wanted. I'm not saying you weren't at fault, too. She *was* young, you should have known better. But Stacey was just as wrong. She wasn't willing to admit that you were still in love with your wife. She only cared about *her* dream. She hurt you, Parker, and she finally figured it out. Don't you remember? That's why she apologized in the letter."

"You don't understand."

"Of course I do. Stacey was my sister. I knew her better than anyone."

"I destroyed her."

"What about what she did to you?" she asked.

He was silent for a long time. Erin kept her hand on his back hoping the physical connection would comfort him. She ached for both of them. For the young woman her sister had been, for the grief-stricken husband Parker had been. They'd both needed something. If the circumstances had been different, perhaps they could have found it together. Or maybe their odd relationship had been destined for tragedy from the beginning.

"You're very generous," he said. "What I did was wrong."

"Yes, but I refuse to believe that a single conversation could destroy Stacey. She was stronger than that."

He spun toward her. "Then why *did* she die? You don't know, do you? I do. She died for the same reason Robin did. Stacey died because she'd lost the will to live."

"Oh, Parker, you've got to let this go." Erin took a step closer and wrapped her arms around his waist. "It wasn't like that. Stacey was doing fine. She finished her classes at college. She even got good grades. Does that sound like someone who has lost the will to live? She died because there was a complication in the pregnancy. It was a one in a million chance that something could go wrong." She tilted her head back and stared at him. "She had a beautiful baby she wanted to live for. She'd seen Christie. How could she see her child and still want to die?"

Their gazes locked. She could see the war being waged in his eyes. Would her words be enough to defeat years of blaming himself?

"It's all there in the letter I gave you. The one Stacey wrote. She apologized, Parker. She knew she'd been wrong. And she said that she wasn't sure whether or not to tell you about the baby. She planned to make a decision after Christie was born. Those aren't the words of someone who wants to die. She had a future, something to live for. She had me. She knew I would support her, no matter what."

"You don't know how much I want to believe you," he said hoarsely.

"Then do. I have no reason to lie about this. I loved my sister with all my heart. She was brilliant and funny and the best friend I ever had. I'll always miss her. But I know her, Parker. I know her dreams and I know what happened to her that summer. She lost her head. So accept your part of the blame, but don't take it all on yourself. Leave some for the rest of us.''

''Are you sure?''

Her heart ached for him. ''Of course I'm sure. Obviously it's the destiny of the Ridgeway women to have a serious crush on you. We're just going to have to learn how to handle it better.''

She spoke without thinking. As the meaning of the words sunk in, Erin wanted to call them back. But it was too late. She stepped away from Parker, then turned her back on him. Oh, Lord, why couldn't she think before speaking?

She could feel the flush of embarrassment climbing her cheeks. At least it was dark and he wouldn't be able to see. She pressed her hands against her face.

''What I meant was—'' she muttered in a strangled voice, then realized she didn't have a quick line to make it all sound right.

''Erin?''

She cleared her throat. ''I think it's time for me to make my escape.''

Before she could leave, he grabbed her arm and turned her toward him. His gaze searched her face. ''Erin?''

Okay, there was no easy way out of this. She would survive the moment. To the best of her knowledge, no one had actually ever died of embarrassment.

She stared at the open collar of his polo shirt. ''Look, it's no big deal. Really. It's just the stress of the situation, and being here. You've been nice to Christie and me. You know, I *am* a single mother. I don't get out much. Socially, I mean.''

She was babbling.

He touched a finger to her chin, forcing her to look at his face. His eyes were bright with an emotion she couldn't read. His mouth curved up at the corners.

''Stop looking at me like that,'' she said.

"Like what?"

"Like I'm Christie, and I've just given you a dopey looking drawing."

"You're nothing like Christie."

Was that good or bad? "This doesn't change anything. I'm not Stacey. I'm not going to get you drunk and seduce you."

"Too bad."

"What?"

He moved a little closer. The finger touching her jaw slid up and caressed her cheek. The sound of the ocean faded to a dull roar.

"Parker, you're not listening to me. I'll admit that I sort of fell for you while I was reading Stacey's diary. I mean she made you sound terrific and I thought...well, I'm not sure what I thought. Anyway, then I got here and you were good-looking and sweet to Christie and I like to think any woman in my position would have reacted the same way. But it's not a problem."

"You're talking too much."

"Huh?" His finger brushed against her skin, moving back and forth. He was making it difficult to think. "I'm saying I can control my feelings. This doesn't have to change anything. You don't have to worry about me."

"I'm not worried."

With that he dipped his head lower and brushed his mouth against hers.

Like a lit match touching dry tinder, fire exploded inside her. Instinctively she clung to him. He wrapped his arms around her waist and hauled her hard against him. His tongue swept against her lips. She parted for him, seeking him as he entered, shivering when he began to explore her mouth.

She was ablaze with heat and long-denied need. She wanted him. All of him. So it took every ounce of will-power to pull back.

"You don't have to do this," she said, her voice trembling. "I don't want you to kiss me because you feel sorry for me."

He laughed. "Erin, do you remember the last time I kissed you?"

She nodded.

"I told you then I was concerned that my attraction to you was making you uncomfortable."

"I thought you were kidding," she whispered.

"Fool," he said gently, then pressed his lips to her forehead. "I didn't want to scare you off. And I didn't want you to think I was using sex to keep Christie."

"You'd never do that."

"I know that. I didn't know if you did. There's something powerful between us. Maybe it's time we stopped resisting and went along for the ride."

She wasn't sure. This could be an elaborate trick to make her feel better about mentioning the crush. Then he pressed his hips against hers and she felt the hard ridge of his desire. That part would be difficult to fake. Okay, he *did* want her. Now what?

"I'm not Stacey," she said, voicing the fear she didn't want to admit she had.

"I know, Erin." He cupped her face in his hands. "You're afraid I just want to relive the past."

"Maybe."

"The only thing I remember about that night is that I wanted to get so lost, the pain couldn't find me anymore. This isn't about that. This is about you and me and how much I want you in my bed. No ghosts this time."

She believed him. Maybe because she wanted to. A thousand questions filled her mind, but she ignored them. She ignored everything but the man in front of her. If she trusted him with her child, then surely she could trust him with her body. She raised herself on her toes and pressed her mouth to his.

Chapter Eleven

She was soft and sweet as she pressed against him. Parker felt his body harden more as she leaned into their kiss. In the past five years he'd been aroused on occasion. There were mornings he awoke with the lingering physical evidence of an erotic dream. A cold shower quickly diluted his need. But not this time. He could feel heat burning away the barriers he'd constructed. This time there was no turning back.

He broke their kiss and wrapped his arm around her shoulders. "I think we need some privacy," he said.

"What?" She glanced around the terrace, then smiled sheepishly. "Oh, we're outside. I'd forgotten."

"Good."

As they crossed to the stairs, she looked at him. "Parker, are you sure?"

"I haven't been as sure of anything in a long time."

"I'm a little nervous."

"Because of everything in the past?" He wanted to reassure her. She was the only woman he was thinking about. Briefly he wondered if that was wrong. Should he still be caught up in the grief of his wife's passing? Then he decided he didn't want to have to think about that right now. Tonight he wanted to feel alive. In Erin's arms, in her body, he could find life again. He could see the colors and do away with the dull gray of his world.

"Actually it's because I haven't, well, done this sort of thing in a while. What if I've forgotten how?"

They'd reached the second-floor landing. A light glowed in the hallway. He turned to her and studied her large, hazel eyes. Confusion dilated her pupils.

"It's been a long time for me, too. I think we can fumble through together." He ran his hands up and down her bare arms. "I did some remodeling on this floor a few years back. Kiki helped. We moved the master and put in different furniture. The bed is about three years old."

She frowned. "Why on earth are you telling me that now?"

"I didn't want you to think—" He paused, not sure how to explain it.

"Oh!" She smiled. "You didn't want me to think that it was the same room and bed you'd had while you and Robin were together."

"Yeah."

"Parker, that's so sweet." She raised on her toes and pressed her mouth to his.

Her lips were hot and slick from their last kiss. He wanted to devour her. Instead he held back, pressing gently, testing the seam until she parted for him.

This time, instead of allowing him to enter and taste her, she thrust into his mouth. She explored him, then teased the tip of his tongue with hers.

Desire ripped through him with all the force of lightning across the sky. The pulsing in his body increased as his erection flexed painfully against the fly of his shorts. He hauled her hard against him, then tilted his head to allow her to go deeper and reach all of him.

She was the aggressor, circling him, retreating, then advancing. Her teeth clamped down on his lower lip and she nibbled the sensitive skin. He was breathing hard. Every muscle in his body tightened. He could feel the blood racing, fed by the rapid pounding of his heart.

He ran his hands up and down her back. The curve of her rear taunted him. He slipped lower and gripped the fullness, squeezing gently and urging her closer. Her belly brushed against his arousal. He groaned and wondered if he would explode right then.

He broke the kiss and leaned close. "The bedroom is about ten feet down the hall. If we concentrate, I think we can make it there."

She giggled. "You think so?"

"I know so." With that he put his arms around her waist and lifted her off the ground. "At last I have you under my control," he murmured.

She was still smiling when he kissed her again. The smile faded as she sighed. This time he was the aggressor. He licked her lips, tracing the shape before dipping inside.

She clung to him, then shifted so she could wrap her legs around his hips. Her hot center pressed against his need. She rocked her hips slowly.

He caught his breath. "I don't think you have to worry about having forgotten a damn thing," he said.

"Oh, Parker." She buried her face in his shoulder. "You make me laugh. I didn't know how much I missed that. I was so scared and nervous but this is going to be fun. Thank you."

"Don't you think you're thanking me a little too soon? It could still be awful."

She raised her head. "No, it couldn't." She kissed the tip of his nose.

He started for the bedroom.

When he kicked the door shut behind him, they were plunged into darkness. Erin's legs were still wrapped around his hips and she still pressed sweetly against his erection. He wasn't sure if he should let her slide down and risk losing control all at once or if he should continue to be tortured to death. He settled on a compromise. He made his way to the bed and sat. She was still close to him, but now she was on his lap and not pressed up against his need.

He reached for the lamp on the nightstand. Soft light filled their half of the room. He could see the faint flush on her cheeks and her hard nipples pressed against her T-shirt.

He brushed her hair back, then fingered the red-brown strands. "You're very beautiful," he said.

"No, I'm not. I'm average."

"I'm the man, and I get to think you're beautiful if I want to."

She smiled. Her hands rested on his shoulders; her thighs hugged his. The night stretched before them, endless in its possibilities. He was in physical pain from desire, but he wanted to go slow. He wanted this to last . . . for both of them.

"I'm the woman and I get to tell you that you're wrong," she said. "But thank you for saying it anyway." She leaned close and kissed his cheek. "Besides, you're the beautiful one."

A faint heat rose on his cheeks. "Men aren't beautiful."

"Oh, but they are. Your eyes, the hard lines of your face, the shape of your chin, your dark hair. I've thought about touching it." She placed her fingers on his head, then fingered the short strands. He'd never thought of his hair as an erogenous zone, but he felt her caress down to his toes.

"What else?" he asked. "*Where* else?"

"Here," she said, running her index finger across his mouth. She repeated the action, this time with her tongue. His hips arched toward her.

"I've thought about touching you here," he said, circling the sweet spot below her right ear. He pressed his lips there and tasted her skin. She shivered.

"Here," she whispered, touching the bottom of the open V of his shirt. Hot breath fanned his skin an instant before she kissed him there. He had to hold back a groan.

"Here," he murmured and touched the puckered point of her breast. Her eyes widened and her fingers tightened on his shoulders.

He dropped his hands to her waist and drew her up until she was kneeling in front of him. He opened his mouth and blew warm air over the small point, then bit her gently through the layers of her T-shirt and bra.

She sucked in a breath and arched toward him. With one quick jerk, he pulled her shirt hem out of her shorts and drew it up over her body. She freed her arms and tossed the garment aside.

Her bra was white and lacy. He could see her pale skin and her rosy puckered nipples. He buried his face between the lush curves.

"I want you, Erin," he groaned. "I can't tell you how good this feels."

"I know," she said, and hugged him close.

As his fingers moved up her spine toward the hooks on the back of her bra, he inhaled the female scent of her. The valley between her curves was a tempting resting spot, but he had other places to be before the night was over. He pressed a kiss to her breastbone, then turned his attention to her generous curves.

He nuzzled her skin. She was warm and as smooth as silk. He licked the first hint of fullness. He found then released the hooks of her bra. Thin straps slipped off her shoulders. The lace inched down, exposing more and more of her feminine flesh until he could see the pink circles around her nipples.

She pulled her bra off her arms and let it fall to the ground. Her full breasts swayed with the action. He caught them in his hands. The lush curves filled his palms. He cupped her gently, then brushed his fingers against the tips. She sucked in a breath and exhaled his name. Her hands tangled in his hair, urging him closer. He opened his mouth and tasted the tight pink peak.

She was sweeter than he would have imagined. Sweet and alive. He circled his tongue around the firm tip, then drew it deeply into his mouth. She surged toward him, swaying in time with his ministrations. Her breath came in tight little gasps, as if she had no control over herself.

He turned his head slightly and found her other breast, his fingers touching the damp heat of the first. He repeated the action, drawing her inside, tasting her, learning what made her stiffen and what made her sigh. She trembled in his embrace.

With his free hand he explored her back, then slid around to touch her ribs. She was all curves and valleys to his hard planes. Even her skin felt different than his, so smooth and supple. He dropped his hand to her bare thigh, then rode the lean length up to the hem of her shorts. He moved over cloth to cup her rear. He could feel her heat as she arched against him.

She whispered his name. She pressed her breasts toward him, urging him to take more, to touch her more. She wanted him and her desire made him drunk with life. He'd forgotten what it was like to hold another person so intimately, to taste skin, to feel flesh rippling with fire. He'd forgotten the intensity of the heat. The few times he'd sought release had been quick couplings without emotional connection. He'd forgotten what it meant to make love with someone. He'd forgotten the soul-healing pleasure of intimacy.

He wanted to bury himself inside her and explode into waiting feminine warmth. But more than that, he wanted to bring Erin to the edge of sanity, then watch her fall off the other side. He wanted her shaking and frantic, out of control.

To that end, he moved his fingers around her leg and up inside her shorts. He sought and found the elastic edge of her panties, then slipped inside. He could feel her need beckoning him.

Moist heat engulfed him. Slick female flesh promised paradise. He explored her, the tender folds, the damp curls, the tight passage that would lead him to ecstasy. He dipped inside of her, fitting first one finger, then two. She spread her knees wider. Her hands clutched his head, holding him against her breasts. Then he slid up until he found the tiny place of pleasure.

With the first stroke of his fingertip, a shudder racked her body. He felt an answering echo down to his groin. He pulled his hand free, grabbed her by the waist and drew her down onto the bed. Her wide hazel eyes watched his every move. Her mouth was parted, as if she was having trouble catching her breath. In the lamplight, her skin glowed. He wanted to cup her breasts and sup on them again, he wanted to love every inch of her with his mouth. But first he had to get the rest of her clothes off.

He made quick work of her shorts and panties. When she was naked before him, he stared at her, at the beauty inherent in the female body. He touched her shoulders, her slender arms, the indentation of her waist and the swell of her hips. He followed a path to the red-tinted curls guarding her feminine secrets, then dipped down to touch her.

Instantly she parted her legs for him. He bent over and pressed a kiss to her belly. His fingertips found that magical spot and slowly began to caress it. The nub swelled under his gentle assault. Her legs spread more and her muscles trembled. Her breathing came in quick panting gasps.

He stretched out, supporting himself on one elbow. He could see the color climbing her chest to her face. Her pupils dilated, her hands clutched at the bedspread. His own need swelled to the point of explosion, but he ignored the pressure. He ignored everything but her pleasure.

Her hips arched against his touch. As he felt her gather herself for that final pinnacle he reached down and drew her nipple into his mouth. He gently nibbled the taut peak. She groaned. He moved his fingers faster, circling around, brushing over, teasing her into mindlessness. He raised his head so he could watch her.

Her body stiffened. Her eyes closed, her mouth parted, but she didn't breathe. Then a great shudder swept over her. Beneath his fingers, muscles contracted and released. She clung to the bedspread and trembled uncontrollably. The flush on her chest and face deepened.

Slowly he circled around that most sensitive place. When the shaking stopped, he drew his hand up her belly. Her skin rippled everywhere he touched. He cupped her breasts, then dropped a kiss on her mouth. When he raised his head, she smiled at him.

"Not bad," she murmured, smiling.

"I could tell."

She blinked as if bringing him into focus. "I think it must be working with the mouse," she said.

He nipped her earlobe. "What are you talking about?"

She turned toward him and pulled him close. They pressed together from shoulder to ankle. Their legs tangled. She smelled of sweet perfume and musky sex. He wanted to devour her. He settled on a couple of deep kisses that left her sighing.

"The computer mouse," she said, kissing his cheek, then his jaw. "All that eye-hand coordination you do every day. That's why you're so good at this."

He rolled on his back and laughed. "I knew all that time at the keyboard had to be good for something."

Erin stared down at him. Dark hair flopped across his forehead. He was handsome enough to take her breath away. Actually her breathing was still a little shaky from her recent release. She'd heard about the earth moving before, but hadn't had the pleasure of experiencing it herself. But with Parker, she'd felt a definite tilt in the universe.

"It was very good," she said, and straddled his hips.

She shifted until her damp center rested on his erection. He groaned softly.

"Keep that up much longer and you're going to make me embarrass myself," he said.

"Good."

She tugged his shirt free of his shorts and pulled it up a few inches. The exposed band of flesh was tanned, muscled and covered with a firm layer of muscle.

"Impressive," she said and touched him. She slid her hands up under the shirt. "Maybe you could take this off."

"No problem." He half sat up and pulled his shirt over his head. It went sailing across the room.

He was as broad and strong as she'd imagined him to be. The pattern of hair began below his shoulders and tapered down to a dark narrow line that disappeared into his shorts. She bent over him. As she touched his mouth, his hands cupped her breasts.

She sought entrance between his lips. He parted for her. Tongues circled. His fingers did the same on her nipples. She brushed him once, his fingers repeated the action. It was unbearably erotic. As she did to him, he did to her. Heat spiraled between them. She rocked against his hardness, the stroking bringing her back to readiness.

Her skin was on fire. Every nerve ending quivered in anticipation of the release to come again. She wanted him, she needed him. All of him.

She broke the kiss and pressed her mouth against his neck. He tasted faintly salty. She bit his shoulder, then traced a damp line through his dark curls until she found his nipples. She circled them until Parker was the one having trouble catching his breath. His hands grabbed her hips and he urged her to rock faster against him. Faster and faster until she was ready to explode again.

He sucked in a breath then held her still. She looked at him. His face was taut, an obvious battle for control waged in his eyes.

"I don't mind," she said.

"I do." He ground out the words between clenched teeth. "I want to be inside you."

Her body tensed with pleasure at the image his words invoked.

"Yes," she said, sliding off him and onto her knees.

He sat up and pulled off his shorts and briefs, then he reached for a drawer on the nightstand. He paused and half turned toward her. "We need to use protection."

"Oh." Erin shook her head. "Oh, my. You're right. I haven't—" She cleared her throat. "There haven't been many—"

He leaned over and touched her cheek. Dark eyes softened with understanding. "Yeah, Erin. Me, too. Fortunately for both of us, Kiki is an optimist. She's been trying to get me interested in one of her friends for years. I never was, but she supplied protection, just in case."

Erin figured this could have been more embarrassing, she just wasn't sure how. "Great."

He pulled open the dresser drawer and drew out a box about half the size of a loaf of bread. They both stared at it. She wasn't sure what she'd been expecting. Something small and discreet. Maybe a little box with two or three condoms inside. The one Parker had set down between them could hold enough protection for an entire football team.

"I'm going to be really sore," she said without thinking.

He grinned at her. "If *you* think it's intimidating, imagine how I feel."

The shared laughter made her feel better. He opened the top. "I don't believe it."

She leaned over to see what he was looking at. A strangled half gasp, half laugh caught in her throat. There were a rainbow colored assortment of fluorescent condoms. Purple, green, orange, yellow.

Parker gingerly picked one up. "They even glow in the dark."

"Let's turn the lights out and see," she said, then clamped her hand over her mouth.

He looked at her, his expression unreadable.

"Sorry," she said, trying to hold back a bubble of laughter. It escaped.

One corner of his mouth tilted up. Then he smiled. Then his laughter joined hers.

Erin sagged back on the mattress. She had trouble catching her breath. "I can't believe she bought those. They're so bright, and there's so many. Where would you buy them?"

"I don't think I want to know." He was still staring at a bright yellow condom. "I don't think I can wear this. Besides, the mood is definitely broken."

She glanced down at the impressive proof of his gender. "It doesn't look broken to me."

Parker moved next to her and wrapped his arms around her. "You think you're very funny, don't you?"

"I *am* very funny. Ask anyone."

He kissed her hard.

Her humor faded and was replaced by desire. "I want you," she said.

"Not as much as I want you." With that, he lowered his head to her breasts and teased her into incoherence. His fingers once again sought and found her sensitive place.

She retaliated by running her fingers up his thigh to the dark crown of curls, then lower to his hard maleness. She encircled him and he groaned low in his throat. She stroked his length, pausing to brush her thumb against the silky tip, and he trembled. She repeated the action and he came up on his knees.

"It'll damn well have to do," he muttered, tearing the package open.

She parted her thighs for him and held her breath as he slid inside. She was tight. He moved slowly, stretching her, pausing so she could adjust to his width and length. When at last he was buried deeply in her waiting warmth, their gazes locked. He braced his weight on his hands and began to move.

She watched his passion grow. Brown eyes darkened. His mouth pulled taut. She knew her face reflected the same sensations as the pressure inside built to an unbearable pitch. She grabbed his hips and urged him deeper, faster. Her skin burned hot, her pelvis surged toward him. In and out he thrust, taking her higher, further, stretching until only a slender thread kept her grounded in this world.

Then he reached between them and touched her core. He rubbed the tiny spot and tossed her out into the wild storm. She exploded into a million parts, each a vibrating, quivering moment of perfect pleasure. She was vaguely aware of his final surge into her, the tight muscles that convulsed in answering ecstasy. Then there was nothing but a shared embrace and the steady thudding of their hearts.

* * *

"Pretty amazing," Erin said as she snuggled closer. She inhaled the scent of his body, knowing she would remember this night forever.

Parker had his arms around her. They tightened briefly. "That's what I thought, too," he said.

She raised her head and rested her chin on his shoulder. "I think it was the condom."

He grinned. "Too bad Kiki won't be getting a report. She'd be thrilled that I finally used one."

"You think she won't know?"

"I wasn't going to tell her."

Erin rolled her eyes. "I was hardly going to announce it over breakfast, but I think she might notice we're both grinning like fools."

"I can control myself," he teased. "You're the one with the crush."

"Oh, yeah? Well, I happen to know you find me very attractive. I've seen the proof."

"Impressive, wasn't it?"

"I swooned."

He laughed, then pulled her up on top of him. Her breasts rested on his chest, her legs slipped between his. He tucked her hair behind her ears.

"Did I hurt your feelings?" he asked.

"About what?"

"Teasing you about the crush. I was just being playful."

"Parker, it's fine. I knew how you meant it." She leaned close and touched her nose to his. "It could be worse. I could be in love with you."

He grimaced. "Please no. Anything but that. Love is hell." He hugged her. "But this is very nice."

"I have to agree." She liked being with him this way. The sex had been wonderful, but the intimacy afterward was better. She liked the closeness and the conversation. She liked that they could tease each other.

"I'd forgotten how good it felt to make love," she said.

"Me, too. We'll have to do it again real soon."

She wiggled her hips. "Hmm, is that a bit of interest I feel stirring even as I speak?"

"Maybe."

"Great." She scrambled off him and leaned over the side of the bed. Condoms were scattered everywhere. "Looks like the box got kicked off. It's a real mess. Do you have a favorite color?"

"You pick."

She grabbed a bright purple one then sat up. "Can we please turn off the lights?"

"Erin!" he growled.

"Is that a yes?"

He frowned, as if trying to intimidate her. She just batted her eyelashes at him.

"Oh, all right. I don't know why I'm agreeing to this."

She moved closer and kissed him. His mouth parted and she tasted his heady flavor. Passion flared between them. He caressed her breasts, stroking them gently as if he were concerned she might be tender from the last time. The combination of his concern and his actions had her trembling and ready in seconds.

He lowered her onto the mattress and slipped his hands between her legs. As he began to work his magic, she sighed. "Now I know why Kiki slips out every night."

"Me, too."

He brought her close to release, then reached for the protection. When he'd slid it on, he stretched up toward the light on the nightstand.

"Yes," she said, trying to muffle a giggle.

He turned the switch, plunging them into darkness. She could see a faint illumination around the edges of the drapes and from under the door. Aside from that nothing in the room was visible, except a bold, bright purple erection.

"It's huge," she said without thinking.

Parker laughed. It bounced in time with amusement. "It's no bigger than it was before."

"Well, it looks bigger and you're not getting anywhere near me with that."

She started to scramble off the bed. He grabbed for her, catching an ankle. She shrieked and started laughing, too. She struggled for leverage, but he was pulling her steadily toward him. She couldn't see any part of him except that which was sheathed in fluorescent purple latex.

She was on her belly as she slid across the mattress. Laughter left her breathless. Then he cupped her rear and laughter softened to passionate sighs. He turned her gently. She parted her legs, allowing him to enter her waiting heat.

Once again he quickly led her to release. In the past she'd had a difficult time with sex, her response had been slower than her partner's. But not with Parker. He seemed to know what she was feeling. He touched her everywhere, leaving her mindless and ready for the ultimate pleasure.

When their breathing had returned to normal, she turned on the light and glanced at the condoms scattered across the rug. "I liked it," she said.

"They're okay for once in a while, but I think I'd like something more normal for the rest of the time."

She looked at him. Was he inviting her to his bed again? She wasn't sure. Then she glanced at the clock and saw it was close to two.

"I'd better head back to my room," she said. "If I stay here, I'll fall asleep. I don't want Christie to wake up in the morning and find me gone."

She stood up. He followed her, unselfconsciously naked and amazingly beautiful. "I wish you could stay," he said.

"But I understand." His dark eyes crinkled at the corners as he smiled. "Thanks for tonight."

She collected her clothes and quickly pulled them on. "Thank *you*." They kissed, lingering until the flickering fire warned her she better leave now or she'd risk not leaving at all. "I'll see you in the morning."

"I can't wait," he said.

She slipped into the hallway. She could feel herself smiling and knew that she'd been right. Kiki would be able to tell what they'd been doing. How embarrassing.

She made it to her room without breaking into song. Once there, she changed into her nightgown then got into bed. Despite the late hour, she wasn't especially tired. Her body was pleasantly relaxed but her mind raced. She relived the events of the evening and wondered if she would regret giving herself to Parker. If they both tried, they could be friends and lovers. Other people did it. She was an adult, she could do it, too.

She got up and crossed to the window. After drawing back the drapes, she stared out at the black night. Stars winked overheard. She could hear the ocean below. She opened the window and inhaled the scent of the salt air.

Restlessness gripped her. She wanted to do something, anything but sleep. She looked around, hoping to find something to read. Her gaze fell on Stacey's diary. She walked over to the dresser to pick it up, then paused when her attention was caught by her reflection.

She stared in the mirror, gazing at the face of a stranger. She didn't know this woman. Her eyes were wide and bright, her face flushed, her mouth swollen from kisses. With her hair in disarray and her nightgown silhouetting her naked body, she was a wanton temptress.

Erin searched for some sign of herself, some hint of the sensible sister, the one who planned and carefully waited her turn, but she was gone. Lost in a fire of passion that had swept her away. Unfamiliar emotions passed across her face. She tried to figure out what she was feeling, but she couldn't focus on anything long enough. But she knew something was different.

She touched the diary, running her fingers across the cool leather cover. Inside her sister's hopes and dreams filled every page. It had been easy to feel sorry for Stacey. Her sister had gotten caught up in a romantic dream that had no basis in reality while Erin had always prided herself on knowing the truth.

She returned her attention to the reflection in the mirror. To the stranger with a deep emotion shining in her eyes. She'd confessed her crush to Parker, and he'd teased her about it. A crush was safe, but love was dangerous. For both of them.

She had been so sensible. She'd waited for her turn; she'd taken only what was offered. She never demanded or grabbed for anything in her life. Hiding had made her world seem safe. Until tonight. Until she'd grabbed passion with both hands and been burned.

She glanced down at her palms half expecting to see singe marks and blackened skin. There was no sign of what had occurred, but she knew the truth.

She'd made the "sensible" decision based on all the available facts, save one. Erin had never made love to a man she didn't think she loved. She couldn't. So if she'd been intimate with Parker tonight, she would have given away more than her body. And she had. Sometime during those hours of passion, she'd handed over her heart.

That's why she looked different. It wasn't about sex, it was about caring. She'd given Parker the one thing he didn't want. Just like her sister, she'd made the fatal mistake of falling in love with him.

Chapter Twelve

Parker woke up feeling better than he had in years. He lay in bed for a moment, trying to remember why. Then it all came back to him. Erin, making love, the glow-in-the-dark condoms. He sat up and grinned. Hot damn, it felt good to be alive.

He threw back the covers and stood up. Plastic packets crinkled under his feet. He glanced down and saw small squares of brightly colored protection scattered on the rug. The empty box sat overturned by the nightstand. One of them must have kicked it off while they'd been otherwise occupied.

He grabbed the box, then started collecting the condoms. As he did, images from the previous night flashed through his brain. Erin smiling, Erin flushed and wide-eyed with passion, Erin gasping his name, Erin touching him . . . everywhere.

He knew his sense of well-being didn't just come from the release provided by sex. It came from the intimacy, the connection between a man and a woman. They weren't strangers anymore. They'd trusted each other enough to share something fundamental. Trust. He shook his head. He didn't have faith in a lot of people and fewer still trusted him. As he picked up the last couple of condoms he wondered if he should warn Erin away. He hadn't done well by the women in his life. Robin and Stacey were both proof of that.

"This is different," he said aloud. It was different because Erin was strong. She didn't need him the way the other two had. They had enjoyed each other as adults, but it hadn't been about being in love. As long as they were friends, everything would be fine.

That decided, he put the box in the top drawer of the nightstand then headed for the shower. As he lathered soap, he started thinking about the program that was giving him so much trouble. If he didn't get an answer soon, he was going to have to scrap the whole thing. He hated to; he'd already invested hundreds of hours. But he couldn't afford to—

He paused in the middle of rinsing shampoo from his hair. Equations and computer codes filtered through his half-formed thoughts. A whisper of excitement rippled through him. Maybe he'd been going at the problem all wrong. Maybe there was another way.

By the time he'd dressed, he'd found the answer. He jogged to the end of the hall and sat in front of his computer. Within minutes, he had the program up and was trying his new solution.

He vaguely heard Kiki come to the door and ask him a question. He waved her away.

"It's going to be one of *those* days," he heard her say.

"One of what days?" Christie asked.

"Your father is working. He's found the solution to his programming problem. Now come along with me. We need to give him plenty of quiet today. Maybe we'll go into town for lunch."

There was more conversation, but he ignored it. A breakfast tray appeared on his desk. He drank the coffee and left everything else. Hours must have passed because there was a second tray, this one with sandwiches. He ate one so he could keep working.

About three in the afternoon, he surfaced for the first time that day. His body was stiff, his mind swirling with more half-formed ideas. He needed a break.

After standing and stretching, he noticed the sun was shining brightly. The ocean was calm and a brilliant cobalt blue. Christie sat in the window seat reading.

"Hi," he said.

She glanced up at him and smiled. "I'm being very quiet. Kiki told me you were working and I wasn't to d'sturb you. I brought a book."

"So I see." He crossed the room and settled next to her. "What are you reading?"

"*The Princess and the Pea*. It's about a girl who doesn't know she's a princess and she sleeps on a pea." Christie giggled. "I wouldn't want to sleep on a pea. That's silly."

"I agree." He tugged on one of her pigtails, then drew her onto his lap. She went willingly, snuggling against him. "What else do you know about this princess?"

"The pea keeps her awake and she gets the prince." Christie wrinkled her nose. "The prince is nice, but I'd rather have you."

Her compliment caught him off guard. "Thank you, Christie." His chest tightened.

"I'm glad you're my daddy," she said. "I used to ask God every night for a daddy and then he gave me you. You're 'xactly what I wanted."

He had to clear his throat before he could speak. "I'm glad you're my little girl," he said. "You're exactly what I wanted, too."

"Really?" She gazed up at him. Her brown eyes were wide and trusting. "Did you ask God for a little girl of your own?"

He shook his head. "I didn't think I would get that lucky. I wish—" He brushed her bangs off her forehead, then took her tiny, perfect hand in his. "I wish I'd known about you before. I would have come and found you."

"Just like in my stories." She patted his chest. "I understand, Daddy. Mommy told me you didn't know about me. I'm sorry my other mommy, Stacey I mean, didn't tell you. Then we could have been together for always."

"That would have been nice," he said. Then he wondered. How would he have reacted to the news of Stacey's pregnancy five years ago? He wouldn't have wanted to believe it was his child and probably wouldn't have until he'd seen the baby. The guilt—it would have overwhelmed him. Sometimes it still did.

What would have happened if he'd known about Christie from the beginning? How would he have acted? Would he have wanted her? All that innocent life might have gotten in the way of his mourning. The last month had taught him he used the pain of losing Robin to remind himself he was alive. If he felt that, he was at least feeling something.

But Christie required more. With her around, the pain disappeared. He had to experience the world, and sometimes he didn't want to. Maybe she would have brought him back to the land of the living sooner, or maybe he would have destroyed her, too.

No, he told himself. Erin wouldn't have let that happen. Erin. Just thinking about her, about them together last night, made him grin. If he'd meet her five years ago, he would never have seen her as her own person. He wouldn't have risked getting to know her, getting close to her. He would have missed the chance to... To what? Care? Did he? Could he? It wasn't safe, not for either of them.

"Do you have to do more work?" Christie asked.

"Yes. I'm finishing up a program. I'll be done either tonight or tomorrow, then I promise we'll spend some time together. Okay?"

She nodded. "Yes, Daddy, it's okay. I'm a big girl. Mommy goes to work at school and you go to work here. When I grow up, I'm going to go to work, too."

She jumped down and started out of the room. At the doorway, she turned back to him. "When Kiki brings you dinner tonight, you eat everything on the tray. Even your vegetables. They make you big and strong."

He grinned. "Yes, Christie. I promise."

She gave him her winning smile, complete with dimples, then disappeared into the hall. He wasn't sure he deserved it, but he'd gotten lucky with her. Pray God, he didn't screw up.

Parker strolled back to his computer and stared at the screen. In a matter of seconds, he was lost in the program.

When next he surfaced, it was dark outside. An untouched tray sat on his desk. He hadn't even heard Kiki come in. He glanced at the clock and was stunned to see one forty-eight. He'd been at the computer since eight that morning.

Weariness descended. He rubbed his burning eyes. He was tired and sore, but it had been worth it. The problem was solved, the program nearly complete. Nothing like a night of hot sex to clear your thinking, he told himself. Maybe he could—

Damn. He'd been in his office all day. He hadn't seen Erin. She hadn't come to see him—at least he didn't remember her coming in the room—and he hadn't sought her out. After last night she was probably expecting something from him. Even something as simple as a polite greeting. He bolted from the room, then paused at the top of the stairs.

"You're a jerk, Hamilton," he muttered aloud. Last night had been terrific, so the first chance he got, he messed it up.

He started up the stairs, then paused. It was nearly two in the morning. He couldn't go barging into her room just to apologize for ignoring her all day. He would have to wait until morning. No doubt she was going to be furious. He deserved it. He'd been an insensitive clod.

He headed down the stairs toward the main floor. Halfway there he noticed a light shining from the study. Kiki would be gone or asleep. Had his housekeeper left a lamp on for him, or was Erin still awake?

He hurried across the hardwood floor and stepped into the study. Erin sat in the leather wing chair reading. The light behind her left shoulder highlighted the red in her hair. She was dressed in a loose summer dress. Skinny straps left her shoulders and slender arms bare. The front dipped low enough to hint at the generous curves below. His fingers curled toward his palms as he remembered touching her there, holding and caressing her.

She hadn't noticed him in the doorway. "Erin?" he said.

She glanced up and smiled. "Ah, life arises from the laboratory. What did you discover today, Dr. Frankenstein?"

He crossed the floor in three long strides. "That I'm a jerk," he said and bent over.

She raised her face and accepted his kiss. Her soft, yielding mouth relieved some of the tension in his chest. When her mouth parted, he swept inside and teased them both into a state of mild arousal.

At last he pulled away and dropped a kiss on the top of her head. "Thanks for not being angry."

"Why would I be? You went to work and got involved with your program. I guessed you had some kind of breakthrough. I think that's great."

He settled on the ottoman in front of her chair and studied her face. Her eyes were clear of any dark emotions, her mouth curved up at the corners.

"Really?"

She put her bookmark in place and set the book on the small table to her right. "Cross my heart." She made an *X* over her left breast.

"I owe it all to you," he said, placing his hands on her knees. "You inspired me."

"I'll take credit for distracting you, but I think inspiration is a little much." Her hair brushed against her bare shoulders. "Quit looking so guilty. I'm not mad. I know your work is important to you. We made love last night. It was terrific for both of us. This morning you found the solution to a problem that's been bugging you for weeks. If anything, I'm flattered. Why can't you accept that?"

"Because I should have brought you breakfast in bed, or maybe a dozen roses."

She raised her eyebrows. "Oh, that would have been subtle. Then no one would have known what happened."

"Yeah, okay, maybe not breakfast in bed. I didn't mean to ignore you today. I don't want you to think I don't care about what happened last night. It was great." He met her gaze. "You were great."

His hands moved up her legs to her thighs. It was late, but they were still awake. Maybe they could—

She wrapped her fingers around his wrists and held him in place.

"Parker, we have to talk."

That particular phrase always meant bad news. He placed his elbows on his knees. "About?"

"Us." Erin shifted in the chair. "The next step. I wondered what you had in mind. Christie and I will be here another five weeks. What happens now?"

"You mean sexually?"

"Was it a one-night thing?"

"I hadn't thought that far ahead," he admitted. "I enjoyed being with you. I'd like us to be lovers." He never thought he would say that again. He never thought he would want anyone. But it was more than just the sex. He liked her and respected her. She made him laugh and forget.

She leaned forward and placed her hands on top of his. Their faces were inches apart. He could see the individual colors in her irises. The blues, greens and golds. He could study the perfect shape of her mouth, the cupid's bow upper lip and the full lower one.

He wanted her. His blood heated and his arousal was instant. He wanted to do everything they had done last night, and a few things they hadn't.

"I know this complicates the situation," he said, "but I think we can work it out."

She laced her fingers with his, then stared at their joined hands. "I'm not that sophisticated, Parker. I wasn't a virgin last night, but I haven't been with a lot of men. I enjoyed what we did." She gave him a half smile. "'Enjoy' isn't quite powerful enough, is it? You were amazing."

"But? Not that I don't appreciate the compliment, but I hear a but."

She nodded. "But I don't think I can be your lover. Not that I don't want to be. It's very tempting. I'm just afraid that in the end, I'll disappoint you."

"That's not possible."

"I can't keep giving my body without my heart coming along for the ride." She met his gaze. "If we continue to be lovers I'll—" She swallowed, but didn't look away. "I'll fall in love with you and I know you don't want that."

He'd known it was too good to last, but the sharpness of his regret startled him. Until she'd actually refused, he hadn't known how much he'd wanted her in his life. It wasn't fair, he acknowledged. A temporary situation gave him everything he wanted, but offered little to her. He knew he was safe, emotionally. He was never going to care about anyone again. He'd learned his lesson a long time ago and he wasn't going to repeat it.

"I understand," he said, and was surprised when regret boiled into anger. He did understand, but he didn't like it. He wanted to be with her. He wanted her in his bed and in his life. For the summer, of course. He wasn't looking for an emotional connection.

"I'm also concerned about Christie," she went on. She gave his fingers a quick squeeze, then released him. "If she sees us acting like a couple, she'll start to think that we're going to be a normal family. I think just staying friends is better for everyone."

"Safer, you mean," he said, fighting the irritation of not getting his way. "Settling for what's offered instead of taking what you want."

She flinched and turned her gaze away. "An interesting comment coming from you. Playing it safe is what you do best, Parker. Isn't that what this entire household is about? Providing you with a place to escape."

Now it was his turn to feel uncomfortable. "This is my home," he said. "Nothing more."

"Isn't it? You don't hide out here so you can keep the world at a distance? I'm surprised you've let Christie in as much as you have. I suppose she's accepted because she's just a child and because her visit is temporary. But an adult woman is more of a risk." She stared at him, her hazel eyes seeing far more than they should. "I believe that you got a brilliant idea this morning and I'm pleased to have had a small part in that inspiration. But I find it interesting that you felt it necessary to seal yourself away from me for an entire day.''

''I have a responsibility to my work.''

''And maybe it was a little easier not to have to face me and what had happened between us.''

''I don't regret what happened.''

She gave him a sad smile. ''That's not what I'm saying. You—'' She hesitated.

''I what?'' he asked, then wondered if he really wanted to know.

''You hold a part of yourself back. You do it with Kiki, with me, even with Christie. I'm sure you held back with Stacey. Did you do the same thing with your wife, Parker? Did you keep parts of your heart from her?''

He rose to his feet. ''You have no right to ask me about her.''

''I have every right,'' she said quietly. ''This isn't about me. I'll survive whatever happens between us. Our relationship isn't important. What matters is Christie. She's your daughter. I won't let you do to her what you've done to the other people in your life. You'd better think long and hard about this. You'd better search your heart and know for sure. If you hold back from your daughter, she'll know. She won't understand that it's about you and not about her. She'll blame herself. I won't let you hurt her that way.''

''I wouldn't do that,'' he said, pacing across the room.

''Not on purpose, maybe, but it's a habit.'' She laced her fingers together and studied them. ''You still mourn Robin. While I can appreciate that you really loved her, I can't help but wonder why you won't let go. Is it guilt, Parker? Is it because she died knowing you held a part of yourself in reserve? Christie is only four years old. You can't let her dream of flying, then let her crash to the ground. She trusts you. Are you going to let her down?''

He stood in front of the fireplace and stared at her. "Never."

She went on as if she hadn't heard him. "The hardest part about being a parent is that you have to give everything and pray that it's enough. Sometimes it's not, but you have to try anyway. You have to be willing to make sacrifices. When we first came here I was a little jealous of your relationship with Christie. She wanted a father and you did everything right. I handled it because being with you was the best thing for her. Now it's easier. I'm glad you two get along. My point is I had to be willing to make a sacrifice and you're going to have to do the same."

Erin jealous of him? But he was just fumbling in the dark with this while *she* did everything right. God, he was so confused.

"I love her," he said.

"That's a start."

A thousand thoughts swirled through his mind. Erin's accusations about holding back a part of himself. Could he be a good parent? Was he capable of giving as much as Christie needed? What would happen to her if he failed?

He turned and left the room. The inky blackness of night called him. He opened the French doors and stepped onto the terrace.

A soft sea breeze caressed him as he stood looking at the ocean. He couldn't see anything beyond the occasional whitecap. He could hear the pounding of the surf, matched the thundering of his heartbeat. It had been so long since he'd fought them that he'd thought he'd conquered the demons. He'd been wrong.

They returned silently, swooping out of the night, attacking him with swords sharpened by regret. They pierced his protective layer of logic, zeroing in on his exposed uncertainties. Robin. Always Robin.

Without closing his eyes he could see her lying in the hospital bed. He'd clutched her hand and begged her not to leave him. It was just pneumonia; she wasn't supposed to die.

He drew in a deep breath and instead of salt air, he smelled the antiseptic scent of hospital disinfectant. He could feel her fragile fingers resting in his, and see the shadows under her eyes.

"Don't go," he'd whispered. "I'll never make it without you."

She'd looked at him then, turning her head until she could see him. "It's better this way," she'd said, every word a labor of breath and energy. "You'll remember me alive. You won't hate me."

"I could never hate you, Robin. You're my whole life. I love you."

A single tear slipped out of the corner of her eye. "Today," she murmured. "You love me today. What about tomorrow? What happens when the disease steals my body? You're so alive, Parker. You would hate the illness and eventually you'd hate me." She paused to catch her breath. A sharp cough racked her thin frame.

"Never," he told her. "I'd be right here. Always."

Then she'd smiled at him. A sad knowing smile that had made him feel like an unruly child. They hadn't talked again. He'd stayed with her, holding on to her until she slipped into a coma, then silently died.

Now, with the night air surrounding him, Parker questioned his commitment to his wife. Had Robin believed he held something back? Obviously she hadn't trusted him to be there for her during her illness. He'd been so angry with her for leaving him. Had he ever forgiven her?

Had she ever forgiven him?

The unexpected question brought a rush of shame. He hung his head and breathed a prayer of apology. To her and to Stacey. Erin was right. His wife had been right. They both sensed a weakness in him.

"I would have stayed with you," he said aloud, speaking to the night. "Always, Robin. I loved you."

As the words caught flight and were carried aloft, even he heard the answering echo of falseness. He loved her, but not with all his heart. He'd held something back. In the end, she'd known the truth. He wasn't enough. He would never have been enough.

He returned to the study. Erin was still in the chair although she hadn't picked up her book. He stood in the doorway. "You're right," he said. "About everything. I understand why you don't want a relationship with me. I don't blame you."

"Parker, that's not what I said. You're twisting my words."

He shrugged. "It's what you meant and that's what's important. I'll do my best with Christie. I can't promise to be perfect, but I want to be a good father to her. I do care about her."

"I know." Sadness settled in her eyes. "That's all anyone can ask for. If you're aware of the problem, I'm sure you can prevent it from happening. Just remember she needs you to love her unconditionally."

"That shouldn't be too hard. Christie is easy to love." He turned to leave, then paused. "I—" Hell, what was he supposed to say to her? "Good night, Erin."

He climbed the stairs and prepared for a long night battling the demons. Maybe this time they wouldn't win.

When Parker walked into the kitchen the next morning, Kiki was already rolling out cinnamon rolls. Christie sat beside her on the counter. She had a small bowl filled with raisins in one hand.

"Daddy!" she squealed when she saw him. She held out her arms.

As Kiki took the bowl from her, he crossed the room and grabbed Christie close.

"Morning, angel. What are you doing?"

"I'm helpin' with breakfast. We're making cinnamon rolls."

"So I see." He swung her around once and set her back on the counter. Her pink shirt matched the glow in her cheeks. Her hair was in its usual pigtails. She was bright and pretty, and he was proud that she was his child, even though he couldn't claim any of the credit.

"How are you, Kiki?" he asked as he got a cup out of the cupboard and poured some coffee.

"Never better," the housekeeper said. This morning her jogging suit was white with red dots. Her athletic shoes were plain white, but the laces had tiny dots on them. "Breakfast will be ready in about twenty minutes."

"I'm not hungry."

"You hardly ate anything yesterday," she reminded him.

"I know." It didn't matter. He's spent most of last night wrestling with all Erin had said and remembering his time with Robin. He hadn't liked some of his conclusions.

"Mommy's not hungry, either," Christie said.

Kiki glanced at him. He read the questions in her eyes. Was Erin's lack of appetite his fault? He knew it was. Their talk had affected her as well.

She'd hinted at a relationship and he'd been interested in an affair.

Hamilton, you're a real bastard, he told himself.

He dropped a kiss on the top of Christie's head. "You're my best girl," he told her.

She grinned. "You're my best daddy."

He wasn't...yet. But he was going to do his damnedest to make sure he turned out that way. He owed it to Christie. Maybe he even owed it to himself.

Chapter Thirteen

Erin was curled up on a chair by her bedroom window
when someone knocked on her door. For a half second, she
hoped it was Parker, that he'd come to sweep her off her
feet, tell her that he was a fool and of course he was madly
in love with her.

"Yeah, right," she murmured.

The person at the door knocked again. "It's Kiki, Erin.
May I come in?"

So much for daydreams. "Sure, Kiki. It's not locked."

The housekeeper stepped inside. "At least you're up and
dressed. I was afraid you'd still be in bed."

"I'm not that far gone. I just needed a little time to myself."

Kiki put her hands on her hips. This morning she wore a
white jogging suit with red polka dots. The cheerful print
matched the older woman's personality.

"You can't hide in here forever."

"I'm not hiding. I'm—" She thought for a moment, searching for the perfect word. "I'm regrouping."

Kiki crossed to the foot of the bed and sat on the cedar hope chest there. "Sounds like hiding to me."

That's because it was. Erin shifted on her chair. She was so confused by everything. Too much had happened too fast. She hadn't slept much. She'd been thinking about everything she had said to Parker and what he'd said back. In truth she was pleased that he'd found the solution to his programming problem. But she was also hurt that he'd ignored her for the whole day. She'd expected some kind of acknowledgment from him.

"Do you want to talk about it?" the housekeeper asked. Her blue eyes were kind, her expression understanding.

"I wouldn't know where to begin."

"Would it help if I told you I knew what happened a couple of nights ago?"

Erin felt a flush heat her cheeks. She stared at Kiki. "How?"

"The two of you spilled the box of condoms and didn't pick them all up. I found several when I vacuumed yesterday." She leaned forward. "Don't feel guilty, Erin. You and Parker are consenting adults. What you do behind closed doors is no one's business but your own."

Then why are we talking about it, Erin wondered, still chagrined that the secret was already out. "It's not as simple as that. The whole man-woman relationship is very complicated. I've been out of the game for so long, I don't know how to play anymore. Not that I ever did."

"It's like riding a bicycle."

"I'm not sure I ever believed that old saying. I rode a bike when I was kid and when I tried one as an adult, I nearly got myself killed." Erin folded her hands on her lap and drew in a deep breath. "Everything is different from what I thought it would be."

"Maybe that's because you've changed. The last time you were involved with a man you were in college. Just a young woman. Now you're a mature adult, a single mother with a child to worry about. That would change anyone's perspective."

Erin stared at her. "You're right. Why didn't I think of it that way?"

The words made perfect sense. Everything *had* changed since she was last in the dating world. She'd grown up, started raising Christie. Her wants and needs were different, but her heart still held on to its adolescent dreams. She was mature, but inexperienced. Most likely, she was doing everything all wrong.

"I can see the truth more clearly," Kiki said, "because I'm not personally involved. I know this is unfamiliar and feels a little awkward, but it will be worth it in the end."

Erin smiled. "You can't expect me to believe that."

"Why not? It's true. Don't *you* think Parker is worth the effort?"

Erin's smile faded. Of course she did. She had to. She'd lost her heart to him. She gripped her fingers tightly together and wondered how everything had gotten so messed up. She'd fallen in love with Parker, then she'd lied about it. She'd told him that if they continued to be lovers, she would become too emotionally attached. The truth was physical intimacy would deepen an already existing attachment. She'd shied away from telling him her real feelings because she couldn't face his rejection.

"I've made a mess of everything," Erin said softly. "And I don't know how to fix it."

Kiki stared at her. "I'm going to tell you something I probably shouldn't, but I've been here too long for Parker to fire me, so I guess it's safe. I'm doing this for his own good, and for yours. Parker is a good man."

"I already figured out that part."

Kiki winked. "I knew you were bright." She thought for a moment. "I don't know how much he told you about his family."

"He mentioned that they never cared about his achievements, or about doing anything with their lives."

The housekeeper nodded. "That's all true. I met his parents once. They came here for dinner. They found fault with everything and admitted being disappointed that we didn't have a television in the dining room so they could watch their favorite game show during dinner."

"A real class act," Erin said. "Didn't they think the house was wonderful? What about the view? What about seeing their son?"

"I don't think they cared. Certainly not about Parker. He's very—" Kiki paused as if weighing her words. "He's very good at what he does. He's brilliant and inventive. He has a gift for figuring out what people are going to want and need before they do. He's made a fortune, but none of that is important to him. He appreciates what the money buys, but if he lost everything tomorrow, I truly believe he wouldn't care except for how it affected those around him. What I'm trying to say is he doesn't see himself as brilliant or gifted. To him, he's just a computer nerd who got lucky."

A computer nerd. She knew someone else who fit that description. "Like Robin."

"Exactly like Robin."

"They had everything in common," Erin said. "He loved her very much. He still loves her."

"Loving Robin is safe," Kiki told her. "She's not here anymore. She can't change or get angry. Their relationship is familiar, but it's not what you think it is. She wasn't a perfect person."

Erin looked at the other woman. "I'm pleased Parker still thinks about her. To me, that shows he has the ability to commit. That's what I want for Christie. I want to know that he'll commit to her, no matter what. I want to be sure that he'll be there for her. He will."

"Parker's relationship with his daughter isn't the reason you're hiding in this room, though, is it?"

Erin sighed. "No."

"You're worrying about measuring up to Robin. Don't think about that. You're two different people, and she's gone forever."

"That sounds like a polite way of telling me I *can't* measure up."

Kiki shook her head. "It's a polite way of saying you wouldn't want to measure up. Robin had many flaws."

"I'm no paragon of virtue, either. I—" She hesitated, then figured she had to confess all to someone. Maybe Kiki could help. "My sister kept a diary while she was here. Most of the entries are about Parker and Stacey's feelings for him. I'm afraid I've taken those entries a little too much to heart."

"So what if you have? You've needed a push in the right direction for a long time. Parker hides behind his memories and his work. You hide behind Christie. You've both been hiding for too many years. Get out, Erin. Get your hands dirty. Risk making mistakes. Remember what it feels like to be alive."

Kiki's words stung. Erin struggled to keep the hurt from showing. "I know exactly what it feels like to be alive."

Kiki smiled. "Do you? What was the last big risk you took?"

"Coming here."

"And before that?"

Erin couldn't remember. She wasn't much on taking risks. *You're going to die waiting for your turn.* That voice spoke in her head again. She tried to ignore it, but it was too loud and truthful. The voice was right; Kiki was right. She'd been waiting for someone to hand her her turn. She'd never taken an uncalculated risk. She'd never grabbed for what she wanted. If she were to die right this minute, her tombstone would read: Erin Ridgeway—a Cautious Person. Is that what she wanted for her life?

"Everything is confusing," she murmured, not sure what to do with her newfound insight.

"Growing isn't always comfortable, but it's worth it in the end." Kiki stood. "I have to go to the grocery store. Why don't I take Christie with me so you can have some time to think? You could take a drive up the coast. Or inland. There are some beautiful houses and scenic routes in the area."

A drive. "That sounds great," Erin said. She rose to her feet and crossed to the housekeeper. "Thanks for the advice."

Kiki patted her arm. "I hate to see you so unhappy, Erin. Life is precious. Enjoy every moment. Grab on to happiness with both hands and refuse to let go."

"I'm not much of a grabber."

"Practice. It gets easier with time." Kiki left the room.

Erin stared after her and remembered that the other woman had suffered the loss of a child, then the disintegration of her marriage. Yet she still talked about happiness and living life to its fullest. Her philosophy made Erin ashamed of her miserly existence.

She grabbed her purse and her camera, then headed for the door. A few minutes later, she was turning her car around in the large circular driveway. At the street, instead of heading south for town, she went north and followed the coast. At the next highway, she headed inland.

The lush green grass springing up on the side of the road, the trees and cool ocean breeze were different from what she was used to. She and Christie lived in the upper desert of Southern California. Palmdale was a high valley, surrounded by open bare land and brown mountains. Dry wind accompanied every season. When it rained, things were green for a few weeks, then gradually died. Homeowners fought a constant battle to keep their small lawns lush and healthy.

She pulled into a park and left the engine running as she stared at the children and their parents. Grown-ups pushed kids on swings. A soccer game took up one side of the park. Children in birthday hats sat around a cluster of picnic tables. Families together.

Erin leaned against the headrest and closed her eyes. Families. She hadn't been part of a family since she was nine years old. She and Stacey had been shuffled from place to place. They'd never belonged, except to each other. Now Stacey was gone and Erin only had Christie. She loved her daughter with all her heart, but sometimes she got weary of being the only one responsible. Sometimes she wanted someone to be there for her.

Was that a heartfelt prayer of a grown woman or the unrealistic desire left over from the dreams of a nine-year-old orphan?

She didn't have an answer. Questions swirled through her mind. Should she take Christie home now, before more damage was done? Then she reminded herself Parker hadn't damaged his daughter. He'd been good to her and for her from the first moment they'd met. Erin was the only one at risk of being wounded and that was because she'd broken the rules. She'd fallen in love when she was just supposed to be his friend.

As much as she would like to run away, it wasn't an option. She and Parker were connected through Christie and they would stay that way for the rest of their lives. She would have to find some kind of middle ground with him.

What had gone wrong? Did she regret making love?

"No," she whispered. "Never."

That night had been magic. She'd forgotten what it felt like to hold someone and be held. The joy of sharing had little to do with the physical rapture she'd found with him, and everything to do with the touching of souls. No matter how much it would hurt her later, she couldn't regret a moment of their time together.

Did she regret loving him?

Erin drew in a deep breath and opened her eyes. A young couple had walked into the park. The man carried a toddler in his arms. He set the child down and watched him weave unevenly on the grass. The man glanced at his wife. For that moment, Erin saw the affection in his eyes, she felt their love as they joined hands, then laughed as their child pointed to a bird and flapped his arms as if they were wings.

Loving Christie had kept Erin alive after the loss of her sister. Love was the best anyone could aspire to. So, no, she didn't regret loving Parker. She just wasn't sure what she was going to do about it.

She backed out of the parking lot and continued down the road. About fifteen minutes later, she came across an old abandoned barn. The roof was intact but boards had come off the walls, and where there had once been wide double doors, a huge hole yawned like a giant's toothless grin.

Erin pulled onto the side of the road. She collected her camera and stepped out onto the dirt path leading to the barn. The air was cool and still, the sun warm. Birds called in the distance, but the barn was alone. An abandoned dark silhouette against a perfect blue sky.

She studied the structure, the shape and size, then walked around it slowly. Visually she explored the possibilities, trying to figure out why the isolation of the building spoke to her. Was it that the building remained standing, despite being alone? Was it the desolation of the scene? She wasn't sure. She only knew that she had to capture the essence of the moment and preserve it.

She loaded the camera and began taking pictures. Some she took quickly, clicking a series of the barn. Others, she set up carefully, finding the right angle, the right play of light and shadows. She felt herself becoming one with her subject. Her mind filled with possibilities. Different shots, different combinations of centering and foreground.

Later, when she'd used up five rolls of film, she glanced at her watch and gasped. She'd spent three hours at the barn. It had felt like fifteen minutes. Exhilaration filled her, along with a sense of having accomplished something. She couldn't answer questions about her future, or deal with potential regrets over her relationship with Parker, but this time away from the house had taught her one thing. She'd been wrong to stop taking pictures.

She walked back to the car and slid into her seat. For a moment she stared at the barn. Once again it was just an abandoned old building, but for those few hours it had been more. It had been her dream.

She headed toward the house, going through town to leave her film at a photo lab. As she filled out the information on the envelopes, she calculated how many more rolls of film she wanted to buy. She was ready to start taking pictures again.

On the way to Hawkin's Point, she thought about what Kiki had told her, and what she, herself, had said to Parker last night. She'd been hard on him, angry because he'd abandoned her. Now she understood him a little better. If he'd felt the same joy in his programming that she'd felt taking the pictures, then she couldn't begrudge him his time away from her.

Kiki was right. Life was to be lived. If Erin were honest with herself, she would be willing to admit that her regrets were rarely about things she said. Her regrets came from opportunities missed. Things she *didn't* do.

She wanted to change that. She wanted to grab on with both hands. The only problem was she wasn't sure what to grab for. Happiness, Kiki had said. What would make her happy? Was it finally her turn, or was the voice right? Would she die waiting for her turn? Was it time to make things happen?

The house came into view. Funny, as beautiful as the three-story structure was, she had no desire to take pictures of it. At first she wasn't sure why, then she realized she already knew this building inside and out. An image of it lived in her heart. She didn't need a static photograph to remind her of home.

That night, after putting Christie into bed and reading her a story, Erin went to find Parker. She went down to the second floor and saw a light shining from his office. After crossing the landing, she paused in the hallway. He was in front of his computer, obviously deeply involved in his program.

She stepped inside the room and quietly made her way to the window seat. She hadn't spent much time in here. She wasn't sure why. Maybe because she knew he'd once worked here with Robin and she didn't want to encounter any ghosts.

Tonight she didn't feel any strange presence, so she settled on the cushion and waited for Parker to notice her.

The office was large, with high ceilings and a wall full of windows. Blinds had been pulled open to allow in the light, and he didn't bother to lower them at night. Erin realized this room faced the ocean. There was no one to look in and disturb his privacy.

His computer desk took up about a quarter of the space at one end of the room. Books and papers were piled high on every available surface, and formed teetering stacks on the floor. The steady clicking of his fingers on the keyboard provided a rhythmic counterpoint to the faint rumble of the surf below.

Dark hair fell over his forehead. He brushed it away, absently. His gaze was focused and intense, his mouth a straight line. He wore a T-shirt over jeans and his feet were bare. Even his watch was an inexpensive sports model available at any department store. Nothing about Parker Hamiliton indicated that he was worth millions.

Nearly a half hour passed before he glanced up and saw her. He blinked. "Erin?"

"Hi."

"Have you been sitting there long?"

She stood and stretched, then settled back on the window seat. "Not very. How's it going?" She motioned to the computer.

"Great. I'm sorry. You should have said something."

"I didn't mind. I like watching you work. It's very intense."

He grinned. "I get completely involved in what I'm doing. With my luck I probably drool or something."

She laughed. "You were fine. You don't even squint."

His smile faded. "Is everything all right? Christie—"

"Christie's fine, too. She's already asleep. I wanted to talk to you for a minute, if you have time."

"Sure." He clicked a couple of keys, then angled his chair toward her. He stretched out long, lean legs and leaned back. "I'm listening."

What had seemed so simple just a short time ago suddenly became awkward. She fumbled for words, wanting to find the right ones. When they didn't appear, she settled on just being honest.

"I'm sorry for what I said last night," she told him. "I was a little hurt and angry that you were so involved with work, but I didn't feel I had the right to complain about that. So I got analytical instead. Feel free to ignore my pop psychology. I'm hardly an expert. It's not my place to say those things about your relationship with Robin. I hope you can forgive me."

"Already done." His eyes darkened. "You were right about everything, you know."

"No, I wasn't. I was lashing out." Fighting the truth and trying not to be hurt because she loved him and he wasn't interested in her feelings.

"Then you have good instincts." He shrugged. "I've been thinking about what you said. About holding back. I don't want that to happen with Christie."

"It won't. You're a terrific father. She adores you."

He rubbed his temple as if he were developing a headache. "Adoration is for rock stars. I want to be a part of her life. But sometimes the responsibility terrifies me. I don't want to do something stupid and mess her up. I have this vision of her twenty years from now, paying a therapist a hundred dollars an hour and it's all because of me."

Erin laughed. "Then make sure you give her a big enough allowance so she can pay for it."

"You're not helping."

She stared at him, at his handsome features, at the concern obvious in his expression. "I know it didn't work out between you and Stacey. Her imagination created a relationship where one didn't exist at all. But she had good instincts, too."

"What do you mean?"

"She picked you to fall in love with, Parker. You're going to do fine with Christie. You'll learn as you go, like the rest of us parents."

"You've had a head start on me."

"You'll catch up."

He didn't respond. Instead he stood and crossed the room to the window seat. He sat next to her and took her hand in his. His fingers were warm and strong. He rubbed his thumb across her palm. She sensed he meant the gesture to be friendly, even comforting, but she found it arousing. Heat skittered up her arm to settle in her breasts and between her thighs.

"I'm sorry about all you lost. All I took from you," he said.

"What are you talking about?"

"Stacey."

"We've been through this. It wasn't about you at all."

"If she hadn't gotten pregnant, she wouldn't be dead." His pain radiated as if it were heat. His gaze met hers. "You have every right to hate me for that. She was your sister. Your twin. That bond, I—" He shook his head. "You still miss her. I hate myself for what I've done to you and Christie."

"Parker, no. Never. Don't hate yourself. I don't hate you or blame you."

"You should."

She turned toward him and squeezed his hand. "I'll admit you should have acted more responsibly that night. It was wrong to make love with my sister. But it was nothing more than a mistake. You didn't set out to hurt her."

"But I did and she died."

Erin leaned close. "I refuse to let you wish that night away. I can't imagine what my life would be like then. Don't you see? Without that night, without that mistake, there would be no Christie. That's what you gave me. I'll always miss my sister. You're right, we did share a unique bond and part of me always feels her loss. But I've gained this beautiful loving child. That was Stacey's last gift to me. Christie is a part of my sister and I won't ever regret having her in my life."

He put his arms around her and drew her close. "I don't deserve you. Most people would want me drawn and quartered for what I did."

"Then most people are wrong."

She leaned against his chest and inhaled the scent of him. His embrace made her feel safe and secure. She wanted to stay here forever. She could hear the steady beating of his heart. For a moment she was tempted to raise her head and kiss him. He would respond. They could share the night, join their bodies, experience paradise in each other's arms.

But in the morning he would walk away and she would be the one left with a broken heart.

He brushed her hair off her face and tucked it behind her ear. "Christie spent some time with me today," he said. "We were using a couple of new programs for kids. I've been thinking of some educational software modifications I'd like to make for her. She's very bright."

Erin smiled. "What else would she be? Look at her parents."

"I guess you're right. It's interesting that you don't share Stacey's interest in computers."

"Twins start out identical, but they grow up to have different personalities. Stacey was always more outgoing than me. She was the risk-taker."

"You took a risk coming here."

She snuggled closer. "I'm glad I did."

At this moment, in his arms, she could pretend it was real. That he cared about her, that everything was going to work out. But in her heart, she knew it was just a fantasy. He wasn't in love with her and he didn't want her to love him. They weren't the perfect family. They'd come close, but it wasn't meant to be.

"Where do we go from here?" he asked.

To bed. But she didn't say the words. She couldn't afford the price. "We don't have to go anywhere. We can stay right where we are."

"Where's that?"

She drew in a deep breath. "Friends. We can be good friends. I could use someone like you in my life, and Kiki's right. You live like a hermit. You need us, too."

His arms tightened, holding her close. "That sounds great."

Actually it sounded horrible to her. Empty and cold and not nearly what she wanted. Still it was better than nothing. She couldn't make him love her. She couldn't force a response he didn't want to make. So they would be friends and she would make it enough. Because the alternative was to confess all and risk losing him completely.

She ignored the voice that whispered once again that she was settling and waiting for her turn. She ignored Kiki's advice of grabbing onto happiness with both hands. Parker wasn't interested. If she tried to grab for happiness, all she would find was smoke, and all she would get was a broken heart.

Chapter Fourteen

The brisk wind caught the edge of the kite and sent it soaring up in the air.

"It's flying!" Christie squealed. "It's flying in the sky."

Parker grinned. "I knew we'd get it right."

He released more string, trying to get the kite up above the cliffs behind them on the beach. Once free of the erratic breeze, the kite really could take off for the heavens. So far it had been a losing battle.

Parker moved upwind and let the kite out a little more. The breeze shifted, the kite sputtered and twisted. The long slender tail drooped.

"It's falling," Christie said and put her hands on her hips. "You stay in the sky, you naughty kite. You're 'posed to fly just like the birdies."

It pitched back and forth, then dropped suddenly and fell to the sand. The yellow-and-blue lightweight material fluttered and danced at the end of the line, but didn't rise. Parker coiled string as he walked toward it.

"I can design programs used by millions of people, but I can't keep a kite in the air," he muttered.

Christie looked at him and laughed. "Daddy, you're so funny."

She flung herself at him, wrapping her arms around his legs. He dropped the string, crouched down and hugged her close. She smelled of salt and summer. When she stepped away, he looked at her face. Despite using a sun block, their time at the beach had left freckles on her small nose. Her arms and legs were sturdy and strong, faintly tanned from long hours of play.

When she smiled at him, he knew exactly where her dimples would appear in her cheeks. He knew the sound of her laughter and her moods. He knew which stories she liked at bedtime, her favorite foods and how much it hurt to see her cry. What he didn't know was how sharp the pain would be when she was gone. It was already mid-August. She and Erin would leave by the first of September. Their perfect summer was nearly over.

He hadn't noticed the passage of time until Kiki had mentioned it that morning at breakfast. The days had all blended together until he'd allowed himself to believe this would go on forever. But it wouldn't. Erin and Christie had a life separate from his. When they left, he would no longer be a full-time father. He would also lose his time with Erin. They would become polite strangers greeting each other across the threshold, passing Christie back and forth like a package.

"Let's do it again, Daddy," Christie said. "Let's make it go really, really high."

"So high we can barely see it," he said, grabbing the string and straightening. He released several feet, then started to run down the beach. His daughter raced behind him, trying to keep up.

The kite danced along, finding the occasional gust of wind, drifting upward, then falling toward the ground. At the end of their cove, he turned and started running toward the stairs. The sun heated him. Waves pounded against the shore. Parker wondered if he looked as stupid as he felt, jogging up and down the small beach with a kite bouncing along behind him.

The breeze flirted with the kite, taking it up a few feet. Once it nearly cleared the cliffs before plummeting to the shore. When he reached the stairs, he turned again. He met Christie halfway. She was panting.

"I can't keep up," she wheezed. "You run fast."

He slowed to a walk. The kite hit the sand. "Maybe we should go up to the cliff and try it," he said. "I don't think we're going to get it flying from here. I'm sure it has something to do with the way the wind acts when it hits land."

Christie flopped down on the sand. "Okay. Let's do that next."

He reeled in the kite and settled next to her. The breeze ruffled her bangs. He studied her face. He saw himself in the child's features. And Erin. He grimaced. No, he saw Stacey. Erin wasn't Christie's biological mother, although she was one in every other sense of the word.

Christie tilted her head, just as Erin would, and smiled. "Why are you looking at me, Daddy?"

"I was just thinking what a pretty girl you are."

She dimpled. "Mommy says that, too. She says it's more important to be pretty on the inside, but pretty on the outside is nice, too." She leaned forward. "Pretty on the inside is about your heart," she said confidentially. "Not the blood and other stuff inside. It's about being a nice person. Mommy's a nice person."

"She's the best," he said, wondering how many other women would have been so willing to share their child with him. Erin had given unselfishly.

He remembered her confession of jealousy and how she'd gotten over it. Those first few weeks must have been hard for her. He and Christie had developed a bond almost immediately. Erin had kept her feelings to herself. She was bright, funny, easy to talk to and just as pretty as her daughter. He wondered why some guy hadn't already claimed her.

Maybe there was a man patiently waiting for her in Palmdale.

The thought made his stomach clench and his hands curl into fists. Talk about being ugly on the inside, Hamilton. You don't want her for yourself, and you don't want anyone else to have her, either. But that statement wasn't completely true. It's not that he didn't want Erin, it's that he didn't—

He leaned back on his elbows and shook his head. Hell, he didn't know what he wanted. One thing was for sure: He didn't want her and Christie to leave in two weeks. He wanted this summer to go on forever. He wanted Erin back in his bed. He wanted to be the kind of man she could respect and care about. He wanted to let the ghosts go.

But were they willing to let *him* go? And even if they did, would anything change? Wasn't he still a threat to everyone he cared about? Wasn't it better for Erin, better for Christie, if they stuck to their plan?

Christie shifted so she lay on the warm sand and rested her head on his belly.

"There's a birdie up there," she said, pointing at the blue sky.

Parker squinted against the sun. "It's just a speck. It must be very high."

"Higher than our kite?"

"Yeah, but that's not saying much."

She giggled.

He laced his fingers behind his head and relaxed on the shore. Christie sighed as if she were drifting off to sleep. It was a lazy afternoon. She sighed again, then turned, and stretched out across his chest. Her eyes closed and her breathing became regular.

The trust inherent in her actions made his heart ache. How he loved this little girl. He would give his life for her. Emotions welled up inside him. They grew until the pressure was unbearable. He wanted to let them out, but he was afraid. Afraid of not being enough. Afraid of hurting her.

Erin's words came back to him. She'd warned him he would have to give with his whole heart. He couldn't hold back, not with Christie. The child would sense the truth. He wondered if that same rule applied to Erin. If he wanted her in his life, would he have to give with his whole heart? After all, she, too, would know if he held back.

But if he did as she asked, they were all at risk. Look at what had happened to Robin and to Stacey.

He had no answers to his questions. Maybe time was the solution. He would be a part of Christie's world for the rest of her life.

But what about Erin?

That was less simple, he admitted. Once she left his house, he would lose his chance. They would return to their own schedules and the reality of getting through the day would gradually wear away at anything they might have had together. That would be best for both of them, but was it what he wanted? Was it what Erin wanted?

He stared up at the sky and realized he didn't know what she wanted. He didn't even know how she felt about him. She'd told him they couldn't be lovers because eventually she might fall in love with him. How long would that take? A week? A month? A year?

Erin in love with him? The thought made his spirits soar. With her beside him, he could do anything. He could— He closed his eyes. He could destroy her.

So when the time was up, he would let her go.

Parker didn't realize he'd drifted off to sleep until a sharp sound awakened him. Christie scrambled off him and jumped to her feet.

"Daddy, Daddy, it's a dog!"

Sure enough a small dirty mutt came over the rocks at the end of the beach. The dog was about ten inches to the shoulder, all matted hair and big brown eyes. A long tail pumped back and forth as if finding people was the greatest joy in the animal's life.

"He's so cute," Christie said, rushing toward the dog.

"Wait." Parker grabbed her arm and held her in place. "Let's make sure he's friendly. Stay here."

"But he wouldn't hurt me."

Parker stared at her. "Christie, this is a strange dog. It might be sick. If it bites you, then you'll get sick, too. It's better to be careful now. Please stay here."

Her mouth drooped as she nodded her head. "Yes, Daddy."

The little brown dog quivered as he approached. It rolled on its back and exposed a skinny belly. Parker let the animal sniff his hand and received a quick lick in return. He touched the dog's stomach. The animal moaned in pleasure.

"He seems friendly enough," Parker said, then frowned as he clearly felt ribs. Had the dog gotten lost or been abandoned? He sure hadn't eaten in a while. He probably hadn't had anything to drink, either. They hadn't had rain in a couple of weeks.

Christie squatted next to him and held out her hand. When the dog licked it, she giggled. "He likes me."

"Of course he does. Rub his belly like this." He demonstrated the back-and-forth motion. The dog writhed and moaned, then jumped up and barked.

Christie clapped her hands together. "You want to play? Daddy, does the dog have a name?"

"Let me check." He felt through the thick fur for a collar. There wasn't one. "No tags. I wonder what happened to his owner."

"Maybe he doesn't have one. Maybe we can keep him. My very own puppy. Please say yes, Daddy, please?" The dog and the little girl stared at him with equally pleading expressions.

"We'll see. For now, let's give him some water."

They'd brought a Thermos down with them. Parker poured water into a plastic cup and offered it to the dog. The animal drank greedily, then barked once and raced toward the steps. When Christie didn't follow, he stopped and barked again.

"I think he wants to play," Parker said.

"I'm coming," she yelled, and ran after the dog.

The two of them played tag. Parker found a stick and threw it. The dog returned it and drank a bit more water. He was friendly and good-natured. Where were his owners?

When Christie and her new friend were tired from running, they started to explore the rocks at the far end of the beach. Parker tried his luck with the kite again. The wind had shifted and this time he managed to get it nearly as high as the top of the cliffs.

He let out more string. "Look, Christie," he called.

There was no answer.

He glanced toward the rocks but didn't see anything—not even his daughter. The piles of boulders were about twelve feet high, the result of a rock slide nearly a century before. He'd never bothered exploring the other side.

"Christie?"

He couldn't see the dog, but suddenly it started barking. He dropped the kite and ran toward the sound. "Christie!"

He searched the boulders and couldn't find them. The barking came from somewhere else. Inside the rocks. But he couldn't get there from this side of the beach. The rocks stretched out twenty feet into the ocean. The bottom dropped quickly and the water would be well over Christie's head.

Parker's heart pounded and fear chilled him. "Christie, honey, can you hear me?"

He scrambled over the rocks, trying to figure out where a four-year-old would want to go. The rough surface scraped his hands and caught his jeans, but he continued searching frantically. The little dog whimpered. He followed the sound, peering between boulders. Then he saw it. A bit of pink lying below him on the sand. Christie's shirt. A foot in front of him was the hole she'd slipped through. She was lying very still.

"Christie!" He tried to fit through the hole but he was too big. Then he saw the dog next to her, tugging at her clothing. Parker realized the tide was rushing in and was nearly up to her thighs.

"God, no!"

He was frantic with dread. He had to get her out of there. In another few minutes, the tide would catch her and carry her out. But how to reach her?

The little dog barked again and Parker realized the animal couldn't have gone through the hole, either. It was too far down. So there had to be another way to that small stretch of beach. The dog had come over the rocks. He could go back the same way.

Parker moved quickly, jumping from boulder to boulder. When he reached the far side, he saw a small cave.

"Christie?"

The dog ran out and tugged on his pant leg.

"I know, boy," he said. "I'm here."

He crawled into the shallow cave. Christie was lying facedown on the sand. Her left arm was bent awkwardly, probably broken. His heart stopped. Dear God, he couldn't lose her, too.

Then she stirred. Her eyes fluttered open. Tears filled them. "Daddy, my arm hurts."

The tide surged in, soaking her to her waist. Her tears became sobs.

He reached for her and gently drew her next to him. She screamed when he touched her arm, then fainted. The little dog led the way out of the cave and back over the rocks. Parker followed slowly, all the while whispering a prayer that his daughter would survive.

The hospital waiting room was a blur of chairs, light yellow walls and a television tuned to a talk show. Parker paced back and forth. His long strides ate up the linoleum floor and he had to turn around every eight steps.

"It's all my fault," he muttered. "Dammit."

The same phrase had played over and over in his mind on the drive to the hospital. He'd carried Christie to the house and had called for Erin. She'd sat with her daughter in the back seat of the Mercedes. Kiki had wished them Godspeed and had promised to see to the dog who had saved their daughter's life.

Erin stood in front of him and placed her hands on his chest. "Parker, stop torturing yourself."

He stared over her head. "She started playing on the rocks. I should have stopped her. I should have been watching her instead of trying to get the kite flying."

"It was an accident." She touched his chin, forcing him to meet her steady gaze. "When she was two, she fell down the porch steps. She cut the back of her head and bled the whole way to the emergency room. I kept telling myself I should have been holding her hand or paying closer attention. She'd gone down those steps a hundred times before and been fine.''

She blinked as if she were trying to hold back tears. ''She's been on that beach before. Neither of us realized she could climb the boulders. Okay, we both should have told her to stay off them, but we didn't think about it. I'm as much at fault. Please don't blame yourself. It doesn't accomplish anything.''

Her words gave him something to think about. He'd had his share of scrapes and injuries as a child. Most children do. ''I'll watch her more carefully next time.''

She nodded. A single tear leaked from the corner of her eye. She sniffed. ''Are you feeling better?'' she asked.

''Yes, thanks. Although when she gets out of here, we're going to have a long talk about the boulders and not leaving the beach.''

''Good.'' She gave him a shaky smile. Her lips quivered, then twisted. Tears filled her eyes. ''I'm trying to be strong, but I'm not doing a good job. Oh, Parker.''

He held open his arms and she threw herself at him. She was shaking. ''She's going to be okay. It's just a break, a clean one from the X ray.''

''I kn-know that's what they said, but what if there's something else? I couldn't bear it.''

He led her over to the chairs and sat. He settled her on his lap, then rocked her.

''You held yourself together long enough to make sure I didn't feel guilty, then you fell apart?''

She pressed her face against his neck and nodded. ''Dumb, huh?''

''No, very brave. You're a hell of a woman, Erin Ridgeway.''

''A real p-pillar of strength.'' A sob shook her.

"Hush." He smoothed her hair and continued to rock her. "She's going to be fine. They'll probably keep her overnight to observe her."

"I'm not leaving her side."

"No one has asked you to. This isn't a busy hospital. I'm sure you can stay."

As long as he lived, he would never forget those few minutes he'd spent looking for Christie. The gut-level fear had permanently scarred him. While intellectually he could say it had been an accident, in his heart he accepted the blame.

"Thank you for being here," she said and straightened.

Tears dampened her face. Her mouth was swollen, her eyes and nose red. He brushed the moisture from her cheeks, then slid his fingers through her hair.

"There's nowhere else I would rather be," he said, and kissed her.

Her lips yielded immediately. The contact was comforting rather than arousing. She clung to him, then buried her face back in his shoulder.

"Tell me again she'll be fine."

"She's a strong little girl. She has a real zest for life. Of course she's going to be fine. She'll have a cast. Just think of how she'll use that to get her own way."

Erin's laugh was muffled against his chest. "She's going to wrap you and Kiki around her little finger."

"I know. You wouldn't have it any other way."

"No, I wouldn't."

They held each other until the doctor joined them. Erin wiped her face, then stood up and held out her hand to the older man. Parker rose and did the same.

"Mr. and Mrs. Hamilton, your little girl is going to be just fine."

Parker was so relieved he couldn't speak to correct the doctor's mistaken assumption that they were married. Erin sagged against him. He put his arm around her shoulders and squeezed. "I told you so."

She smiled up at him. "Those are the nicest words you've ever said to me."

The doctor chuckled. "As I told you before, it was a clean break. She's already in a cast. Because she was unconscious for a few minutes, we're going to keep her overnight to observe her. If everything is fine, and we expect it to be, then she can go home with you in the morning."

"I want to stay with her," Erin said.

"Me, too," Parker told the doctor.

"That's not a problem. Most parents stay with their children. If you come with me, I'll take you to her room."

The next morning Erin hovered anxiously as Parker carried Christie up three flights of stairs to her room. He held the girl easily, as if she weighed nothing. Kiki had hurried ahead and pulled down the bedspread.

"But I'm not tired," Christie said as she was set on her bed. "I don't want to sleep."

"You don't have to sleep," Erin said. "Just rest. The doctor said you should take it easy today. You can get up and play tomorrow."

"Can't I rest downstairs and watch television?"

Erin smiled, relieved to have her child home. "This afternoon. For now, you're going to stay in bed."

Parker sat next to her and smoothed her bangs off her forehead. "It's not so bad, kid. We'll all keep you company."

Christie stared at him. Her lower lip trembled. "I'm sorry, Daddy. I didn't mean to go on the rocks. I won't do it again."

Erin saw the guilt on Parker's face. He still blamed himself for Christie's injuries. She wished she could make him believe it was just an accident. She didn't think it was his fault, but he wouldn't believe that, either. Maybe with time he could see the truth.

"Are you hungry?" Kiki asked.

Christie wrinkled her nose. "I just had breakfast. They gave me pancakes, but they weren't as good as yours. The nurse was nice, but I'm glad to be home."

"We're glad to have you back."

Erin touched her daughter's wrapped arm. "How does it feel?"

"It hurts a little."

Erin glanced at her watch. The doctor had said Christie could have children's pain reliever every four hours. It was nearly time.

"I'll get you some medicine," she said.

"I'll come with you." Parker started to follow her from the room.

Kiki moved to the bed and asked if Christie would like some stickers for her cast. They were out of earshot before the girl answered.

Erin headed for her room. Parker stopped her just inside the door.

"Are you doing all right?" he asked. "I know you didn't sleep last night."

She glanced at him. There were shadows under his eyes and lines of weariness by his mouth. "You didn't, either."

"I guess we were both worried."

"It's going to be fine, now," she said. "Christie is a healthy child. She'll heal quickly." There was a faint scratching from the end of the hall. She looked in that direction, then shook her head. "I can't believe she's finally won that battle with me."

Parker grinned. "You can still change your mind."

"No, we owe her for saving Christie's life."

"Now?" he asked.

"Sure. You get the surprise, I'll get the pain medication."

Erin measured out two chewable pills, then secured the top of the container. Parker met her in the hall. He held a leash. The skinny little dog that had saved Christie's life walked beside him.

Kiki had taken the animal to the vet. According to him, it had been on its own for nearly a month. Kiki had checked old newspapers and asked around town, but no one was missing a dog. As near as they could tell, someone had just dumped the animal on the beach and abandoned it.

After getting the dog a clean bill of health and a bath, Kiki had bought a leash and a collar.

"Christie is going to be thrilled," Parker said.

Erin sighed. "At least she's small enough not to be too much trouble."

She went in the bedroom first. Christie took her pills. "Where's Daddy?" she asked when she was done.

"He's in the hallway. We have a surprise for you. Now you can't get out of bed until after lunch, but if you promise to behave, you can have your surprise now."

Big eyes got bigger. "What is it, Mommy?"

"Parker?"

He walked in with the little dog at his side.

Christie squealed. "My doggie! Mommy, it's my doggie! Oh, he's so clean and pretty."

"He's also a she," Parker said.

"A girl doggie?"

"You'll have to take good care of her," Erin said. "Walk her and feed her. You can't ignore her because you have something better to do. She's your responsibility."

Tears filled Christie's eyes. "I'll be her mommy. And I'll be as good a mommy as you."

The dog jumped up on the bed and licked Christie's face. The girl giggled. Before Erin could order the animal off, she circled twice, then settled next to Christie. The look in her little dog eyes said this was exactly where she belonged.

"Oh, I love her so much," Christie said, gently stroking the dog's head.

"She needs a name," Kiki said as she leaned against the foot of the bed. "Take your time and think up a good one."

Erin glanced around the room. The joy and happiness here were as tangible as the furniture. Parker moved close and she took his hand. He squeezed her fingers. They were in this together for the sake of their child.

Christie was safe and finally had her precious puppy. Parker was close; everything was as it should be. Erin wished she could hold on to this moment forever with only one small change. She wanted to tell Parker she loved him and she didn't want to leave him. She wanted to have the courage to admit she wanted them to be a real family.

But she didn't say the words. She couldn't force him to love her back. He was still withholding a part of himself. Until he learned that some risks were worth taking, until he saw that only by giving everything would he get all he needed, the clock continued to count down the time until she had to leave.

Chapter Fifteen

Parker stepped into Christie's darkened room. The night-light by the door cast a faint glow over the left side of the bed. He could see his daughter asleep on her back, her teddy bear clutched in her good arm. The cast was supported by a pillow and her new dog curled up by her feet.

He bent over and petted the animal. "How you doing, Laverne?" he whispered. She licked his fingers, then settled back down and gave a contented groan. Between her full belly and Christie's affection, her doggie life was complete. Parker wondered if she minded being called Laverne. They'd discussed other names, but Christie had insisted.

He crouched by the little girl and gently touched her fingers. They curled around the end of the cast. Her skin was warm and soft. Her chest rose and fell in time with her breathing. How fragile she seemed at night. It terrified him to think how easily she could have been taken from him.

A sharp pain sliced through him. He gritted his teeth to keep from calling out. Dear God, he would never have survived that. Not just the guilt, but the sorrow of not seeing her smile or knowing she was alive to brighten the world.

"I'm sorry," he whispered. "I should have watched more closely, or told you to stay off the rocks. Give me a chance and I'll do better."

She slept on. He stared at her and wondered how anyone could know her and not love her. Her presence in his life was a gift. He'd done nothing to earn it. He could only accept graciously and do his best to make her happy and help her grow.

Erin had warned him about holding back. At the time he wasn't sure he could give everything. Now he knew he didn't have a choice.

"I'll make it right," he said softly. "I swear. I'll always love you, Christie. No matter what. I'll love you with all I have."

The act of speaking the words caused the last barrier in his heart to break free. Emotion flooded him, overwhelming him. Love, sorrow, regret, pain, pleasure and need all swirled together until he found it difficult to breathe.

He wanted to weep for the past and how he'd messed everything up. Robin had been right not to trust him. He wanted to stand up and scream that he'd finally changed. It was all right now.

But it was too late. Shame filled him. The change had come because of his wife's death, not in spite of it. Had she lived, he might never have learned to truly love. He missed her but it was time to make peace with her passing. He would always love her, but now it was time to say goodbye.

He squeezed his eyes closed and wondered when it got easier.

"Parker?"

He raised his head and saw Erin standing in the doorway. He rose and walked to her.

"What's going on?" she asked.

He stepped into the hall. She followed. "Nothing," he said. "I was checking on Christie. I..." He swallowed. "You were right. I was holding back from her. In these last couple of days I've seen how much she means to me. We came so close to losing her."

She took his hand and pulled him into her room. There was a chair by the window. When he was seated, she knelt in front of him and placed her hands on his thighs. Her gaze was intense, her expression ernest. "I wish I had the words to convince you it was just an accident. No one is to blame. Otherwise they would be called deliberates."

God knows he wanted to believe her. But he couldn't, he knew the truth. "I should have watched her better. I should—"

"No. I should have come with you to the beach instead of staying inside to finish writing my letters. I should have sensed something was wrong."

"That's ridiculous," he said. "You couldn't know something was going to happen. The odds of her going up on the rocks, then falling through are—"

She cut him off. "Exactly my point. Or are you saying only you can accept unreasonable blame?"

"I..." He stared at her. She had him there. If he told her it was just an accident, then he had to believe it himself. The guilt lingered, but not as strongly as before. Maybe she was right. Maybe it was just one of those things. He gave her a half smile. "You're pretty smart."

"Thank you, sir."

They stared at each other. A subtle awareness filled him. She was close and she was touching him. He hadn't stopped wanting her. But she'd been the one to put the brakes on their physical relationship and he was determined to respect that.

She leaned forward. "I'm glad you were with me through this. I would have fallen apart if I'd been alone."

"You're too strong for that. You would have been fine." He touched her face. "I have a confession. In the hospital, I wasn't sure she was going to make it. I was just as scared as you."

"I know. You were very brave."

"I didn't feel brave. I felt more like a coward."

She took his hands in hers. "Parker, just for tonight, please let me love you." She brought his fingers to her mouth and kissed them. The soft touch burned, but not as hotly as her words. That simple sentence had seared a path to his soul.

"Erin?"

She sighed. "I know you don't want me to feel that way about you, and I won't—tomorrow. But for tonight, accept my heart and my body. Let me love you and pretend that you love me back."

He pulled his hands free and leaned toward her. He gripped her shoulders. "What are you saying?"

Her smile was pure surrender. She reached for the buttons on his shirt and unfastened them. "Make love to me."

A gentleman would have refused her, but he had always known he was a bastard. Desire raced through him, boiling his blood and pooling in his groin. Questions swirled through his mind. She spoke of love. It couldn't be true. She couldn't love him. He didn't deserve it. Except maybe for tonight. While it was dark out and nothing was real, he could accept her gift.

As he pulled her to him, she came willingly, molding herself to him, wrapping her arms around him and pressing her lips to his. The hunger was instant. He tasted her sweetness and wondered how he'd survived this long without her.

"I've missed you," he murmured against her mouth.

Her tongue touched his and she groaned. "Me, too. More than you can imagine."

She pulled his shirt free and touched his chest. He tensed with pleasure as her fingers traced circles on his skin. His muscles rippled, his erection throbbed. He wanted to be in her, touching her everywhere.

He buried his hands in her hair and angled his mouth more firmly on hers. He plunged inside, exploring her, recalling the pleasure he'd found here before. He kissed her until she was trembling. Only then did he reach for the zipper at the back of her short-sleeve dress.

It lowered easily. While he traced a damp path along her jaw, he drew the dress down her arms. The fabric pooled at her knees. He urged her to stand. She rose awkwardly, her thighs shaking. She wore nothing but panties and a bra, pale peach against her honey tanned skin.

Her stomach was at his eye level. He leaned forward and kissed the smooth, flat skin. She sucked in a breath and balanced herself with her hands on his shoulders. He moved lower, kissing and licking until he reached the lace panties, then he slipped down to her guarded secrets and breathed in the scent of her.

She exhaled his name. Her fingers kneaded his muscles. She vibrated with desire and that aroused him more. He liked her that way. He liked knowing he could reduce her to mindlessness with just his touch.

He looped his fingers under the elastic around her thighs and tugged the triangle of lace free. She stepped out of the panties and shifted, parting her legs slightly. He dipped one finger into her curls. Moist heat enveloped him. Slick skin beckoned. Gently, carefully, he opened her, exposing the tiny place of pleasure. He leaned forward and touched his tongue to her. She jumped.

He stroked her, tasted her, loved her until she was shaking too much to stand. When she collapsed, he carried her to the bed and placed her on the spread. He removed her bra. She was flushed and panting. Her nipples stood at sharp attention, her fingers curled into her palms.

Parker quickly tugged off his shirt, then reached for the button fly of his jeans. Rational thoughts intruded.

"Tell me you have protection up here," he said.

She raised her head and focused on him. "What? Oh, no, I don't. I didn't think—"

He gave her a quick kiss. "I'll go get some downstairs. Save my place." He started for the door.

"Parker, wait." She rolled toward the nightstand and pulled open the top drawer. "Kiki is very thorough. She might have... Oh, my. I guess she did." She held up a small box of condoms. "Thank goodness it's not the jumbo-size container."

He took them from her and grinned. "Not a multicolored fluorescent one in the bunch."

"Gee, that's too bad. I kind of liked it with the lights out."

He dropped the box on the bed and swooped down to pull her into his arms. "Figures. Next you'll be wanting me to wear an animal print G-string."

He rolled onto his back, pulling her on top of him. She straddled him and winked. "Only if it's a leopard print. That's my favorite."

As she laughed, her breasts bounced. He caught his breath at the sight, then reached up to cup her fullness. "Erin, you don't know what you do to me."

She arched her head back and moaned as his fingers found her taut nipples. "I have a good idea." She rocked her hips against him, arousing him to the point of pain.

When they both couldn't stand it anymore, he pulled off the rest of his clothing and quickly put on the protection.

Then she was under him, her legs spread in welcome, her eyes closed, her face flushed. As he entered her, he reached between them and found her place of desire. He rubbed his thumb in time with his thrusts. In a matter of seconds, she was straining against him, then she convulsed into release. Her tight muscles contracted around him, plunging him into ecstasy, bonding him to her as surely as if they'd been handcuffed together.

Erin woke sometime after midnight. She didn't bother looking at the clock. Time wasn't important. Her body ached pleasantly from their lovemaking. After the first time, Parker had explored her with his mouth, then she had done the same to him. Now, in the darkness, she could see the faint outline of him next to her under the covers. She could feel his heat and hear his breathing. Her heart swelled.

"If you knew how much I loved you, you would be terrified," she whispered. "Thank you for tonight. I'll treasure it always."

Then she slid out of bed and crossed to the closet. After slipping into her robe, she walked quietly out of the room and across the hall to check on Christie.

Laverne raised her head as she came into the room, stretched, then curled back up and closed her eyes. Erin petted the little dog. At last Christie had her pet. She leaned over and watched her daughter sleep. There was no sign of pain. She adjusted the pillow under the girl's broken arm, then returned to her own room.

Parker slept on, unaware that she was awake. She studied him as she'd studied Christie, but instead of contentment, she felt confusion.

What happened now? The night was safe, but soon it would be morning. Would he be angry that she'd admitted loving him? Would he feel an obligation? Even if he simply accepted what had occurred, could they go back to being just friends? Could she?

I want more. The voice in her head was very clear. She wanted it all. She wanted to be his best friend and his lover. She wanted to stay with him. She wanted more than a part-time arrangement, or temporary cohabitation because they shared responsibility for a child.

She reached out her hand and grasped thin air. Her dreams had eluded her for years.

Another voice filled her head, this one harsh and mocking. *You'll die waiting for your turn.*

Was it true? Would she die waiting for her turn? Waiting had always been her pattern. She closed her eyes against the questions, but that only increased their intensity. She walked to the chair by the window and sat down. Scenes from her past filtered through her mind, long-forgotten memories, snippets of conversation.

Stacey demanding, Erin waiting. High school when they'd both wanted a new dress and there had only been money for one. Or two if they'd sewn them themselves. But Stacey hadn't wanted to sew hers and Erin had agreed. After Christie was born, withdrawing her application to graduate school. Parker asking why she needed a degree to take pictures. Her guidance counselor telling her teaching was a "safe" profession.

Stalling. Settling. Selling out. Being afraid to try for her dream. Being afraid to fail.

The truth was sharp and ugly. She'd always avoided what she wanted for fear of not being good enough. She'd used her responsibilities to hide from her dreams. If Christie hadn't come along she probably would have found another way to avoid what she loved most—taking photographs.

She leaned her head against the chair and fought tears. They wouldn't do her any good now. The question wasn't how to survive the pain of regret, but what she was going to do now that she'd learned the truth about herself. How was she going to change? She'd spent so long waiting for her time and her turn that she'd lost sight of the real goal. She'd forgotten that life was a journey. She kept waiting for tomorrow, all the while wasting a lifetime of todays.

"Not anymore," she whispered forcefully. "No more waiting. I'm going to make this my time. I'm going to seize opportunities with both hands. I'm going to risk falling and getting hurt. I'm going to risk failing." She stood up and walked to the bed. "I'm going to risk loving you," she told a sleeping Parker. Then she dropped her robe to the floor and crawled in next to him.

Shortly after dawn, Parker walked down the stairs. Erin was still sleeping. They had a lot to talk about, but he figured it could wait until she woke up. The extra time would allow him to plan exactly what he was going to say.

After a quick shower, he was just as confused as he had been before. What was right for Erin and Christie? What was right for him? He knew love was dangerous and unpredictable. Had Erin meant it when she'd used the word last night? If she had, what was the next step?

The smell of coffee drew him to the first floor. He walked into the kitchen and found Kiki cutting up fresh strawberries.

She glanced at him and grinned. "You look as if you haven't slept much. Is this good not sleeping or bad not sleeping?"

"Define good not sleeping," he said as he moved to the cupboard and pulled out a mug.

"Good meaning spending the night doing the wild thing?"

"Hmm." He poured coffee, then sat on one of the tall stools across from Kiki. She continued to cut strawberries into a colander in the sink.

"A noncommittal grunt doesn't answer the question," she said.

"I know."

She winked. "You wouldn't be so discreet if you'd been up working, so I'm going to assume things went well. Yes?"

He looked at her. The weather was still warm. A pleasant breeze blew in the open kitchen window. Instead of her usual jogging suit, Kiki was dressed in a sleeveless white shirt and tailored blue shorts. She was tanned and healthy. Her face glowed. She was happy. He was miserable. They'd both spent the night having sex. What was wrong with this picture?

He wanted Kiki's advice. But when he opened his mouth, instead of asking about Erin, he blurted out, "I should have been paying more attention to Christie. I should have kept her safe."

Kiki put down the small knife and wiped her hands on the towel next to her on the counter. Her blue eyes darkened with compassion.

"I've been there, Parker. Guilt is hell. It eats you up inside until there's nothing left and you want to die." She glanced at the counter for a moment, then returned her attention to him. Her mouth pulled straight and the lines on her face deepened. "You turned your back for a moment. Every parent does it. We're not perfect. We love our kids, but we're still just people who make mistakes."

"So you're saying let it go," he said. "I don't know if I can. I keep thinking about Robin. If I'd loved her more, maybe she wouldn't have died. She was afraid I would grow to hate her because of her illness. She sensed my inadequacies."

"Is that what she told you?"

"Yeah." He stared at his coffee. "She said I would grow to hate her. It was easier if she died of pneumonia."

"And you believed her?"

"What? Why would she lie?"

She came around the island and stood next to him, then placed one hand on his shoulder. "Did you ever stop to consider that *she* was the person who wasn't strong enough? Maybe she couldn't face her own disease. Dying gave her a way out."

"No, it wasn't her."

"Can you be sure?" She smiled. "Believe me, I'm intimately familiar with the frailty of the human psyche. I've experienced it firsthand. After I lost my son, my world faded to black. I was so depressed I literally didn't care if I lived or died. It took a lot of hard work and some medical attention to help me want to live again." She squeezed his shoulder. "You've been given a second chance, Parker. Not many of us get those. You've got Erin and Christie, now. Don't blow it."

"That's what I wanted to talk to you about. I've been thinking about Christie leaving. I don't want her to go. Erin has dreams. She wants to go to graduate school and study photography. I was thinking about asking her if Christie could stay here permanently."

"What?"

"I know it will mean more work for you. Having Christie around is more responsibility. I have to work and—" He paused. He wasn't saying this right.

"Erin isn't going to give you custody of her daughter."

"I know. That's not what I meant. Christie could stay here while Erin went back to college. There are several close by. She could live here on weekends."

Kiki stepped back and moved around the island. She picked up the knife and grabbed a strawberry. "You know, Parker, for a computer genius, you're really dumb when it comes to women."

"I take it that means you don't approve of my idea."

She laughed. "Oh, that's one way of putting it. You're completely missing the big picture."

"Which is?"

"First, Erin isn't going to give up her child. Not even temporarily. She's not going to let you support her while she goes back to college. Frankly I don't think she wants to go to college."

"But—"

"Let me finish."

"All right." He sipped his coffee. Maybe talking to Kiki had been a bad idea.

"Second," she continued, "you're fooling yourself with all this talk about Erin going to school and wanting to keep Christie around. Of course you care about your daughter. But she's not the point. You're in love with Erin and if you think you can let her go, you're even dumber than I thought. Third—"

But he didn't hear what was third. Her second point rattled in his brain like the echo of a gunshot. Kiki thought he loved Erin. Loved her? Love?

It couldn't be true. He knew better. He knew the risks involved. He knew how he could destroy.

But what if Kiki was right? What if he hadn't been responsible for his wife's death?

He rose from the stool and headed for the stairs.

"Parker?" Kiki called after him, but he kept on going.

He climbed to the third story and walked into Erin's room. She was still in bed. As he crossed the floor, she turned and opened her eyes.

"Morning," she said. "You're up early."

She stretched. The sheet slipped, exposing part of one full breast. Heat raced through him and with it the realization that Kiki was right. He couldn't let Erin go.

He sat on the edge of the bed and stared at her. Her eyes were dark in the dim room. Her mussed hair tumbled across the pillow. She reached up and touched his mouth.

"You're frowning. What's wrong?"

"Nothing. Everything." He tried to collect his words. "Do you still want to study photography?"

"That's an odd question."

"Do you?"

Instead of answering, she slid across the bed and got out on the other side. She walked naked to the closet and returned with a shopping bag. After closing the door and flipping on the light, she upended the bag on the bed.

Hundreds of photographs spilled onto the rumpled sheets. He picked up one at random. It was of an old abandoned barn. The stark light and bright blue sky illuminated every broken board and smashed window. The isolated building looked as if it had been tossed aside without a second thought. Physical pain swept through him as he stared at the picture.

He grabbed another snapshot. Christie smiled up at him. She was caught in a moment of pure joy and he found himself smiling back.

He dug through the pile, looking at photo after photo. All were excellent, some even brilliant in their composition and ability to evoke emotion. Erin was far more gifted than he'd realized.

She pulled on her robe and sat next to him. "What do you think?"

"You deserve the chance to study," he said slowly. "These are amazing."

He drew in a deep breath. It would be so simple. Tell her his plan. She could pursue her dream; he would take care of Christie. Everyone would be happy.

He took her hands in his. "Erin." He paused. Letting her go was the right thing to do. She would be safer without him. He had nothing she wanted or needed.

He stared at her face, then squeezed her fingers. He had the right words now. He could tell her to go.

"Don't leave me," he said without thinking. "God, it's not right or fair to ask you to stay, but I don't want you to go. Kiki's right. I am stupid about relationships, but I do know one thing. I love you. I can't survive without you. But you're so talented. I don't want you to give up your dream. You wanted to take classes or—"

She pressed her fingertip to his mouth. Her smile quivered at the corners. "Hush. My dream has always been in my heart. You were right. I've been afraid to take pictures. I didn't need an education. I needed courage. You've given me that. You've given me back something I've always enjoyed. It was never about not having the right training, it was about being willing to expose my vision of the world."

A single tear slipped out of the corner of her eye. She brushed it away. "Last night I swore I was going to grab on to happiness with both hands, so here goes. I lied to you, Parker. I didn't just love you for those few hours we were intimate. I've loved you for a long time, and I plan to keep on loving you. You don't have to worry about me leaving, because I'm not going anywhere. We belong together."

The joy and love tangled together, leaving him breathless with relief. He cupped her face and stared at her familiar features, then pulled her close to him. "You'll stay?"

"For always." She reached for the buttons on his shirt and started unfastening them.

He touched her cheek, her shoulders, her breasts, not sure he was going to get everything he'd ever wanted. He was still cautious. The fear lingered, but he knew they could work it out. Later they would talk more about Robin and Stacey, about second chances and taking responsibility. But for now, it was enough to love and be loved.

"You're sure?" he asked.

She laughed. "Yes, for the first time in my life, I'm very sure."

Several hours later, they heard a light knock on the door.

"It's me," Christie said. "Kiki says I can't come in yet, but we're all getting married and going to stay here. We're going to be a real family."

Erin snuggled closer. Parker stroked her hair, wondering what he'd done right this time. He didn't know this much happiness existed in the world.

Then he frowned. "Did I ask you to marry me?"

Erin glanced up at him and smiled. "Not exactly."

"Will you marry me, Erin? I swear I'll love you forever."

She sighed with contentment. "Yes. A thousand times, yes. You're all I've ever wanted."

"Kiki's right," he called to the little girl. "We're getting married and living together as a family."

"Goodie!" There was some muffled conversation, then, "I gotta go. The cookies are ready. Bye. Oh, you can't get married till my cast comes off. I want to wear a pretty dress."

Her voice faded as the housekeeper ushered her down the hall.

Parker lazily stroked Erin's breast. "We should probably get up and talk with her."

Erin rolled onto her back and pulled him down on top of her. "Later," she murmured against his mouth. "She's got cookies to eat and we've got something of our own to take care of."

He chuckled and stretched over the side of bed. "Look what I've got," he said, holding up a bright purple condom.

She grinned. "Great. I'll pull the drapes while you put it on."

She started to get out of bed, but he tugged her back, trapping her beneath him. He stared at her. "I love you, Erin."

"I love you. We're going to be wonderful together."

"We already are."

Epilogue

Five years later

The gallery was crowded with the usual opening-night crowd dressed in cocktail dresses and tuxedos. Champagne flowed freely, diamonds glittered as brightly as the conversation.

Erin drew in a deep breath.

"Nervous?" Parker asked.

She glanced up at her handsome husband and smiled. "You'd think I'd be used to this by now, but I'm not. It terrifies me. I always worry that I've lost my touch."

"Judging by the number of red Sold dots on your pictures, I wouldn't worry about it."

She followed his gaze and saw that most of the photographs had already been purchased. The relief was sweet.

"Our accountant is going to be whimpering," she said.

"Don't worry about him. The money goes to a good cause."

Erin donated most of the proceeds from the sale of her pictures to a foundation she and Parker had set up to help young unwed pregnant women get support and stay in school.

"Daddy, up."

Erin smiled as Parker bent over and picked up two-year-old Sam. His miniature suit was rumpled and stained, and bits of cookie clung to his mouth.

"Your son already found the buffet line," Parker said.

"*Your* son needs cleaning up."

Parker kissed her cheek. "Let me take the monster to the men's room and I'll fix him right up." He strolled through the crowd.

Erin stared after him for a minute, and wondered how she'd gotten so lucky. She didn't know there was this much happiness in the world. The past five years had flown by.

"This is an important collection," she heard a familiar but young voice say. "Not only because of the theme but because of the departure from the artist's usual subjects."

She turned around and saw Christie talking to an elderly man. Her nine-year-old had grown up. In her taffeta dress and patent leather shoes she looked more like a teenager than a little girl.

She strolled over and held out her hand. "Hi, I'm Erin Hamilton. I see you've met my daughter."

"A very knowledgeable young lady," the man said and adjusted the glasses perched on the tip of his nose. He was short and squat, with white hair and a beard.

Erin touched her daughter's shoulder, then glanced at the pictures. Usually she took photographs of children and families, but the collection on the wall was a study of different carousel horses.

"How much for all of them?" the man asked.

"They're not for sale," she said and pointed to the small sign explaining that.

"I'll give you a hundred thousand dollars for all eight."

"Sorry, I can't."

"Two hundred thousand. They're for my wife."

Erin stared at the man for a moment. "I can't sell these particular photos, but I still have the negatives. I would be willing to do up prints for you. Fifty thousand for all eight."

"Done," the man said eagerly.

"Write your check to the Stacey Ridgeway Foundation," she said.

The man pulled out his checkbook.

Parker came up behind her. Sam looked a little cleaner. He was already getting sleepy. The boy rested his head on his father's shoulder and yawned.

"You're not selling the horses are you?" Parker asked, placing his hand on her swollen belly. Their next child, a girl, was due in a month.

"A copy of them. I have to keep the originals."

"I know," he said.

She leaned against him and sighed in contentment. Parker knew everything about her. He understood that the horses reminded her what was important. That she had to grab on to happiness with both hands, then hold fast. If she was willing to risk everything, her dreams could come true.

She covered his hand with hers, glanced at Sam, then drew Christie close. She looked up at her husband. "You've been the best time of my life," she murmured.

Ignoring the crowd milling around them, he kissed her. "It's only going to get better," he promised.

And she knew that he was right.

The first book in the exciting new
Fortune's Children series is

HIRED HUSBAND

by *New York Times* bestselling writer
Rebecca Brandewyne

Beginning in July 1996
Only from Silhouette Books

Here's an exciting sneak preview....

Minneapolis, Minnesota

As Caroline Fortune wheeled her dark blue Volvo into the underground parking lot of the towering, glass-and-steel structure that housed the global headquarters of Fortune Cosmetics, she glanced anxiously at her gold Piaget wristwatch. An accident on the snowy freeway had caused rush-hour traffic to be a nightmare this morning. As a result, she was running late for her 9:00 a.m. meeting—and if there was one thing her grandmother, Kate Winfield Fortune, simply couldn't abide, it was slack, unprofessional behavior on the job. And lateness was the sign of a sloppy, disorganized schedule.

Involuntarily, Caroline shuddered at the thought of her grandmother's infamous wrath being unleashed upon her. The stern rebuke would be precise, apropos, scathing and delivered with coolly raised, condemnatory eyebrows and in icy tones of haughty grandeur that had in the past reduced many an executive—even the male ones—at Fortune Cosmetics not only to obsequious apologies, but even to tears. Caroline had seen it happen on more than one occasion, although, much to her gratitude and relief, she herself was seldom a target of her grandmother's anger. And she wouldn't be this morning, either, not if she could help it. That would be a disastrous way to start out the new year.

Grabbing her Louis Vuitton totebag and her black leather portfolio from the front passenger seat, Caroline stepped gracefully from the Volvo and slammed the door. The heels of her Maud Frizon pumps clicked briskly on the concrete floor as she hurried toward the bank of elevators that would take her up into the skyscraper owned by her family. As the elevator doors slid open, she rushed down the long, plushly carpeted corridors of one of the hushed upper floors toward the conference room.

By now Caroline had her portfolio open and was leafing through it as she hastened along, reviewing her notes she had prepared for her presentation. So she didn't see Dr. Nicolai Valkov until she literally ran right into him. Like her, he had his head bent over his own portfolio, not watching where he was going. As the two of them collided, both their portfolios and the papers inside went flying. At the unexpected impact, Caroline lost her balance, stumbled, and would have fallen had not Nick's strong, sure hands abruptly shot out, grabbing hold of her and pulling her to him to steady her. She gasped, startled and stricken, as she came up hard against his broad chest, lean hips and corded thighs, her face just inches from his own—as though they were lovers about to kiss.

Caroline had never been so close to Nick Valkov before, and, in that instant, she was acutely aware of him—not just as a fellow employee of Fortune Cosmetics but also as a man. Of how tall and ruggedly handsome he was, dressed in an elegant, pin-striped black suit cut in the European fashion, a crisp white shirt, a foulard tie and a pair of Cole Haan loafers. Of how dark his thick, glossy hair and his deep-set eyes framed by raven-wing brows were—so dark that they were almost black, despite the bright, fluorescent lights that blazed overhead. Of the whiteness of his straight teeth against his bronzed skin as a brazen, mocking grin slowly curved his wide, sensual mouth.

"Actually, I *was* hoping for a sweet roll this morning— but I daresay you would prove even tastier, Ms. Fortune,"

Nick drawled impertinently, his low, silky voice tinged with a faint accent born of the fact that Russian, not English, was his native language.

At his words, Caroline flushed painfully, embarrassed and annoyed. If there was one person she always attempted to avoid at Fortune Cosmetics, it was Nick Valkov. Following the breakup of the Soviet Union, he had emigrated to the United States, where her grandmother had hired him to direct the company's research and development department. Since that time, Nick had constantly demonstrated marked, traditional, Old World tendencies that had led Caroline to believe he not only had no use for equal rights but also would actually have been more than happy to turn back the clock several centuries where females were concerned. She thought his remark was typical of his attitude toward women: insolent, arrogant and domineering. Really, the man was simply insufferable!

Caroline couldn't imagine what had ever prompted her grandmother to hire him—and at a highly generous salary, too—except that Nick Valkov was considered one of the foremost chemists anywhere on the planet. Deep down inside Caroline knew that no matter how he behaved, Fortune Cosmetics was extremely lucky to have him. Still, that didn't give him the right to manhandle and insult her!

"I assure you that you would find me more bitter than a cup of the strongest black coffee, Dr. Valkov," she insisted, attempting without success to free her trembling body from his steely grip, while he continued to hold her so near that she could feel his heart beating steadily in his chest— and knew he must be equally able to feel the erratic hammering of her own.

"Oh, I'm willing to wager there's more sugar and cream to you than you let on, Ms. Fortune." To her utter mortification and outrage, she felt one of Nick's hands slide in-

sidiously up her back and nape to her luxuriant mass o
sable hair, done up in a stylish French twist.

"You know so much about fashion," he murmured, eye
ing her assessingly, pointedly ignoring her indignation an
efforts to escape from him. "So why do you always wea
your hair like this...so tightly wrapped and severe? I'v
never seen it down. Still, that's the way it needs to be worn
you know...soft, loose, tangled about your face. As it is
your hair fairly cries out for a man to take the pins from it
so he can see how long it is. Does it fall past your shoul
ders?" He quirked one eyebrow inquisitively, a mocking
half smile still twisting his lips, letting her know he was en
joying her obvious discomfiture. "You aren't going to tel
me, are you? What a pity. Because my guess is that it does—
and I'd like to know if I'm right. And these glasses." He
indicated the large, square, tortoiseshell frames perched on
her slender, classic nose. "I think you use them to hide be
hind more than you do to see. I'll bet you don't actuall
even need them at all."

Caroline felt the blush that had yet to leave her cheek:
deepen, its heat seeming to spread throughout her entire
quivering body. Damn the man! Why must he be so infuri
atingly perceptive?

Because everything that Nick suspected was true.

* * * * *

To read more, don't miss
HIRED HUSBAND
by Rebecca Brandewyne,
Book One in the new
FORTUNE'S CHILDREN series,
beginning this month and available only from
Silhouette Books!

Made in MONTANA

by Jackie Merritt

The Fanon family—born and raised in
Big Sky Country...and heading for a wedding!

Meet them in these books from
Silhouette Special Edition® and
Silhouette Desire® beginning with:

MONTANA FEVER
Desire #1014, July 1996

MONTANA PASSION
That Special Woman!
Special Edition #1051, September 1996

And look for more MADE IN MONTANA titles
in 1996 and 1997!

Don't miss these stories of ranching and love
only from Silhouette Books!

™

MONTANA

MILLION DOLLAR SWEEPSTAKES

SWP-M96

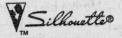

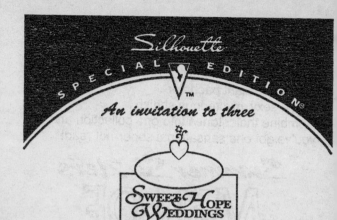

Silhouette

S P E C I A L E D I T I O N™®

An invitation to three

Sweet Hope Weddings

from Amy Frazier

Marriages are made in
Sweet Hope, Georgia— where the
newlyweds-to-be are the last to find out!

New Bride in Town
(#1030, May '96)

Waiting at the Altar
(#1036, June '96)

A Good Groom Is Hard To Find
(#1043, July '96)

 Marital bliss is just a kiss away!
Celebrate the joy—only in
Silhouette Special Edition.

There's nothing quite like a family

REUNION

HANNAH MICHAEL KATE

The new miniseries by
Pat Warren

Three siblings are about to be reunited.
And each finds love along the way....

HANNAH
Her life is about to change now that she's met
the irresistible Joel Merrick in HOME FOR HANNAH
(Special Edition #1048, August 1996).

MICHAEL
He's been on his own all his life. Now he's
going to take a risk on love...and
take part in the reunion he's been
waiting for in MICHAEL'S HOUSE
(Intimate Moments #737, September 1996).

KATE
A job as a nanny leads her to Aaron Carver,
his adorable baby daughter and the
fulfillment of her dreams in KEEPING KATE
(Special Edition #1060, October 1996).

Meet these three siblings from

Silhouette SPECIAL EDITION®
and

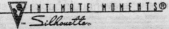

INTIMATE MOMENTS®
™ *Silhouette*

Look us up on-line at: http://www.romance.net

You're About to Become a *Privileged* *Woman*

Reap the rewards of fabulous free gifts and benefits with proofs-of-purchase from Silhouette and Harlequin books

Pages & Privileges™

It's our way of thanking you for buying our books at your favorite retail stores.

PROOF OF PURCHASE
Offer expires October 31, 1996

SSE-PP159

**Harlequin and Silhouette—
the most privileged readers in the world!**

For more information about Harlequin and Silhouette's PAGES & PRIVILEGES program call the Pages & Privileges Benefits Desk: 1-503-794-2499

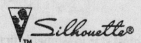

SSE-PP159